**Also By Joseph Redden**
*Emotional Overload*
*Odd Faces*—a coffee table book
*Love's a Crime*
*Secrets Can Kill*
*Poisoned at the Party*
*The Vineyard Murders*
Nonfiction coauthored with his parents:
*Delaware Then and Now,* and *More Delaware: Then and Now*

*To Eileen,*
*I hope you enjoy my mystery!*

# LETHAL
# GLITCH

## (A DETECTIVE LOGAN MYSTERY)

*Warm Wishes,*
*Joe*

## JOSEPH REDDEN

To Mom and Dad,

Thank you for all your help with all my writing and photography projects. I would never have been able to do all this without your love and support.

# CHAPTER 1

Claire Morgan cringed when she heard children shriek with laughter outside. She peered out her bedroom window and saw them dart across the footbridge over the creek. High school boys played volleyball nearby. Couples strolled across the grounds. People sat with drinks under umbrellas on the patio.

Memorial Day weekend was supposed to be the start of a fun-filled summer. After a brutally cold winter, Claire felt a chill now. She was usually the life of any party—but not today. She wiped away her tears with the palms of her hands as she gazed at everybody having fun. She heard the muffled voices of her guests downstairs.

She had to remain calm for Trent—at least for this afternoon. She went into the bathroom and soaked a washcloth with cold water before holding it to her large blue eyes. She touched up her makeup and checked her frosted hair. It wasn't so bad, she thought. There was no sign of gray.

At fifty, she was an attractive woman who exercised regularly. She had a statuesque body and a regal look about her. People were dazzled by her class and elegance. She was so insecure, however, that she didn't think she was especially beautiful.

She had always been obsessed with her looks. She feared that she was losing her appeal. She constantly reminded herself that she was imagining it.

"Any man would want me, right?" she asked the air. "Why doesn't he want me?"

Dissolving into tears again, it took her about ten more minutes to calm down. She tugged at her pink sundress until it accentuated her cleavage and walked hurriedly out of the room.

Meanwhile, Trent chatted with guests on the back porch at the east end of the house, which dated back to the eighteenth century. At the left, there was a stone fireplace. Guests sat on wicker furniture and rocking chairs and engaged in lively conversation. He glanced at his wristwatch and wondered where the hell Claire was. He had run out of excuses for her absence by now.

He spent practically every waking hour consumed with the publishing business. It was always on his mind. He had insight. He had vision. He turned struggling newspapers into thriving publications within months by hiring tech-savvy college graduates. They had drive, just like he did at their age. They were as hungry for success as he was then.

Trent was restless and could never sleep more than four or five hours a night. He'd lay in bed awake, constantly making mental notes about an idea. He was always on the go. He could never have achieved his success without making some sacrifices. Unfortunately, the sacrifices created a major ripple effect on his marriage. He was always at work. Lately, he hadn't been fitting in quality time with Claire. And he hadn't played golf with their son, Bill, in months. At fifty-five, he exuded strength and power.

At nearly six feet tall, he had an athletic frame with feathered salt and pepper hair and a distinguished looking face. He had dark eyes and a firm jaw. Despite his hectic schedule, he fit in regular workouts at the gym.

He looked up to see Claire walking hurriedly through the dining room toward the entryway that led to the porch. "Where have you been? You said you would be right back. That was almost an hour ago."

"I'm sorry, dear."

"The Prescots have been asking for you."

She followed him into the family room at the other end of the house and saw the Prescots mingling with guests. It was a large room with sky-lights built into an arched ceiling. A pianist played classical music at a grand piano in front of French doors with white lace curtains. There was a gigantic half-moon window above the doors. On either side of the doors, there were large windows that offered an excellent view of the patio and the magnificent rolling wooded grounds. White leather sofas and chairs formed a circle around a glass coffee table. Wildlife prints brilliantly illuminated by track lights were the only color on the white walls. A mammoth flat-screen TV hung on the longest wall.

Open steps with beige carpeting led to a lounge upstairs. On the second floor, a laptop computer sat on a desk, paperwork stacked neatly across it. There was an antique globe at the left. Wooden train models figured prominently on a shelf. There was a slanted desk in the corner and a ladder-back chair next to it.

Feigning a cheerful grin, Claire put on all the charm as she brushed past the Prescots. She had to have a drink to answer their nonstop questions. She went to the wet bar by the large pillar by the entryway and poured a glass of Merlot. She was not in the mood for their nonstop cheerfulness.

Claire sneered as she watched them saunter toward her. Lucinda had on a navy-blue outfit with white polka dots that clashed with a silk scarf with white stripes. To make matters worse, Lucinda wore a pink hat with a large purple flower in front. As they drew closer, Claire could see dark roots under layers of bleach-bottle beauty. Tom could have been spotted a mile away with his gaudy orange-checkered pants and equally appalling shirt in varying shades of red.

The Prescots crowded up to her, all smiles. "You must be pretty proud of Trent!" Lucinda exclaimed.

Claire forced a smile. "You'll never know how proud I am, Lucinda."

"How many newspapers does he own now?"

"At last count, fifteen newspapers and five magazines," Claire answered sharply.

"How do you feel, being 'Man of the Year'?" Lucinda asked Trent, who had followed Claire to the bar.

He grinned, his eyes sparkling. "Elated."

Claire clamped her jaws and acted like she was interested. She had heard it too many times to count.

Detecting her irritated mood, Trent said, "Claire, I'm sure the Prescots would love a grand tour. Why don't you show them around?"

"Certainly." Her voice sounded strained. "Do you want to come?"

He shook his head.

"I've been dying to see the place!" Lucinda cried. "Come on, Tom."

Claire went through the French doors, which led out onto the patio. The Prescots waved at the guests under the umbrellas. Their plates were piled to the hilt with fried chicken, hamburgers and hot dogs, and a lot of delicious desserts.

Trent scowled as he watched Claire descend the patio steps, followed by the Prescots. Claire was pointing, and they nodded appreciatively. They walked toward the greenhouse.

At that moment, he felt a sharp slap on his right shoulder. He looked up to see the *Main Line Chronicle*'s managing editor, Todd Stevens, towering over him. At twenty-six, Todd was tall and lanky with long, shaggy dark hair and piercing blue eyes. He had on blue jeans and a red polo shirt. He was a workaholic who over the course of three years had transformed the newspaper, which had been on life support, into a thriving competitor of e-magazines and e-newspapers.

"Is she all right, Trent?" Wilkins asked.

"You know how she gets."

"I bet you couldn't wait to get her out of here."

Trent rolled his eyes and grunted. "She detests these parties."

"Even to support your award?"

Trent nodded.

Their colleague Mac Yeager came over to them, waving the latest edition of the newspaper. He was a burly forty-eight-year-old, with thick red hair and a large ruddy face. He had on tan Dockers and a mustard tweed jacket with patches on the sleeves.

Yeager had tens of thousands of followers on his various blogsites. Over the years, he had made a lot of friends and even more enemies. He had a reputation for being a vicious critic. He could make or break any theatrical production, whether on film or on stage, with a single sentence. Readers formed their own opinions about Yeager. A lot of people thought that he had a massive chip on his shoulder. Others thought he was truly demented.

Others referred to him as the devil incarnate. He got tons of hate emails—and the snail mail variety, as well. Yet readers stuck to him like a drug that they couldn't pull themselves away from. They had to get their latest fix of Yeager's opinions about a new flick or stage play. They couldn't wait to see which movie star he would rip to shreds next. They had no shame. And neither did Mac Yeager.

Yeager slapped him on the shoulder. "Congratulations, Trent!"

"Thanks, Mac."

"Is Michelle coming?" Yeager asked.

"She's running late as usual. But she'll be here."

Trent yanked the newspaper from Mac's hands and scanned the review. In bold letters, the headline read, "**Model Can't Act; Play a Bomb.**"

Trent handed the newspaper to Todd and said, "I hope that Michelle hasn't seen it yet." He looked back at Mac. "Can't you say anything good about people?"

"You pay me to be blunt, Trent. And I tell it like I see it."

Trent was about to respond when he saw the gardener staggering across the lawn.

Marty Brown had gotten there early that morning to do last-minute work before the party and must have taken a break in the shed with a few drinks. Trent mumbled something under his breath and went down to have a word with him.

"Marty!"

But Marty kept walking. Trent quickened his pace. He came up from behind and slapped Marty's shoulder. The old man slid the flask into his jacket pocket and turned to face him. He hoped his boss hadn't seen it.

"Hello, Mr. Morgan."

Trent smelled the liquor on his breath. Marty's eyes were blood-shot, and he could barely stand up straight.

"I'm losing my patience, Marty! You promised that you would stop drinking on the job."

"I'm sorry. It won't happen again."

"I should have fired you weeks ago," Trent grumbled. "I want you out of here once and for all!"

"Please, give me another chance."

"I've given you a lot of chances!"

"Please, I won't do it again. I swear!"

Trent glanced over at the house. Guests were staring.

"Very well then. This isn't the time or place for an argument." He shook his left index finger at the older man and added, "This is your final warning. If I catch you drinking on these premises again, you'll be terminated. Am I making myself clear?"

"Yes, sir. I'm sorry."

Trent shook his head. "No, you're not. If you were sorry, you wouldn't have done it." Trent left the gardener standing there and marched across the lawn toward his guests on the patio. A few minutes later, he went back into the family room and talked to some other people.

Mac and Todd sat in the lounge, facing the balcony rail where they had an excellent view of the activities going on in the family room below. Instead of discussing business, they gossiped about Michelle du Prix and Trent Morgan like they were in junior high school. They exchanged knowing looks with people who heard them from downstairs and giggled naughtily as they looked back at Trent. Fortunately, he was too busy talking to guests across the room to pay attention.

✻ ✻ ✻

Claire led the Prescots out of the greenhouse, and they walked down to the pond. There was a two-seated rowboat tied to a small dock. Claire pointed to the shell of a burned-out farmhouse almost hidden from view behind some trees. They went to take a closer look and were fascinated to see moss growing inside it.

After a while, they headed back toward the house and smiled at a guest stretched out in a hammock. They followed the tiled footbridge across the creek. Claire smiled at some guests who were sitting out on lawn chairs as she led the Prescots toward an old stone pump house at the left, which had been built in the 1700s. Beside the original section of the house, it was the only structure still standing from that time period. The air felt cool as they followed her inside. Tom looked around and shook his head in amazement at the beer bottles and sodas floating in the water.

Claire led them to the front yard garden with its dazzling array of lilies, gladiola, and many other beautiful flowers. The flowers blended together in magnificent splashes of reds, pinks, blues, purples, violets, and oranges. She pointed out historical details about the construction of the original eighteenth century section of the house. The additions had been built about ten years ago. It looked like three individual pitched-roof houses in one. The front door was at the center. At the right, stood the original stone house with two gigantic chimneys. There were chimneys on the other sections, as well.

They heard a car barreling down the road and turned to look. A white stretch limousine was approaching the house. Claire tried to conceal her disappointment, but she was not a very good actress. She always managed to let her true emotions shine through. She scowled, secretly cursing the horrible events in her life lately. She could not conceal the hurt in her eyes.

"Is everything all right?" Lucinda asked her. "You look pale all of a sudden."

"I'll be okay," she replied flatly. While the Prescots admired the spectacular scenery, Claire's mind was on the limousine.

＊　＊　＊

Michelle du Prix blew in like a hurricane and created such a stir as she marched through the front door that she aroused a wide range of emotions for anyone standing in her path. People gawked at her in awe, their friendly conversations stopped in midstream. Men leered at her, their eyes slowly moving up and down her body and staring at her tight-fitting white leather skirt and chiffon blouse. They gazed at her unusually long legs and the leather boots that stretched to her knees. Others just stood there with dopey grins, their faces beaming.

The wives and girlfriends made cursory mental notes about her fashion sense. Their eyes fixed on her Armani handbag and diamond necklace. (They had no idea that Trent Morgan had given it to her last Christmas—with his wife there!) They thought that the flat white leather cap that covered her hair looked adorable. Her arms were crazy with bracelets. In a split second, they mentally picked her apart, like everyone does when they watch a beauty pageant, whether they admit it or not. She was anorexic thin, with a flat chest and sunken blue eyes. Her face was pale. Twin dabs of rouge could not bring her cheeks to life.

The women's admiration for the super-model turned to anger in a blink of an eye. They glared at their men for looking at her that way, like she was a piece of meat.

Michelle had grown accustomed to those reactions. She always dressed to get attention, but she always felt uncomfortable when she felt men's eyes bearing down on her like that. She pulled off the cap, exposing a platinum-blond crew cut. She flung the hat toward the staircase newel, and it fell into place.

"Let the party begin! Michelle's here!"

She breezed into the family room and made a beeline for the bar. She poured a glass of white wine while guests clamored to talk to her. Every so often, she erupted into shrieks of laughter. She was definitely the life of the party.

Bill Morgan hid behind tall potted plants across the room, watching men ogle her. As the afternoon dragged on, he had heard the guests gossiping about her alleged relationship with his father. He hoped that his mother hadn't heard what they were saying. Bill didn't know how she would handle it in her current "fragile" emotional state. His father was too wrapped up in himself to notice.

Bill knew the rumors were true, and he couldn't wrap his brain around it. He was only a year older than the woman that his father was dating, for crying out loud. Bill couldn't contain his anger and resentment, knowing full well that Michelle was not interested in him. He wondered what she saw in his father anyway.

At twenty-six, Bill was ruggedly handsome with dark eyes and wavy brown hair. He had a firm mouth and rippling muscles on a tall frame. He wore checkered blue shorts and a T-shirt with a Key West sunset on it.

Out of the corner of her eye, Michelle saw him lurking behind the plants. She gave him an icy glare as he worked his way over to her.

"What are you doing here?" he asked angrily.

"Your father invited me," she answered coldly.

He grabbed her wrist and pulled her out of the room.

"Let go, you're hurting me!"

He shoved her into the hall. No one was there, so they could talk privately.

He let go of her wrist. "You have no right being here."

"I'm tired of hearing it. Now leave me alone!"

Trent appeared suddenly and ordered his son to go away. Bill stomped up the hall steps. Trent gave Michelle a hug and kissed her gaunt face. She had just leant in to kiss him on the lips when guests shuffled into the hall and he shrugged her off. Open displays of affection were out of bounds for the time being. Trent put his hand around Michelle's waist and said, "It's so nice to see you, Ms. du Prix. I'm glad you could come."

She ran her hand along his shoulder and lowered her voice. "Really Trent, darling, do we have to be so formal? I'm sure everybody knows about us."

He smiled at the guests and whispered, "They will if you talk loudly enough. Just keep cool."

"But Trent," she whined.

He resumed his regular tone when the guests moved into the dining room at the right.

"I'm sorry about that," Trent said. "Did he hurt you?"

"I'll be all right. I was having a blast until he put me in a mood."

Bill leaned on the second floor rail and glowered as his father. "I think what you are doing is sick and twisted."

"This is none of your concern, Bill."

"You only invited her here out of spite for Mother!"

"I'll deal with you later. Now get the hell out of here!"

Bill silently watched. Then he stomped back to his bedroom to return a text from a business associate.

"I have something to show you in my study. This way, Ms. du Prix."

Trent put his hand on her shoulder and guided her upstairs. They turned left, and Trent led her to his office at the back of the house.

A laptop computer sat on Trent's mahogany desk by the window. There was a pile of paperwork next to it. A stone fireplace was centered on the wall to the right. On either side, hardback books lined the shelves. Journalism awards and medals hung on the opposite wall.

Across the room, Trent and Michelle lay in each other's arms on the overstuffed maroon leather couch. He kissed the back of her neck, his heart racing. His hair was sticking up.

"Six weeks is too long to wait," he said, out of breath. "I didn't think I would ever be able to kiss you again."

She pulled away, folded her arms, and pouted. "Did you tell her?"

"Not yet." He leaned forward to kiss her again, but she got to her feet and headed for the door.

"I'm not going to kiss a married man. You won't see me again until you're divorced."

He went over to her and put her hands in his. "Give me another chance, please."

She glared at him. "You lied to me. You said she wouldn't be here today. Boy was I mistaken. I feel like a fool! I'm tired of being a laughingstock. I'm sure everybody knows about us. I'm tired of being the other woman. It's gone on long enough. Tell Claire you're leaving her, or we're through! I mean it this time."

He wrapped his arms around her. "I'll tell her first thing tomorrow morning."

"If you don't tell her, I will!" She opened the door and marched back down into the family room.

"Damn!" he shouted.

\*   \*   \*

Claire and the Prescots climbed the brick steps that led to the back porch. The couple waved at the guests as they followed Claire across the room. Claire pointed to a white door at the left with a black latch that led into the living room. Lucinda peeked her head in and beamed when she saw the beautiful antique furniture. Though the rest of the house was modern, it was nice to keep the old section the way it might have looked back then.

They went through the door to the dining room. Tom's mouth watered when he saw the massive array of cuisines spread across the long table. Meatballs and lasagna for meat lovers; vegan and gluten-free alternatives were in aluminum chafing dishes. Bread, salads, and desserts were at the right. Guests wouldn't leave hungry.

Tom piled his plate with fried chicken and a hamburger and then went for the meatballs. He sat at a barstool in the family room and shoved a forkful of baked beans in his mouth. He still tried to save room for chocolate cake and blueberry pie.

Lucinda spotted Trent across the room and went over to him. She waved her hands in excitement. "I just love your grounds! You may have new neighbors."

He chuckled and said, "The more the merrier."

Claire scowled at Michelle from across the room. Michelle rolled her eyes and forced a smile.

"Why hello, Mrs. Morgan!" Michelle bellowed. "Lovely bash you have here!"

Trapped, Claire was forced to go over to talk to her. They kissed each other on the cheeks and exchanged phony pleasantries.

"It's been too long," Michelle said.

Claire gritted her teeth and clutched her stomach. "You're so right. Pardon me, Ms. du Prix. I'm suddenly feeling as if I might vomit. Please excuse me." She hurried up the steps and walked hurriedly down the hall toward her bedroom at the right.

Lucinda Prescot cornered Michelle over by the bar. "Poor Claire. I didn't think she looked quite right."

"Maybe she ate something that didn't agree with her. Pity."

Lucinda frowned. "It's too bad."

Conversation shifted to Michelle's modeling career.

"I bet you go to a lot of exotic locales," Lucinda said.

Michelle grinned. "It's true. Why, I just came back from Milan a couple of months ago to do a play in Philly."

Lucinda gushed. "You were in Italy?"

"Yes, and it was so beautiful there. It was a blast! But coming home was a nightmare. The plane sat on the tarmac for two hours! All because of terrorists and all the ultra-tight security."

"That's too bad."

"I was exhausted when I got home, that's for sure."

"I enjoyed your play, by the way."

Michelle's face brightened. "Thank you! It's nice to finally have some recognition."

"How do you have time to be in plays and travel around the world?"

Michelle put her hand daintily to her mouth and leaned close to Lucinda. "I bore easily. I'm the type who has to always be doing something."

Lucinda leaned forward and put her hands around Michelle's arms. "I'm the same way! It must be so exciting, doing what you do!"

"It's wonderful!"

Michelle smiled and gently nudged her right arm free. She moved toward the patio, but Lucinda held out a napkin and asked, "Could I have your autograph, Ms. du Prix?"

"I thought you'd never ask," Michelle replied cordially. She reached for a pen in her jacket pocket and flashed a big grin. "How shall I make it out?"

"To Lucinda and Tom."

She wrote, "To Lucinda and Tom, love Michelle," and handed it to Lucinda. "Here you go."

"Thank you, Ms. du Prix."

Tom went over to them and said, "Let her have some breathing room, Lucinda. Michelle, I'm sorry about that."

Michelle winked at him. "That's okay, Tom. I'm used to it." She glanced at the newspaper under his arm and asked, "Is that today's *Main Line Chronicle*?"

"Yes, do you want to look at it?"

"May I? I've been worrying myself to a frazzle about a certain story in it. I didn't have time to get a copy before I left to come here. And it hasn't been posted on the website yet."

"Go ahead." His eyes glazed over. Then he looked down at his wife and maintained a poker face.

Lucinda frowned, her eyes darting from her husband to the supermodel. "Come on, Tom. Can't you see she's a busy woman?" She grabbed his arm and pulled him toward the dining room.

\* \* \*

Michelle went into the study to read Mac Yeager's review. She clenched her fists, hoping beyond hope that there would be one nice thing written about her performance. But there were no nice comments. All that hard work down the drain! She had spent many long hours rehearsing with the cast. How dare he write such trash! All he had to do was sit on his fat ass and criticize for his lousy column! Mac Yeager had destroyed her role in the play which had taken her weeks to prepare for.

She sniffled, tears rolling down her cheeks. Memories of horrible words her stepfather had uttered when she was a young girl came flooding back. Overwhelming feelings of insecurity hit her hard.

"Damn you, Mac!"

She stormed out and looked for him in the crowd. He was in the dining room, laughing as he stuffed his face with fried chicken. His nose was bright red.

Mac looked up and silently mocked her as she stood in the doorway. He leaned toward Todd and said, "Oh, jeez. Here she comes."

She pushed through the crowd, crumpled the newspaper, and threw it in Yeager's face.

"What's the meaning of this? What do you mean I can't act? What the hell is a wooden performance?"

He rolled his eyes, a pious expression on his face. "I call it like I see it, babe."

"I worked like a dog doing this play, and you tore me apart!"

Trent went over and nudged them to the back porch. Michelle raved hysterically. Yeager held his hands on his chest to ward off her angry jostling. Guests crowded around them to view the ugly incident firsthand. Others peered out the window, shocked by what was unfolding in front of them.

"I tried not to let you see it, Michelle," Trent said. "I'm so sorry."

"You're sorry! That doesn't cut it!"

"You gave a lousy performance," Mac replied coolly. "I'm sure in time, you'll—"

She slapped his face and shouted, "You arrogant son of a bitch! I oughta—"

"Break it up, you two," Trent said in a quiet tone. "You're embarrassing me. The guests are watching. Try to be civil and you can work out your differences in the morning."

"I want you to print a retraction, Trent!" Michelle insisted.

"Reviews are the objective opinions of the writer," Mac said.

"Of a baboon is more like it! I want a retraction, Trent."

"I'll see what I can do."

"It's a fine day in journalism when a newspaper owner gives in to the whims of his mistress!" Yeager cried.

"You're fired!" Trent shoved Mac toward the ledge, knocking over a pot of red Petunias in the process. Mac got up and pushed Trent into the shrubbery.

*　　*　　*

Bill sat at his desk in his bedroom, talking to his client on his smartphone. He looked in amazement at all of the cars parked on the front lawn. He heard a loud commotion coming from the family room and politely ended his call. Then he logged off his laptop computer and rushed out to see what was happening. He was soon in the thick of it. He pushed his way to the center and acted as a referee while guests helped separate Trent and Mac. Bill's voice was firm. "Come on, you guys. You're acting like two-year-olds!"

"I'll get you for this, Mac!" Michelle screeched.

"With the help of your lover boy!" Mac shot back.

Guests dragged Yeager toward the back door. Michelle picked up a potted plant from the cement rail and threw it at him. It missed him and hit the window as the door closed. Bill shook his head and grumbled as he marched back inside.

"Come on, you're acting childish," Trent said.

"How dare you!" Michelle shrieked. "I thought you would be on my side!"

"I am, but you're acting like a prima donna."

She waved her arms and raved. "What do critics know? They don't know how hard actors work to put on a show. We busted our butts! It's not my fault there were so many mistakes! It was just the dress rehearsal, for crying out loud! We still had a few kinks to work out."

He patted her shoulder and said, "I know. It's okay."

He looked up and saw Claire watching from her bedroom window. He hoped she had not witnessed the ugly incident. He put his hand around Michelle's waist and led her across the lawn.

Michelle folded her arms and dug her right heel into the ground. "Do you believe the nerve of that moron?"

"Just go back inside and cool off. I'll throw Mac out. It will all be over with soon, I promise."

She went around to the front entrance so she would not have to face the guests. Then she went upstairs to his study, locked the door, and lay on the sofa. Tears streaked her cheeks.

# CHAPTER 2

Claire Morgan had always been consumed with herself. As a middle child, she never got the proper attention from her parents, Edward and Kathleen. Though she worked hard to measure up to their expectations, it was never quite enough. She was jealous of her sister Maggie, who was two years older. Maggie could do no wrong in their parents' eyes. They adored her. Maggie always got what she wanted. She maintained good grades at their private school. She had money handed to her. Claire had always resented her for that.

Susan was three years younger—the baby of the family. She was the cutest and most precocious. In high school, she was popular. Boys flocked to her side. Claire was afraid to bring boyfriends home to meet the family for fear that Maggie would snatch them away from her, like she so often did. And if it wasn't that, Susan would rave about her budding social life and make Claire seem dull in comparison.

In time, Claire blamed her lack of popularity on her looks. She studied hard so she didn't have to think about her awkwardness. She always felt more at ease around the servants. From an early age, she confided in them, not her family. The rift between her and her sisters continued into adulthood. Maggie moved to Manhattan and married a wealthy businessman. Five years later, she married the attorney who handled her divorce. It had been years since Claire had spoken to her.

Susan squandered her inheritance as she gallivanted around the world. Claire cut her off when she asked for handouts. Her childhood wounds never healed. Old resentments remained. She was angry that Susan was so irresponsible with her finances.

Claire now had everything she had ever dreamed of. She lived in a beautiful home on spectacularly beautiful grounds and had a lot of money. She could go anywhere she wanted at any time. But for the past few years, she had been traveling solo. Trent was too caught up in his work to take time for vacations. Interestingly enough, it didn't take much for him to drop everything as far as Michelle du Prix was concerned.

She locked her bedroom door and lay on the king-size bed that had satin sheets and a burgundy quilt and faced a window overlooking the backyard. She watched an old black-and-white movie on the large flat-screen TV across the room, so lost in her thoughts that she refused to come out to talk to concerned friends.

Every so often, she glanced at her sixteen-by-twenty sepia-toned wedding portrait over the bed. They had been so happy and in love then. She wondered what had gone wrong.

A little while later, Claire's eyes trained on the oil paintings of her parents on either side of the door. The expression on her mother's face was a constant reminder of the woman who had criticized Claire on a regular basis. She was never satisfied with anything Claire ever did.

When she heard the doorknob jiggle, Claire looked up to see her housekeeper, Elizabeth Ashton, holding the keys. She was heavyset, with curly red hair and dark eyes full of wisdom. She was a compassionate friend and confidante.

"Are you okay, Claire? We've all been worried about you."

"I'll never be okay! Never!"

Elizabeth sat at the edge of the bed and patted her shoulder. "What's wrong?"

"He's going to leave me! I know it."

"It's out of our hands now. We just have to deal with what we're given."

Claire reached for her tortoiseshell comb on the bedside table and sat at the vanity across the room. She stared at her reflection in the oval mirror, concentrating her attention on her face as she combed her hair. Was that a new wrinkle on her chin? Had her face drooped? "Do I look old?"

"No, you're fine."

"Then why is Trent leaving me for that tart?"

"Maybe he's going through a midlife crisis."

"Maybe I should find a younger man."

"Don't do that," Elizabeth advised.

Claire ran her fingers through her hair, concentrating on the frosted highlights. "Maybe I should bleach my hair."

Elizabeth's eyes widened in astonishment. "Why do you want to do that? You look fine just the way you are."

"What does Michelle have that I don't have?"

"I can't think of anything offhand."

"My thoughts exactly. Just take one look at her. She's ugly in a plain sort of way. I don't really understand what men think of as attractive in women. She's thin as a rail! I have a figure, don't I? I mean, I haven't lost my figure, have I?"

"You look just fine."

Claire pressed her fingers to her chest and sucked in her stomach so her breasts would stick out a little more. "I have breasts. Men like that in women, don't they?"

"People come in all shapes and sizes."

"I really don't see what he sees in her."

And so the conversation went.

*　　*　　*

About 3:00 p.m. on Monday, Claire opened a cabinet drawer and reached for a bottle of peroxide. She looked at her hair and grimaced. She had to do something about those unruly locks! About thirty minutes later, she showered to get rid of the bleach aroma. She toweled off and blow-dried her hair. Then she meticulously combed it. But it still was not right, so she grabbed the scissors and began trimming like mad. She stepped back into the stall and washed the loose hair off the back of her neck. She repeated the preening ritual. She went back into the bedroom and sat at her vanity. She peered into the oval mirror as she once again meticulously brushed her hair with the tortoiseshell comb.

At this hour, sunlight cascaded through the room. To the left of the vanity, there was a love seat with an embroidered pink rose pattern. An antique porcelain baby doll in a dress from the 1800s was on it. Bric-a-bracs from various travels were in a glass display case in the corner. On the other side of the room, ladder-back chairs stood around a marble coffee table. A tall bureau with framed photographs of family members was to the right. A watercolor painting of an old house out in the country hung over it.

When she was finally satisfied with her coiffure, Claire went through the entryway leading out of the room and stepped into her walk-in closet at the right. It was probably big enough for ten people to stand in. She searched for an outfit that was one size too small and threw it on. She looked at herself in the full-length mirror and checked her upper torso. The smaller dress accentuated her breasts. She hoped that Trent would notice.

She went downstairs and sat at the dining room table. Elizabeth Ashton stood there, her mouth agape.

"I'll have my tea now, Elizabeth." She began reading the newspaper.

Bill stared at his mother in astonishment as he entered the room. He pecked her on the cheek and asked, "What on earth did you do to your hair?"

"Does it make me look younger?"

"No, it makes you look foolish." He sat facing her and checked the stock market listings. "Are you feeling better now?"

"Yes, dear, thank you for asking."

Elizabeth began serving dinner when Trent arrived. He reached for the remaining sections of the newspaper, too busy to notice Claire's new hair color. They engaged in small talk, each too busy reading to actually hear what the other person was saying.

At half past seven, Trent shoved the last forkful of roast beef in his mouth and said, "It was great, Elizabeth."

She smiled and said, "I'm glad you liked it, Mr. Morgan." She collected dirty plates and went into the kitchen.

"Did you fire Mac Yeager?" Claire asked Trent.

"I would rather not get into it," he said without looking up.

Bill laid the newspaper down and glared at his father. "You really embarrassed me yesterday. All because of Michelle."

"Don't talk about it here," Trent urged.

"Like you don't think Mother knows about her."

"Enough!" Trent shouted. "Bill, I want to discuss something with your mother. Would you leave us alone for a few minutes?"

Bill looked over at his mother, and she nodded. He went into the family room, though he could still hear them talking.

Elizabeth finished clearing the table and heard tidbits of the conversation. Though she tried not to pay attention, it was impossible not to. She heard them arguing as she put food away. They were so noisy that she heard their screams over the dishwasher's resounding roar.

"You don't think I'm attractive anymore."

"Oh, Claire, you're overreacting."

She yanked the newspaper from his hands. "Look at me. What do you see?"

It was the first time that he noticed her new hair color. Or what hair was left. He scowled, his forehead creasing. "What the devil did you do to your hair?"

"You didn't even notice that I bleached it!" she squealed. "I'm not appealing anymore! That's why you're seeing her, isn't it?"

He slapped his forehead and muttered, "Holy cow."

"How can you do this to me?"

Trent put his hand on hers and said, "Claire, we need to talk. This has been going on too long, and I can't take it anymore. We don't have a marriage. I want a divorce."

"So you can hook up with that bitch!"

She threw an empty coffee mug at him. The pottery shattered at his feet. She stood there raving.

"How could you? I spent hours fixing myself up to be more desirable! She's no good for you! She's only out to get your money! Correction. My money! It was my family's money! I made you what you are!"

He slammed his fist on the table and yelled, "Damn you, Claire! I'm marrying Michelle."

She pounded his chest and screeched, "Damn you!"

He held her hands in place and said, "Get a grip. It's over."

"It will never be over! I'll get you for this!" She stormed out and scrambled upstairs.

Elizabeth Ashton entered the room carrying a dustpan. Without looking at him, she went about her housekeeping ritual. Trent reached out to help, but she shook her head.

"I'll get that, Mr. Morgan."

"I'm sorry for that outburst. I didn't want anyone to hear."

Elizabeth frowned and said, "Just give her time to get it out of her system."

Bill appeared in the doorway and stared at his father in disbelief. "How could you leave Mother for Michelle?"

Trent leaned down and flicked a pottery shard from his loafers. "It's none of your concern, Bill. It's between your mother and me."

"You're old enough to be her father." Bill stomped into the hall.

Trent poured coffee into another mug and stood there holding it in trembling hands. "I can't seem to do anything right, Elizabeth."

She pretended not to hear him and finished cleaning the mess. Then she went back to the kitchen.

Trent went into the living room and eased into the navy-blue wing chair. He gazed out the window, sipping his coffee. When he had had time to calm down, he reached for his smartphone on the marble end table and dialed Michelle's number at the bed-and-breakfast inn down the road.

"Did you tell her?" she pressed.

"Yes."

"How did she take it?"

"Not well," he replied gravely.

"You did the right thing. Hey, I'm really sorry about the party. I've had time to cool off. I'm sure if I talk to Mac, we can patch things up."

"It's too late. I fired him."

She smiled to herself. "Well, you're the boss. When can we see each other?"

"Not now. I have a meeting at the *Main Line Chronicle*."

"Can we meet for lunch?"

"Make it a late lunch." He fell silent a moment and went over to the window.

"Trent, are you there?"

"Yeah, sorry, babe. I thought I heard something. I have to go. I'll see you at Starbucks at two o'clock."

"Love you."

"Likewise."

He hung up and went back over to the window. He saw their gray Mercedes-Benz pulling out of the driveway. Then he saw Bill running toward the garage.

He reached for the mug and spilled coffee on his shirt.

He went upstairs to change into another one and noticed that Claire's bureau drawers were wide open. Her closet door was open, and clothes were not on their hangers. Her suitcase was not there.

"Damn!" he shouted.

*　　*　　*

The sun was setting when Trent Morgan turned onto the back road heading toward home. He was oblivious to the Beethoven violin concerto that was blaring on the radio. His thoughts were on Claire. Though their relationship had grown strained over the years, the fear of losing her triggered feelings that had faded long ago. Little things brought back memories of a time when they had been in love.

He blamed himself for the destruction of his marriage. He believed that people could have anything that they wanted if they worked hard enough. His desire to succeed had created a rift in their relationship.

His parents, Eleanor and Raymond, were demanding. They had had to work for everything they got in life. Raymond had worked his way through college. Afterward, he had gotten a job at an engineering firm in Queens. He had worked long hours and was never at home. In time, he had worked his way up to a high management position, and they had settled into a comfortable lifestyle.

Trent had worked hard to meet their approval but had never quite gotten it. They would never give him things. He had had to earn his own way and learn to be independent.

His little brother, Peter, received all the attention. Trent had to be the responsible one. At eleven, Peter had been hit by a car and wound up disabled. What little attention his parents had given Trent until that point had then been spent on Peter. The strain had created tension in their parents' relationship. They'd divorced when Trent was in college. Two years later, Raymond had married a younger woman—only six years older than Trent.

Trent had sworn that he would not repeat his father's mistakes. Unfortunately, he was doing just that. He was a workaholic who had alienated his wife and son. In a few weeks, he planned to divorce Claire and marry a younger woman. He didn't care what people said. Michelle du Prix made him feel twenty years younger.

He pulled into the driveway and pressed the button to open the garage door. He went into the house, checked the mail, and headed up to his bedroom. Claire's suitcase was still missing. He yanked off his tie, kicked off his shoes, and slipped into a black nylon jogging outfit.

On his way downstairs, he saw Bill doing paperwork at the desk in the computer room. He looked at his father and said, "Mother hasn't returned."

"I know. Where did she go?"

"I don't know," he replied angrily.

Trent's jaw stiffened. He waved his hands and said, "She's done this before. She'll be back." He went downstairs and looked out at the garden.

Bill leaned on the balcony rail. "I don't think so. You really blew it this time!" He gathered his papers and walked hurriedly to his bedroom.

Trent went into the foyer and opened the front door. He gazed out at the country road that ran beyond the driveway. In the background, he heard the rattling of plates as Elizabeth Ashton set the table. A few minutes later, she rang the bell, and Trent went to the dining room. He ate alone. Bill decided to take his meal to his bedroom.

About half an hour later, Elizabeth reached down to collect Trent's dirty plate. He had barely touched the shrimp scampi.

"Have you heard from Mrs. Morgan?" he asked her.

She shook her head. "No, sir. I would have told you if I had."

"She took her suitcase. Where could she be?"

"I don't know, Mr. Morgan." She bit her lip to avoid saying something she shouldn't. She went into the kitchen and came back carrying a plate of strawberry shortcake. She placed it at his spot, but he shoved it away.

"I've lost my appetite. It's nothing personal. Maybe I could eat it later."

"I'll wrap it up for you." She smiled and leaned over to pick it up and went back into the kitchen.

At eight o'clock, Trent went back to the front door. The sun was setting. It would be dark soon, and he wondered where Claire was.

# CHAPTER 3

It was a slow week at the Townsend Police Department. While officers were on their beats, plain-clothes detectives hovered over their desks, catching up on paperwork.

Detective Frank Logan typed reports, waiting for a juicy new case to come his way.

At thirty-five, he was blessed with a youthful appearance. He could pass for a college student, if need be. He was five feet nine inches tall, with short brown hair and dark eyes. His stomach was flat, his chest firm.

He had grown up in a working-class neighborhood in Philadelphia. His mother, Vera, worked in a department store. His father, Francis, was on the police force. Even when he was a child, Frank had dreamed of following in his father's footsteps. Then, when he was twelve, his father was killed while pursuing a robber. Tragedy struck again two years later, when Vera was killed in a car accident. Frank was raised by his grandfather, whom he affectionately called Gramps.

Losing his parents at such a tender age hardened him to life's harsh realities. He was a straight arrow. He worked hard and got good grades. After high school, he graduated from the police academy, and was assigned to the same police station where his father had worked. Unfortunately, they could not serve alongside each other. He worked hard knowing that Francis would have been proud of him. He was pushing thirty when he made detective.

Five years ago, he had transferred to Townsend after a close colleague was gunned down. Townsend was a small rural community that provided a well needed change of scenery. The slow pace took a bit getting used to though. As a police officer, he had dealt with rape cases, homicides, suicide, robbery, prostitution, and drug dealing. He had never tackled anything as terrifying as getting married.

His on-again-off-again relationship with his fiancée Penny Lane had been a roller coaster that hadn't always been as thrilling as the amusement park ride. He knew she was the kind of woman he wanted to be around from the first time he laid eyes on her.

They had different versions about how they met. Penny claimed that he had been stalking her on his beat while she hung out with friends in a coffee shop. He assured everyone he talked to that he handed her a parking ticket—not necessarily just as an excuse to talk to her. Well, maybe he just wanted to talk to her. Her story was partly true. He had been checking her out for quite some time and thought that she seemed like a nice girl whom he wanted to meet. He was drawn in by the light that emanated from her dark eyes and heart-shaped face. Her features were soft and delicate. He had no idea at the time the affect she was going to have on him.

What happened after they met led to years of anguish for both of them. Frank wasn't a people person. It wasn't in his nature. He kept his emotions bottled up. He worked long hours to put criminals behind bars. He told Penny from the start that was the way it would always be. He would never change. She worked at a bank and hung out with her coworkers. Penny got fed up that he never spent time with her.

Anger and resentment heated up Frank and Penny's relationship after his move. They barely saw each other. Her frequent weekend visits were enjoyable, but she felt like he was being forced to squeeze her in when he was in the middle of a case. Eventually, they broke up, and he got jealous when she started dating a coworker. Then they patched things up, and she moved in with him.

Detective Joe Flosky bounced a Nerf ball into a hoop hanging on their cubicle wall. It didn't make it, so he tried again. Another miss. He burst into laughter and tried it again. He was always laughing about something.

Flosky had lived in Townsend his whole life and knew the residents really well. He had no great desire to move onto bigger and better career opportunities in Philadelphia. At thirty-four, he had become set in his ways. He spent most of his free time with his law-enforcement buddies at Barney's. His expanding waistline was evidence of his overindulgence in the beer department. At five-foot-four, he had a crew cut of dark hair and a ruddy complexion. There was a gap between his front teeth. He was extremely opinionated and irritated them all with his answers to the world's major problems.

He was always hopeful that he would meet the right woman someday. Once in a while, he'd abandon his pals at their usual spot at Barney's and set his charms on women who just happened by. They really seemed impressed listening to him talk about the fascinating murder cases he had helped crack.

Logan finished typing the report and laid it on his desk. He went over to pick up the Nerf ball and tossed it right into the net. He grinned at Flosky and said, "It's all in the wrist, my friend."

"Wanta try it again? Double or nothing?" Flosky flung the ball into the net, and they high-fived each other.

"Way to go!" Logan shouted. He reached for the ball and sent it flying into the hoop one last time. Then he went across the room to pour another cup of coffee. He eased back into his chair and gulped the hot liquid down too fast.

"Ouggh!" he cried.

"Are you okay, Logan?" Flosky asked.

"I'll survive," he grumbled.

They sat sipping coffee, waiting.

Logan yawned. "Sitting around here is boring. I need some excitement."

"That's for sure."

Logan eyed the telephone and said, "Come on, ring. Do something already."

They resorted to tossing the Nerf ball again. When the telephone rang, they raced to answer it. Logan grabbed it first. A competitive trait. He jotted down the message and said, "Trooper Johns spotted a wrecked vehicle on County Road 355. Come on!"

"Now we're in business!" Flosky shouted after him.

✳  ✳  ✳

Flosky was blabbering about something and Logan was glad when he pulled next to the state police vehicle that was parked in a meadow. They got out and saw the smashed front end of a gray Mercedes-Benz wedged against a large oak tree near a pond. Sunlight bounced off Lieutenant Harry Winters's shaved head as he inspected the damage with Trooper Patrick Johns.

At fifty-five, Winters was tall and trim with a wavy mustache and cold harsh dark eyes. He had a lantern jaw and a coarse complexion. There was a scar above his right eyebrow. How he got it was up for speculation. He claimed that he got it breaking up a drunken brawl at Barney's, while his friends came up with other juicy stories about how he got it.

At twenty-three, Trooper Johns was lanky with bright blue eyes and a crew cut of red hair. His feet and fingers were large to match his tall frame.

Winters saw Logan and Flosky coming toward them and said, "Take a look at this, you guys."

The front grill looked like crumpled metal against the tree. The rest of the vehicle appeared unscathed. Logan peered inside and saw keys in the ignition. A pearl necklace was on the floor on the driver's side. There was a pocketbook on the passenger seat. Glass slivers were scattered next to it. There were red splotches on the white leather upholstery.

"It looks like blood spots," Winters said. "And it looks like there's some blood on the trim."

Logan nodded his agreement. "Okay, so we have what looks like blood inside and out."

Flosky pointed to the ground. "And it looks like there are some blood spots on the grass by the driver's side door."

The passenger's side door was unlocked. Winters leaned down to open the pocketbook and checked the driver's license. He went over to Logan and said, "The purse belongs to a Claire Morgan. Her credit cards and other important cards are still in it. There doesn't appear to be any sign of robbery. She had a hundred dollars in cash in her wallet. And her smartphone is there too."

"It's odd," Logan said. "Why would she leave her credit cards and money?"

Winters shrugged his shoulders. "I don't know."

Logan opened the glove compartment and checked important papers. "It's registered to Trent Morgan. Nothing seems out of place—except the damage from the accident."

Flosky popped open the trunk and whistled. "Look what we have here. A suitcase!"

Logan and Winters went over to take a look. It was packed so tight, the sides bulged.

"It looks like she was planning a long trip," Logan said.

"It doesn't look like she made it," Flosky added.

"It's the damndest thing I've ever seen!" Trooper Johns exclaimed. "Where did she go?"

"I don't know," Logan muttered.

Flosky opened the suitcase and sifted through the contents. "Evening dresses, a suit jacket, bras, panties, makeup, and personal women's stuff. It's packed to the hilt."

He tried shutting it, but the zipper got stuck and wouldn't go all the way around. He leaned down and pushed hard to zip it. It was bulkier than before.

He turned to face Logan and said, "Okay, so we got what looks like some blood. But everything else is intact, and there doesn't look like any sign of a struggle."

"Maybe she lost control of the vehicle and hit the tree," Logan suggested. "Maybe she wandered off in a daze."

"There aren't any footprints," Trooper Johns added. "And you would think there would be some footprints at the edge of the pond."

"Especially with the mud on the banks," Winters pointed out.

"So what do you make of it?" Trooper Johns wondered.

Logan shook his head. "It's a puzzle. I can see why she left the luggage behind. But why would she leave her pocketbook if she wandered off?"

"She obviously left in a hurry," Trooper Johns replied.

Logan grunted and said, "Maybe she went to get help."

At that moment, criminologist Lynne Tulley pulled up next to Harry Winters's vehicle. She was about forty with a medium build. She was fair-haired with a wan complexion and pale blue eyes. Her expression was intent. She went over and examined the red splotches on the car seat.

"What do you make of the stuff she left behind, Lynne?" Logan asked.

"She must have been in shock and wandered off," she said.

"That's what we were thinking. But where did she go? She would have left footprints. It didn't rain last night, so they couldn't have been washed away."

"There are some houses nearby," Winters said. "We'll have to go door to door and ask folks if they saw anything."

Tulley photographed the inside and outside of the vehicle. She took pictures of the suitcase and shut the trunk lid. Then she removed a switch blade from her evidence collection kit and took out a razor blade. She sliced a small square section of the front seat upholstery with the red splotches and placed it in a baggie. She labeled, initialed, and dated it. When she was finished dusting the jewelry for prints, she leaned down next to the vehicle and carefully cut grass with the red splotches on it next to the driver's side door.

\* \* \*

Trent Morgan went to the guest bedroom at the other end of the house, hoping that Claire had returned. She usually slept there after they had a knock-down, drag-out argument. The bed was made, and her bags weren't there. She still had not come home.

He ate breakfast quickly and went to the garage. He got into the front seat of his BMW, pressed the garage door opener, and pulled into the driveway. He sped down the road and cursed when he ran into the traffic piled up east of town.

He shook his fists and shouted, "Damned construction workers!"

He turned left and followed the detour three miles. Fortunately, he knew every back road to Philadelphia. The road narrowed, and he slowed down to avoid making a too-sharp turn on the winding road. Then he sped up and went down a hill. He reached the top of another hill and sped around a bend. An Amish horse and buggy loomed in front, and he slammed on the brakes. He rocked forward as the vehicle swerved into a ditch.

"Damn!" He took several deep breaths to calm down. Then he pulled back onto the road.

He could not pass the Amish farmer because it was a solid yellow line. He had to drive at a snail's pace for another mile. The road was too narrow and hilly to attempt passing the buggy, which he might otherwise have done, despite the solid line. At length, the buggy pulled into a lane that led to a farm. Trent floored the accelerator.

At the top of another hill, he looked down on the meadow and saw police cars near the pond. He slowed down and peered out his window to get a better look. Then he saw the gray Mercedes-Benz!

He parked next to a blue van marked "Criminologist" and raced over to see what was happening. He saw the smashed metal frame and cupped his right hand over his mouth for a moment.

"Oh my God! Oh my God! Claire!"

Logan looked over to see what the commotion was about. He saw a man standing next to the BMW. He was about fifty, with feathered salt-and-pepper hair. He had on a black suit jacket and white button-down shirt. He wore black pants and loafers.

Logan went over to him and asked, "Do you recognize this vehicle, sir?"

"It's—it's mine."

"Do you know a Claire Morgan?"

"She's my wife. I'm Trent Morgan. Is she—is she all right?"

"We can't find her, sir. Maybe you can help fill in some missing pieces. When did you last see her, sir?"

"Last night."

"What time was that?"

"About eight o'clock. We had just finished eating dinner."

"Was she planning on going somewhere Mr. Morgan?"

"No."

"Did she tell you where she was going?"

"I didn't know she had gone. I was on the phone and saw the car pulling out of the driveway. I went upstairs and found the room in disarray. Her bureau drawers were open and—and her suitcase was gone!"

"Was she mad at you?"

He grimaced and said, "She was furious."

"Were you having marital problems, sir?"

Trent looked over at the pond and watched the trooper traipsing through the reeds. He looked back at Logan and told him they had gotten into a nasty argument when he asked her for a divorce.

"Is there another woman involved?" asked Logan.

Trent nodded his head reluctantly.

"Do you have any idea where she might have been going?"

"I'm afraid not." After a long silence, he said, "We have an apartment in Manhattan. Maybe she was headed to the airport when she hit the tree. Maybe she wandered off to get help or something."

"That could be. Nothing was taken. Can you look at her belongings and see if anything is out of place?"

Trent checked the wallet, the purse, and the suitcase and said, "I don't know what she has in her handbag. And I don't know what she might have been taking with her. I can't believe her phone's still there, and she didn't even call me last night. There are plenty of bars on it."

"It doesn't look like robbery," Logan said. "There's money still in her wallet. But there are those red spots on the front seat."

"Maybe she cut her hand and went to get help. It's the only thing that makes sense. I expect she'll return when she comes to her senses."

"I hope so. If we have any more questions, when is the best time to reach you at home, Mr. Morgan?"

"About eight o'clock." He reached for his wallet and handed him a business card with both his cell and home phone numbers. "I was just on my way to a business meeting in Philadelphia. And then I have to meet someone at two o'clock. Please keep me posted."

"I'll contact you if we find out anything new," Logan assured him. "Maybe she just went to get help."

"I hope so."

✻ ✻ ✻

Trent canceled his date with Michelle on account of Claire's disappearance. He sat at the stockholders' meeting, unable to concentrate. He wondered if the car wreck was just another one of Claire's stunts to get attention. Maybe she was really hurt. Where could she have gone?

When the meeting adjourned, he collected his paperwork and headed to his car. He turned on the radio and listened to Mozart as he sat in rush-hour traffic. His mind was on Claire. He blamed himself for her unhappiness. He wished he had spent more time with her.

He arrived home about seven o'clock, settled into his easy chair in the den, and read the newspaper. He was soon fast asleep.

Michelle du Prix leaned down and tapped his shoulder. He opened his eyes and looked up at her.

"I came as soon as I could. I'm sorry to hear about Claire."

He rubbed his eyes and grimaced. "It's one of her little tricks again. Damn her!"

Her voice sounded soothing. "Come on. The food is getting cold. Just relax and enjoy the candlelit dinner that Elizabeth set up."

"I can't eat now. Claire has ruined my appetite."

"Come on." She took his hand and nudged him out of his seat. Then they headed into the dining room.

A few minutes later, Trent laid his cloth napkin over his empty plate and shoved it aside. He poured more Cabernet into his glass and took a sip.

"You know there's more to her disappearance, or you wouldn't be so upset," Michelle said.

"I'm sorry. This just isn't the time."

They changed the subject. A few minutes later, they moved into the family room. Trent poured more wine into his glass and did the same for Michelle. He sat next to her on the sofa and asked her about her photo shoot in Los Angeles a few days ago. Anything to keep his mind off Claire's disappearance.

⁎   ⁎   ⁎

The next morning, Logan gasped in disbelief as he drove up the long driveway that led to Morgan House. It looked like three houses in one. His eyes darted around the spacious front yard and the beautiful flowers in the garden.

He knocked on the door and told Elizabeth Ashton the reason for his visit. He followed her across a beige tile floor with floral patterns and glanced at hunting prints on the walls. Next to the door on the right, there was a pewter umbrella stand. He looked up at a staircase that wound around to a balcony on the second floor landing. His eyes trained on framed photographs of horses that hung on the walls going up the stairs.

Elizabeth turned right at the end of the hall and led him into the living room. He looked to his left as he came through the door and saw white wooden steps. The treads were steep and narrow and twisted to the upper floor. The walls were built of stones of varying sizes and shapes, and there was a large stone fireplace between the two front windows. He sat on a Chippendale chair and looked out the window while she went to get Trent Morgan.

He glanced at framed family photographs on the fireplace mantel. Claire and Trent's wedding portrait figured prominently in the center. They looked like a happy couple, a vast meadow stretching behind them. Strands of luscious light brown hair stuck out beneath her veil. Sunlight dappled her face. Trent was an imposing figure in his white tuxedo. His expression exuded power. His hair was jet black back then. Their names were on baby pictures to the left. On the right, there was a baby portrait of their son. There were snapshots of him at various ages next to it. In one, he was hamming it up for the camera, while his parents stood next to him. He was snaggletoothed, with a huge grin. A Christmas tree was in the background. In another one, they were waving snow skis and laughing. There were pictures of him at high school athletic events. A portrait of him in his cap and gown was jammed in at the edge of the mantel. He looked over at an antique roll-top desk by the entryway. A Tiffany lamp was on top. Knickknacks were arranged next to it.

Trent appeared in the doorway, a young blond woman by his side. Logan's eyes trained on her short, tight-fitting pink skirt. He thought she looked dreadfully thin.

He smiled cordially at them and said, "Hello, Mr. Morgan. Ma'am."

Michelle held out her hand and introduced herself to the detective.

"I guess you're their son's girlfriend," Logan said.

"No!" Then she shot an accusatory look at Trent.

Logan smiled, realizing his error. "I see. So you're the other woman?"

"I'm not ashamed to admit it. She never loved him."

"You just referred to her in the past tense, Ms. du Prix. Is there something you know that the police don't?"

She refused to dignify that with an answer.

Trent changed the subject. "Did you find out anything?"

"We talked to residents who live near the pond, but no one saw anything. The good news is that we didn't find her body when we dragged the pond. The bad news is that she just disappeared without a trace. Tell me, Mr. Morgan, how can a grown woman disappear in the middle of a meadow?"

"I haven't a clue."

"There were no track marks, so she could not have been abducted. No footprints."

"Maybe she was abducted by aliens," Michelle said under her breath.

Logan looked over at her. "What was that, Ms. du Prix?"

"Nothing."

A look of desperation flashed on Trent's face. "Then what happened to her?"

"I wish I could tell you."

"Keep me posted," Trent urged.

"I'm sorry I couldn't have given you better news." Logan showed himself out.

Trent went to the bar and reached for a bottle of Jack Daniel's. His hands trembled as he poured the bourbon into the glass. He forced it down and shouted, "Damn!"

# CHAPTER 4

Logan slammed his car door and went over to an old man on a tractor. He waved, and the man turned off the motor. The farmer's overalls were caked in dirt. His hands were coarse, and his face was red from being in the sun all day.

"Can I help you?" the old man asked.

Logan showed him his badge and handed him a photograph of Claire Morgan. "Do you recognize this woman, sir?"

The old man scratched his head and said, "Isn't she that rich lady that lives in that big house down the road?"

"Yes. Her car went off the road by the pond. I think it happened about eight o'clock Monday night. Did you see or hear anything?"

The old man grunted. "I'm afraid not. I quit work about seven that night. I wouldn't have even heard you if I hadn't seen you coming toward me."

Logan handed him a police sketch of her new hairstyle. "She recently cut her hair and bleached it. She doesn't look like she did in this snapshot. She looks more like she probably does in this drawing. Did you talk to anybody who might have seen her?"

"You might try the tavern down the road. Folks are coming and going there all night."

Logan thanked him and took the road to the neighboring farm. He talked to some field hands, but they were not much help either. At eleven o'clock, he drove to the Greenback Tavern in Angola. At this hour, there was an eerie stillness in the room. There were only three customers in the restaurant section. That would change when farmers and construction workers piled in for the lunch rush.

Logan handed the snapshot to the bartender. "Do you know her?"

The man put on his glasses and said, "Never seen her."

Logan showed him the police artist's sketch. The bartender studied both pictures and said, "Maybe she's been here once or twice. But I could be wrong."

"Who was working here on Monday night?"

He checked the roster. "Earl and I were here most of the time. And Randy and Keith."

"Could I talk to them?"

The bartender went into the back room and shouted, "Keith! A cop wants to talk to you!"

"I didn't do anything!"

"Come on. He's looking for some woman."

A moment later, a lanky man with stringy blond hair pushed through the door. He was in his early twenties with hostile dark eyes. His T-shirt was moist from sweat. His blue jeans had holes in the knees. A dragon tattoo was on his right forearm. He definitely did not want to be working in a kitchen.

He went over to Logan and said, "You wanted to talk to me?"

Logan showed him the picture. "Have you seen this woman?"

Keith grunted and said, "I'd remember if I had. She's got some bucks."

"Do you know her?"

"She comes in here once in a while with her old man. They don't really fit in here, if you know what I mean. Acting fancy and all."

Logan repeated information he had about the car accident. "Did she come in here Monday night?"

Keith shook his head.

A couple of minutes later, Randy pushed through the swinging door and came over to him. He was a little older with short blond hair, and he wore a black muscle shirt. Logan asked him the same questions, and he got similar answers. Randy had been so busy that he didn't step out of the kitchen on Monday night.

"I'm going to hang the photo on the bulletin board," Logan told the bartender. "Please make sure customers see it."

"Will do."

"If anybody recognizes her, have them call Frank Logan at the police station." He handed him his card and headed out.

\* \* \*

Bill Morgan had endured a strict upbringing. Though he learned how to behave around important rich people, he had gained a reputation for being a wild child. He did everything he could to get back at his father for working so much. He drove fancy sports cars and dated beautiful women. As long as he was discreet and no one blabbed his indiscretions to the press, he could live his life the way he wanted, without worrying what others thought.

After college, he went to work for a thriving financial firm in the Big Apple and burned out quickly. After spending years sowing his wild oats, he calmed himself down. He started a graphic design business called WJM, Inc. and worked out of his bedroom in his parents' house. Two years later, his business took off. It was an internet success. He was a fierce competitor.

Now that he was making money, Bill could not afford to act so reckless again. He spent more time on his smartphone than communicating with his father, and he liked it that way. As an entrepreneur, Bill enjoyed the life of Riley. He was his own boss. He had freedom to come and go as he pleased. He could support the lifestyle he had grown accustomed to. He could play golf and tennis. He could travel the world, and decorated his bedroom with knickknacks from his various trips out west. His graphic artwork figured prominently around the room. A charcoal portrait that he had drawn of Michelle was on the wall by the door. He just left it there to make his father angry.

He stared at his laptop screen, unable to concentrate on the ad he was designing for a Philadelphia hotel. He had been on the phone all morning, and there was still no word about his mother's whereabouts. He made a backup copy of his layout and watched the news on the flat-screen TV across from his bed. There was still no word about his mother.

He slipped into his tennis shorts and headed out. A few minutes later, he wandered down the cobblestone path that led away from the garden. For the next hour, he slammed his ball against the courtyard wall, working off unwanted tension. He reached for his towel and wiped his forehead. Then he returned to the house.

\* \* \*

After lunch, Logan once again drove down the wooded lane that stretched about half a mile to the Morgans' estate. He traipsed across the lawn and up the brick steps. He rang the bell, admiring the scenery. The door opened, and Elizabeth Ashton looked at him through the screen.

"Mr. Morgan isn't here," she said.

"I'm not here to see him. I need to ask you some questions. Do you mind?"

"All right, but you'll have to talk while I'm working."

"Okay."

He glanced at paintings on the walls as they walked to the other end of the hall. Then he followed her through the dining room door at the right. There was a long table with a white silk cloth and six chairs around it. The cushions were crushed maroon velvet with pink roses embroidered on them. China plates and glasses were stacked on a glass shelf against the wall. Knickknacks stood on a rack in the corner closest to the hall entryway. The window overlooked the wooded backyard.

Elizabeth turned a door latch at the right and led him into the kitchen. It was a sizable room with a high ceiling, a substantial island in the center, and plenty of counter space. There was a brick oven and a two-door refrigerator. Copper pans and kettles hung from hooks above a large stove. A spice rack was on the wall opposite the window. The cabinets were painted white with black latches.

Elizabeth opened the utility closet door, pulled out a broom, and swept the slate floor with vigor.

"Did Mrs. Morgan seem upset the night she left?" Logan asked.

"She was very upset."

"Do you know why?"

"I heard Mr. and Mrs. Morgan arguing. I try not to listen, but it's hard not to. I hear bits and pieces of conversations when I come in and out of the kitchen." She fell silent, concentrating on her sweeping.

"What were they fighting about?"

She told him that Claire threw a coffee mug at Trent when he told her he wanted to get a divorce.

"Did you see her leave?"

"No, I was busy in the kitchen."

"When did you know she was gone?"

"Later that night. About nine. That's usually when I put everything away and get ready for bed."

She leaned down, collected dust in the pan, and tossed it in the trash bin. She went over to the sink, washed her hands, and dried them on her apron. Then she pulled up a chair facing Logan and offered him tea. He accepted, and she poured a cup for both of them.

"Mr. Morgan told me Claire took her suitcase. I didn't say a word. I awoke about six o'clock and prepared breakfast. Mr. Morgan was worried and told me she didn't come back. She often goes off like that and comes back a few hours later. But she didn't come back this time, and we were really worried."

"Did Mrs. Morgan ever confide in you?"

"All the time," Elizabeth acknowledged.

"Did she ever tell you she thought her husband was sneaking around?"

Elizabeth leaned forward, her hand resting firmly against her right cheek. "We knew it for a fact! It was no secret that he was messing around with Miss du Prix. Poor Claire! She was always trying to please him, but he was too busy to notice."

"Do you think Mrs. Morgan was unstable?"

Elizabeth carefully mulled over her answer. "She isn't unstable. I think she acted as any normal woman would when she knows her husband has a mistress. But she was always fretting about her appearance. She would always ask me if I thought she looked fat. And I'd tell her that she looked fine, but she wouldn't believe me. Then she'd ask me if I thought her hair looked too gray, and I'd say she looked fine. That's why she bleached it. She wanted to look younger—to be more appealing to Mr. Morgan. I think she wanted to look more like Miss du Prix."

He looked keenly into eyes full of wisdom. Her face was warm and inviting. Clearly, she was the glue that held the Morgan clan together. She was the one they came to with problems. Surely, she kept their secrets. Would she be willing to reveal them? Had Claire told Elizabeth her latest travel plans? Was she telling him everything she knew?

"That's interesting," he said.

"She was extremely upset the day of the party."

"When was that?"

"The day before she went missing."

"What happened?"

"Michelle happened, that's what. Claire spent most of the time crying in her room. Then she saw them on the patio, holding hands. It wasn't what she thought it was—well, it was partly what she thought it was."

"I don't understand."

She recounted in vivid detail the ugly incident between Trent and Mac Yeager. "They had to be separated. Imagine that!"

"Who is Mac Yeager?"

"He's a critic at Mr. Morgan's newspaper in Philadelphia."

"Can you think of anything else?"

"No. I hope I was of some help."

He smiled. "You were a lot of help. If you remember anything else, call me at the police station." He let her get back to work.

\* \* \*

Marty Brown felt sweat burn his eyes as he trimmed hedges by the porch. His T-shirt was dripping wet and clung to his chest. He laid down the clippers and wiped off his moist face with a towel. His face and nose were red, but it wasn't necessarily from the sun. The rest of his skin was golden brown. His complexion was leathery from working out in the hot sun for so many years. He had callused fingers and chapped hands. He had unruly white hair and was in need of a shave.

At sixty-eight, he was too old to spend hours on his hands and knees doing landscaping. It was work for a younger man, but he would never retire. He had always loved working with his hands in the great outdoors.

He looked up to see a young dark-haired man descend the front steps and walk toward him. The man introduced himself as Detective Logan and asked Marty about Mrs. Morgan's disappearance.

"I don't see how I can be of much help," Marty said.

"You'd be surprised what seemingly useless information can be important. Did you see Mrs. Morgan leave Monday night?"

"No, I was putting equipment back in the shed."

"Did you see her on Tuesday morning?"

Marty shook his head.

"Were you here Sunday afternoon?"

"I worked till the party started."

"Were you at the party?"

"No, I had the rest of the day off." He neglected to mention that his boss caught him drinking on the job.

"Did Mrs. Morgan seem upset on Monday?"

"It's hard to tell with her. She's moody. Always into her looks. I can't blame her though, with that model hanging around. She's a knockout!"

"Does Michelle du Prix come here often?"

"She practically lives here! Christ! Have you seen her? She's a knockout!"

"I thought she looked sickly. Anyway, did you sense any trouble brewing on Monday?"

"Are you kidding? They weren't talking to each other. I was doing some trimming around the dining room about seven. The bay windows were open, and I heard them yelling."

"Could you hear what they were saying?"

"No, but I heard breaking glass. They like to throw things."

"Can you think of anything else?"

"Not off-hand."

"Can you think of any place she might have gone?"

"They have a couple of other places. Maybe she went back to the Big Apple."

Logan thanked him and walked briskly to his police car. He was about to get in when he saw a man with wavy dark hair coming toward him. A towel was draped over his right arm, and a smartphone was sticking out of his tennis shorts. When he got closer, Logan recognized him as the young man in the cap-and-gown portrait over the fireplace mantel. His shoulders were slightly larger now, and his face was more filled out. He had a sunburn on his forehead.

Bill removed his sunglasses and introduced himself. Logan did the same.

"We've been on the phone all day to New York, and no one has seen her," he said quickly. "My mother has just disappeared off the face of the earth."

"Is that unusual?"

He shook his head. "Sometimes she goes off for a few hours, but she usually returns by morning. It's gotten to the point that we just ignore her. It's her way of getting attention. But it's different this time."

He sat at a table on the patio, and Elizabeth brought them out mugs. She poured coffee into them and went back inside. Bill added cream and sugar and stirred briskly. Logan drank his black.

"Detective Logan, I'll pay you any amount of money you want to find my mother."

"It's police business."

"I insist. Any amount of money can't hurt." He looked squarely into Logan's dark eyes. "Give it to me straight. Do you think she will be found?"

"I don't know," Logan admitted. "I've never handled a case this unusual. I talked to neighbors, and they didn't see her. I left her picture at the Greenback Tavern. Maybe a regular customer saw her."

"I hope so. What do you think?"

Logan sipped his coffee and wiped his mouth with a cloth napkin. "I think your mother was really upset. I understand that your parents were having marital problems."

Bill nodded and told him about his father's affair with Michelle du Prix. "What do you think?"

"How would a woman feel, knowing that her husband is leaving her for another woman? I don't know how I would feel if my fiancée betrayed me that way."

Bill sneered. "It feels like a knife twisting in your gut."

"You've been jilted?"

"I'd rather not talk about it!" he snapped, then apologized. "I'm really getting worried. If she had gotten into an accident, why didn't she call to tell us she was all right? Where could she have gone?"

"We're looking into it."

"My father is a very important man. All he has to do is offer a reward on social media and in the newspapers. And he can go to radio and TV news stations across the country. Money is cheap. Someone out there must have seen something."

"Maybe she doesn't want to be found."

"I can't believe it." He sipped his coffee and was quiet a moment. "Well, at least we know that she wasn't in the pond. Maybe she wandered off and hitchhiked."

"That's what I suspect. You'd better be prepared for the worst."

"She's okay. She has to be."

"Do you know anyone who might have wanted to hurt her?"

Bill shook his head.

"How did she act at the party on Sunday afternoon?"

"She was upset. Especially when that witch Michelle arrived. Mother spent most of the afternoon in her room. I'm not sure, but I think she was crying."

"Was there some kind of incident that day?"

"You mean the fight of the decade between Mac Yeager and my father?"

"Why did they get into the fight?"

He shrugged his shoulders. "I don't know. I was in my bedroom and heard people shouting. I rushed downstairs to see what was happening and saw everyone standing on the patio crowding around them. It was chaos! They were really going at it. My father pushed Michelle aside and started hitting Yeager. I had to help separate them."

"You don't say?"

"Michelle was upset that Mac had panned a play she was in. I went to the opening night and couldn't agree more. She can't act. She should definitely stay off the stage."

"It sounds like she didn't take it well."

"That's an understatement. She was livid!"

"Did your mother see what happened?"

"I think so. Their bedroom overlooks the backyard patio. I think she must have seen my father comforting Michelle. And I guess that must have really upset her."

"I can imagine."

"It's all because of Michelle!" He clenched his fists, the veins in his neck protruding. He got up and walked swiftly over to the French doors. He looked back at Logan and said, "Please keep me posted."

✻ ✻ ✻

Two days later, Logan was typing police reports for another case when the telephone rang.

"This is Trent Morgan. Do you have any leads?"

"I'm afraid not, sir. My colleagues and I have been talking to farmers who live near the pond. They didn't see a thing."

"What about at the Greenback Tavern? You told my son that you dropped off a picture of her there."

"That's true, but the regular clientele didn't recognize her. Neither did staffers."

"You must do something, Detective Logan!"

"I've done all that I can do, Mr. Morgan. From what I understand, your wife has a need to get attention. And this isn't the first time she has pulled a stunt like this."

"That's true, but—"

"I'm sure that she will show up eventually."

"Why do I have a feeling that you are going to stop looking?"

"I get the feeling she doesn't want to be found."

"What about the blood? Somebody has taken her!"

"I don't think so, Mr. Morgan. I believe she cut her hands when the front window shattered. Maybe she wandered off from the shock of it all."

"Then you really must look for her!"

"I'm sure there are some places we haven't checked. There are a lot of back roads in this neck of the woods."

"So you'll continue looking?" Trent pressed.

"I will for a little while. But I still think it's a marital problem. Good day, Mr. Morgan." Then he hung up.

# CHAPTER 5

Throngs of newspaper reporters and TV news crews waited outside the *Main Line Chronicle* building. Trent Morgan was late for his 10:00 a.m. press conference. Thirty minutes later, he came out the front door and someone shouted, "There he is!"

Cameras flashed one after another as he approached them. He had not shaved, and his eyes were red. He started speaking, coughed, and started over again. His hands trembled as he read a prepared statement. His voice sounded hoarse.

"Good morning, everyone. Thank you for coming. I called you all here to announce the disappearance of my wife, Claire. One week ago today, she packed her suitcase and left our home near Lancaster, Pennsylvania, about eight o'clock that night.

"Local police found our 2015 Mercedes-Benz abandoned near a pond about ten miles east of our home. She had apparently hit a tree, and the front of the vehicle was severely damaged. The front window was smashed. Police reported seeing slivers of glass on the front seat, along with bloodstains. She left the keys in the ignition. Her pocketbook was on the front seat, but nothing was stolen.

They also discovered her suitcase in the trunk. They checked its contents, and nothing seemed to be missing. In fact, there was a large sum of money inside.

"The police dragged the pond and did not find my wife's body. They interviewed farmers who live nearby. They hung up snapshots of Claire at a local tavern. So far, no one has seen her. And no one heard the car hit the tree. I am offering a $25,000 reward to anyone who has information about my wife's whereabouts. Thank you very much."

"Do the police suspect foul play?" a reporter shouted.

"They won't say."

"When was the car found?"

"It was discovered about six thirty the next morning."

"Do the police have any leads?"

"Not at this time. They believe she may have wandered off. Maybe she was disoriented. Or maybe she hit her head and lost her memory. That is why I have asked you all here. I am begging for your help. If anyone has seen her, please call my office. Thank you all for coming."

He went back into the building with reporters at his heels. They were frantically pumping him for more information. He fought his way through the door and shouted, "Nothing further! Thank you for coming."

\* \* \*

The next morning, a large photograph of Claire Morgan was on the front page of the *Main Line Chronicle* with a headline that read:

**"Publisher's wife missing; Police suspect foul play"**

PHILADELPHIA—NEWSPAPER publisher Trent Morgan is offering a $25,000 reward for anyone with information about his wife, Claire, who has been missing for over a week.

*"Main Line Chronicle"* critic Mac Yeager was seen arguing with fashion model Michelle du Prix during a party at their home in Townsend, Pennsylvania, on May 24. According to eyewitness accounts, a fight erupted between Morgan and Yeager.

"Michelle was angry about a play I panned," Yeager said. "She started hitting me and Trent came to defend his girlfriend—I stand by my critique. She should stick to modeling."

Guests watched twenty-six-year-old William Morgan rush in to help break up the fight. "My father was livid. I'm sure the fight has some bearing on my mother's disappearance. It must have been devastating when she saw him with another woman. Michelle has designs on my father. She's pressuring him to file for divorce."

Trent Morgan declined to comment."

Newspaper headlines across the country were just as crazy with stories about the mysterious disappearance of Claire Morgan with headlines that read: **"Publisher's wife crashes car and disappears," "Claire Morgan Missing; Her husband offers $25,000 reward," "Slashed tires; Woman Vanishes."**

It didn't take long for the story to go viral on social media. Trent Morgan's plea for help was on cable news stations morning, noon, and night. Local TV news stations also picked up his pleas for help: "I am offering a $25,000 reward to anyone who has information about my wife..."

Detective Joe Flosky was buried behind the newspaper when Logan arrived at work. Frank leaned over his shoulder and read the front-page headline. He yanked it out of Flosky's hands and went over to his desk.

"Hey, I was reading that!"

"You'll get it back." Logan groaned as he read it. "I don't believe this! Did you see this?" The headline on the paper he shook at Flosky was **"Pearls found by Claire Morgan's car!"**

"I was afraid you'd see it."

"I never said that."

He scanned the story and grumbled. "Where did these fiction writers come up with this crap?"

"Take it easy. I'm sure that newspaper reporters across the country have gotten things off a bit."

"I can't believe this. Trent Morgan has nerve enough to badger me about the case, and then he leaks incorrect information to the press."

"It might not have been him. Maybe the reporters got it wrong."

Logan shook his head. "I don't know. If it wasn't so slow around here, I'd drop the case and do something else." He went back to his desk and continued reading the article.

"We haven't been bombarded with cases lately, Logan."

"So I have to deal with this jerk."

"Look on the bright side. Maybe somebody will be robbed, and we'll be back in business."

"Whatever."

"You gotta admit it's a really strange case."

Logan nodded his agreement. When he finished reading the article, he dumped the newspaper in the trash can where it belonged. Flosky went over and scooped it up and read the rest of it.

"Maybe Trent bumped Claire off and dumped her body somewhere," Logan blurted out. "And he set up this whole thing with the stuff we found in her vehicle."

"You could be right. In cases like this, a husband or wife usually does it. This one involves another woman. He probably wanted to get her out of the way so he could marry his hottie girlfriend. Have you seen her? She's gorgeous!"

"It's something to think about," Logan agreed. "Maybe we should call in dogs to search the woods."

\* \* \*

Todd Stevens knocked on Trent's office door and popped his head in. "Are you busy?"

"You must be kidding. What can I do for you? Make it quick."

Todd sat across from him. Trent was checking national search databases. He signed off and turned to face him.

Todd handed him the *Golden Star*, a competing newspaper. "I don't like being the bearer of bad news, but here goes."

Trent scowled at the front-page photo of Michelle du Prix entering his Madison Avenue condominium.

"That son of a bitch. Their photographers must have been following her. It's the only way they could have gotten a shot like this."

"It didn't take Mac Yeager long to go to another newspaper."

"If you can call the *Golden Star*, a real newspaper. Take it away!"

"I'm sorry."

Trent fumed as he sifted through the stacks of mail on his desk.

"Do the police have any leads?" Todd asked.

"No," Trent replied without taking his eyes off the mail.

Todd got to his feet. "I'm sorry I bothered you." He closed the door on his way out.

# CHAPTER 6

Penny Lane hadn't been this happy in a long time. At thirty-four, she had endured years of ups and downs with Detective Frank Logan. He had finally popped the question at their favorite Italian restaurant in Philadelphia. For the past couple of years, she had been reminding him that she wasn't getting any younger. She tossed out subtle hints about all her friends who were getting married, but he always changed the subject or pretended that he didn't know what she was talking about. She knew he wasn't that dense. He had a sharp mind and solved the most complex homicide cases. He was just conveniently playing dumb, and they both knew it. All that didn't matter now. They were getting married!

She knew what she was getting when she started dating him. His quiet intensity drew her in—as it did with everyone else who crossed his path. Their relationship hit a rocky patch, and they broke up. Then they got back together only to break up again. He didn't fit in with her coworkers in Philadelphia. He acted like a bull in a china closet when she got him to do anything cultural like going to exhibits at art museums or attending parties with her coworkers at the bank. She got irritated that he only wanted her to hang out at Barney's with his pals from the police station. He never hung out with her friends from work, and she called him on it.

After many years of listening to her parents telling her to steer clear of Frank, she refused to listen. He took baby steps to the altar. Asking her to move in with him was a major step in the right direction, despite the fact that she had to make the long commute back and forth from an exciting advertising job in Philly. He spent long hours at work, and they only saw each other at night and weekends. They had discussed moving halfway but stayed in his cramped apartment in Townsend.

Two years ago, they got to spend more time with each other when her boss at the advertising firm was poisoned at a party held in her honor at their home on the outskirts of Townsend. She played office spy and helped Frank crack the case.

The one thing that they had in common was their desire to help people. Despite his often gruff exterior when he was upset that a case wasn't going anywhere, he basically was a giver. That's what made her stay with him despite their struggles.

Fortunately for her, it had been a slow summer in Townsend. For some unknown reason, the crime rate had gone way down. Residents had grown fearful after a series of mysterious murders of members of a prominent Townsend wine-making family last winter. There were wild rumors and gossip for months. The stories took on a life of their own.

Now wild stories circulated about the mysterious disappearance of Claire Morgan. Her photograph was plastered all over the internet and TV and newspapers and magazines. Every alleged sighting was more bizarre than the one before it. Reporters clung to the story because there was nothing better to write about at the moment.

The usual Saturday night crowd hovered on bar stools watching the Phillies game as they drank their beers. Instead of talking about sports and politics, they couldn't stop talking about Claire Morgan's disappearance. They were not the least bit shy sharing their theories with Logan and his colleagues. The persistent rumor that just wouldn't go away was that Trent Morgan had murdered his wife and hid her body.

Frank didn't want to discuss the case. He had had enough. He was tired of listening to crackpots telling him they saw her. He had more important things to worry about.

He looked across at Penny and grinned dumbly at her. Flosky was mouthing off about his theory about what happened to Claire Morgan. Joe's voice was booming when he got started on something. "She was definitely abducted by aliens!"

Frank rolled his eyes. "If that happened, don't you think people would've reported spotting mysterious bright lights in the sky?"

It was a miracle. At last, Flosky shut his big mouth. "Then what the hell happened to her?" he finally asked.

"I don't know, and I don't care," Logan said. "We've done all we can do at this point."

"Frank, I'm surprised at you," Gwen Winters said. "I've never known you to give up on something like that before."

"If she skipped town, there's nothing we can do."

"We can just listen to geniuses like Flosky, here," Harry Winters said.

They all erupted into fits of laughter. Joe shook his head in disgust.

"But it's true what Joe said," Penny said. "I read all about it in the *National Inquirer*. And there were pictures too."

They all burst into uncontrollable laughter.

"Not you too," Frank grumbled.

"Well, if it's in the *National Inquirer*, it has to be true," Joe said.

Frank took a swig of beer and looked at Joe. "Didn't your mother ever tell you to use an inside voice?"

"Yeah. I could never figure out what she was talking about."

"You're too damn loud, man!" Frank cried. "Tone it down a bit."

Gwen looked at Penny and grinned. "So your big day is coming soon."

"I can't wait!" Penny exclaimed.

"I bet."

"It's good that things have been so slow around here lately. You get so cranky when you're working on a case, Frank," Penny said.

"You knew what you were stepping into when you started going out with me," Frank said. "We discussed it in great detail, as I remember."

"Well, you deserve a vacation after the vineyard murders."

Frank groaned. "Don't remind me."

"Well, at least one good thing came out of it," Penny said.

"What good thing could have possibly come out of such a grisly case like that, Penny?" asked Gwen.

"I got proposed to."

Gwen grinned. "Oh, right."

"I had no idea there was so much involved in getting married," Penny added.

"You didn't listen to me when I said we should just go to Vegas and get hitched in an Elvis chapel or something," Frank said.

"It figures you would think of something like that," Gwen said. "That's not at all romantic. If you're getting married, you need to do it right. Lots of people you know in a big church."

"I keep worrying that I'll be walking down the aisle with my dad, and Frank will be called out on police business just as I get to the altar."

Joe winked at Penny. "Or maybe you'll run out of the church and vanish like Claire Morgan."

Penny's eyes sparkled. "I would never run out on the man of my dreams."

"You'd better not," Frank said.

A George Strait song blasted on the radio. Gwen and Harry got up to dance. Frank and Penny followed them onto the small dance floor. Joe leaned back in his seat and swigged his beer. He looked at the flat-screen TV over the bar. Another picture of Claire Morgan flashed on the screen. He ventured over to the bar and avidly watched another wild story about her disappearance. Then it was on to local news. He grinned dumbly at the woman behind the bar and swigged his beer.

☆   ☆   ☆

Rob Watkins was a wiry twenty-three-year-old reporter from the *Lancaster Times*. Although he worked out, he still looked thin. He was not meant to be a body-builder. He grew a mustache to look older, but it did not take hold. He looked ridiculous and had to endure ribbing from friends. He compensated for his slim physique by acting tough. It was the only way people would take him seriously. The tough act didn't pan out either. It wasn't in his nature to be tough. He had an annoying squeaky voice that didn't come off as tough either. It smelled like he had taken a bath in cologne. He had on lime-green shorts and a red-checkered shirt with a pen and notepad in the pocket. He wore tan Docksiders on rather large feet.

He entered the police station and waved at Holly, the dispatcher. She rolled her eyes. "Hi, Rob."

"Hi, Holly. How's it going?"

"It could be better."

"Is there anything exciting going on?"

She yawned in his face. "It's been a slow week."

"Has Detective Logan found out anything new about Claire Morgan's disappearance?"

"No."

"That's too bad." He leaned on the counter and asked, "Are you busy Friday night?"

Holly opened her purse and flipped through her date book. She looked back at him and frowned. "I'm afraid so, Rob."

"How about Saturday or Sunday?"

She looked at the schedule. "It's a real bad time for me, Rob. Maybe we could try it next week." She liked him, but she did not want to hang around him. He wasn't her type.

She started talking about why she was so busy. Then the telephone rang, and she took a message. Rob heard Logan yelling in the office. The search dogs were unable to locate Claire's allegedly missing body. So they were back to square one. Logan's patience was fragile at this point.

"So the dogs weren't able to pick up a scent."

"Maybe we should call in a psychic." It was Detective Flosky talking now. Rob would recognize that annoying nasal accent anywhere.

"At this point, I'm ready to try anything," Logan said.

"There has to be a logical explanation."

"Well, right now there doesn't seem to be one. Every day, Trent Morgan calls us for updates, and we don't have anything to tell him!"

"Or his son calls," added Flosky.

"It's as if she vanished off the face of the earth. I've talked to farmers up and down the road. They didn't see her."

"I've been giving it some thought. I think I know where she might have gone."

"Clue me in, pal!"

"This place is crazy with Amish farms."

"That's for sure."

"An Amish family lives down the road from the meadow where Mrs. Morgan crashed her car. Their house is down a long dirt road. It can easily be missed when you're driving."

"Do you know how to get there?"

"I can take you there. But it might be best if I just give you directions. They're private people and might not like it if we're both there." He drew a map and handed it to Logan.

"Thanks, Flosky!"

He headed out the door and Flosky yelled, "Watch out for horse manure!"

Logan smiled at Holly and Rob on his way out.

"I don't mean to be rude," Rob said quickly. "But I've got a deadline! I'll be back, Holly!" Then he chased after the detective.

Logan was halfway to his car when Watkins caught up to him. He waved Rob off like an annoying bug as he got in his car. "No comment!"

"Just one question, Detective Logan. Have you found out anything?"

"Leave me alone!" He turned on the ignition and sped out of the parking lot.

✢   ✢   ✢

A few minutes later, Logan pulled down a winding dirt road that went on for two miles. He parked next to a red barn and went over to it. He did not heed Flosky's warning and stepped in a pile of horse manure. He stood on his right foot while holding up his left one. At that moment, an Amish man came out of the barn and went over to him. He had a long white beard and glasses. His hands were rough. His clothes were plain.

He looked at the newcomer in astonishment, suppressing a laugh. "I can get my wife to clean your shoe."

Logan looked down to avoid embarrassing himself further. He was obviously a city boy. "I'd appreciate it."

"I am Zeb Yoder. What can I do for you?"

"I'm Detective Logan. I need your help."

They walked silently to the house, and the old man invited him to sit at the kitchen table. His wife, Sarah, took one look at Logan's shoe and suppressed a laugh. It must have been hard not to. She looked like a truly happy woman. Her eyes sparkled the moment the stranger entered the room. Her cheeks were plump and rosy. There seemed to be pure joy in her eyes.

She collected a bucket and went out to the pump. Logan handed Zeb the police sketch of Claire Morgan. "Have you seen this woman, sir?"

"No," the old man said quietly.

"You would remember seeing someone from my world around these parts, wouldn't you?"

"That is so."

Sarah returned carrying a bucket of water. She laid it on the floor and went over to the washbasin to get brown soap.

"May I have your shoe, sir?" she asked.

Logan peeled it off and handed it to her. She leaned over the sink and scrubbed hard.

"Are there other Amish families around here?" Logan asked.

"The Swarzentrubers live across the way," she said.

"Did any of your family members see anything?"

Zeb nodded. "My son Jacob lives just down the path. He told me about a woman he saw that night who was hurt. We always try to help people in times of trouble. Maybe you should talk to him."

Sarah handed Logan back his shoe, and he thanked her. They went back outside, and Zeb pointed to a small wooden house. Logan shook his hand and thanked him again. Then he started toward Jacob's house with a wet shoe.

*   *   *

Logan knocked, and a young woman clad in a purple-cotton dress and white bonnet opened the door.

"May I help you?" she asked.

He explained his situation. Then he showed her the police sketch. "Have you seen this woman?"

She shook her head. Just then, a robust man with a flaming red beard and equally plain attire stood next to her. He looked down at the sketch. "I have seen this woman you are looking for."

"That's great!" Logan exclaimed. "When did you see her?"

"It was about two weeks ago. I was riding my buggy down past the pond and saw her sitting by her vehicle."

"What time was that?"

"The sun was setting. It was getting dark."

"Was she in pain?"

He scratched his beard and grunted. "Yes, she cut her head. And her hands were bleeding. I went to help her, but she said she was all right."

"Did she say anything else?"

"She was worried about the vehicle. Her head was bleeding, and I took her back here so my wife could care for her."

"Then what happened?"

"My wife was not here. She was helping the women make a quilt for my sister's wedding. So I put a cold cloth on her head and told her to rest. Then I went to put my horse in the stable, and she was not here when I came back."

"Did anybody see where she went?"

"It was dark by then."

"Thank you, Mr. Yoder. You've been a lot of help."

Logan went out, looking down the whole way back to his police car. He did not want to step in anything an animal left behind.

\* \* \*

Back at the police station, Logan had to contend with Rob Watkins again.

"I know you went to an Amish farm," Rob said. "I overheard you talking to Detective Flosky. What did you find out?"

"If I tell you, will you promise to leave me alone?"

"All right."

He told him what he found out from the Amish farmer. Rob jotted notes.

"Anything else?" Watkins pressed.

Flosky went over to them and said, "I've been getting phone calls all day. Apparently people from neighboring towns spotted a mysterious veiled woman wandering around that night. It's probably just a hoax."

Logan groaned. "You think?"

"Why didn't they say anything before?" Rob wondered.

"That's what I'd like to know," Logan agreed. "Did you follow up on it?"

"I thought we could do it together."

"You suffer from an acute case of separation anxiety, Flosky. You can't do anything without me there to tell you what to do. Come on, let's go."

Rob Watkins raced after them. Logan sped down the road, trying to lose the pesky reporter. Try as he might, the annoying kid reporter stayed on his tail.

A few minutes later, Rob pulled next to Logan's patrol vehicle, and walked hurriedly after them. Logan went over to him and set some ground rules.

"If you insist on hanging around me, Rob, just don't get in my way," he growled. "You got that?"

"Don't worry, I won't say a word," Rob promised.

They went into a diner at the height of the lunch rush. Flosky hunkered down at a barstool and asked customers if they had seen Claire Morgan. Logan went up to a heavyset woman with red hair tied in a bun. He showed her the police sketch and asked if she had seen her. Rob stood by his side, pad in hand.

She adjusted her reading glasses and studied it a moment. "I think so."

"When did you see her?" Logan asked.

"Well, I was coming out of the grocery store, when I saw this woman go by. She was odd-looking, that's for sure. She had a veil on. I couldn't get a good look at her face, but I'm pretty sure it was her."

"Do you know who she is?"

"Isn't she that rich lady that lives up by Townsend?"

"Looks just like the woman they've been showing on TV, right?" She nodded.

"You never actually saw her, did you?"

The woman hesitated a moment and shook her head.

"You just heard a lot of wild gossip around town, right?"

"Yeah."

Logan thanked her and went on to other customers.

"How'd you know?" Rob asked him.

"It's the reward. People are coming out of the woodwork now that they know there's money involved."

Logan soon realized it was a colossal waste of time. Customers thought they had seen her but really could not be sure. At that point, he and Flosky talked to people on opposite sides of the street.

An old man leaned on his cane, staring at the police sketch. He grunted before saying, "Yeah, I saw her."

"When did you see her, sir?" Logan asked.

"I saw her wandering down the street Tuesday…no, I was playing bingo that night." He scratched his scraggly beard, lost in thought. "Wait a minute. It was Wednesday night. My doctor told me I need to exercise. My legs aren't like they used to be, you see. He said I need to exercise."

"What time did you see her?" Logan asked patiently.

"Who?"

Logan pointed to the sketch, maintaining his calm tone as he said, "This woman, sir. What time did you see her?"

The man shrugged his shoulders. "I would've remembered seeing her. She's beautiful! No, I don't think it was her. The woman I saw had a veil over her face."

"Now we're getting somewhere. Did you see where she went?"

The old man pointed to the street corner. "I just saw her wandering around like she was lost. She passed by me twice."

"Did she say anything to you?"

He scratched his head. "Not that I can think of. It was the strangest thing. She just came out of nowhere and waited till I saw her. Then, she just disappeared into the night like a ghost."

Logan thanked him and met Flosky back at the car.

"What did you find out?" Flosky asked him.

"Not much. How about you?"

"It was a total waste of time. I'm sorry I dragged you out here."

Logan grunted and got in the car. Flosky slid next to him.

Rob Watkins made a mad dash back to the newspaper office to crank out his story. But it was old news by the time it hit the newsstand the following week. The story went viral on social media. National newspapers and magazines treated the story like it was gold. Americans could not get enough. It got wilder every time people picked up a newspaper or magazine. Headlines screamed for attention with tantalizing teasers:

**Amish farmer spots publisher's wife; She wandered off.**

**Mysterious veiled woman seen in neighboring towns; Mrs. Morgan rumored to be okay.**

**Mrs. Morgan seen by Amish farmer; vanishes.**

**Veiled blond woman seen in Richmond.**

**Lady in black seen in Memphis.**

**Publisher's wife seen in San Antonio.**

Have you seen Mrs. Morgan?

Police call off search for New York socialite; Trent Morgan still looking.

Claire Morgan abducted by aliens.

Have you seen me?

# CHAPTER 7

Logan had grown accustomed to his cramped apartment. He wasn't there enough to notice. That all changed when Penny moved in with him. He was ecstatic that she agreed to live with him, but it made the limited surroundings more noticeable.

He was a man of simple needs. The only thing that mattered was that he had a place to stay and food to eat. His entertainment center consisted of a new small flat-screen TV, a stereo, and a laptop, plus some old VCR tapes and DVDs. He got most of his furniture from Goodwill or other thrift stores. Some of it had been there when he moved in, and some of it came from his old apartment in Philadelphia. Penny's personal touches included plants on the window ledge and large ones hanging above it. She replaced the curtains with lacy navy-blue ones. Framed pictures of her family were on the bureau and end tables. An eleven-by-fourteen color portrait of the happy couple figured prominently over the sofa. He had on his police uniform. She looked stunning in a burgundy evening dress.

The rest of the apartment had a definite Logan flair about it. Portraits of Frank and his father in uniform with the American flag behind them were side by side. He proudly displayed his police academy diploma next to the one his father earned four decades earlier, along with various awards and medals they both received over the years. Framed snapshots of Frank's friends at the Townsend Police Department hung next to them. There were pictures of Joe and Harry horsing around at the station. There was one of Frank behind bars. The kitchen was smaller than cramped for one person and was that much worse with two people rustling around to cook meals.

Their family pictures hung on opposite walls in the bedroom. A collage of Penny's childhood and early adolescence was in a large frame at the center. Pictures of her brother and sister were in similar frames at either side. None of them were spared from snapshots of their gawky stages. The typical Sears family portrait for the grandparents' Christmas gift figured prominently above Penny's collage. No one had to know that they had gotten into a nasty tiff just before the portrait was taken when she was thirteen. Graduations and other important events filled out the wall.

Hanging by the window, there was a framed picture of Frank's mother at the beach when she was in college. Next to it was the last picture taken of him with his parents. It was taken when he was a gawky kid. In between them, there was one of Frank in his mother's arms when he was six months old. There were other ones of his father in uniform. He added ones of Sergeant Tony Mancuso, his former partner in Philadelphia, and a couple of other ones with his colleagues that he found in a box in his closet. He had learned so much from working with them. The skills he acquired there carried over to his life at the Townsend Police Station.

On Saturday morning, he stepped out of the shower and dried off. He went over to his bureau and pulled open the second drawer from the bottom. He reached for a maroon T-shirt with a police academy insignia on it. He looked at the framed picture on the bureau of Penny in his arms at the beach as they hammed it up for the camera. She had on a sexy bikini and he looked like a macho man without his shirt on. A framed photo of Penny wearing a Santa Claus hat was to the right. Her effervescent grin always put him in a cheerful mood. In the middle, there was a gold framed picture of him when he was twelve with his grandfather that had been taken on a fishing trip. They had on fishing getups and were holding rods.

He got dressed and wandered into the kitchen to make coffee. He rubbed his eyes and looked at the wedding magazines scattered across the dining room table. Penny jotted notes in a thick notebook, while her mother, Maribeth, and her sister, Lois, helped her go over the last-minute wedding arrangements. They were so engrossed in what they were doing, that they had no idea he was there.

He went over to Penny and kissed her from behind. "My, my. Aren't you busy beavers?"

Penny looked up at him and beamed. "Good morning."

He looked at Lois and Maribeth. "My God, you're here early!" He glanced at his wristwatch. "It's almost nine."

"We decided to make a day of it," Maribeth said. "How are you doing, Frank?"

"Not too bad."

"Any interesting cases?" Lois asked.

"Fortunately, not at the moment. Just the missing lady case."

"I've heard a lot of wild stories about that one," Maribeth said.

"And they get crazier every time you pick up the paper," Lois added. "Have you made any progress with it?"

Frank shook his head. "We've been looking, but I don't have a clue where she is. She seems to have dropped off the face of the earth after the Amish farmer saw her. And don't get me started about the mysterious veiled woman that townspeople reported seeing."

"Maybe she was abducted by aliens," Lois suggested.

"Oh no, not you too!" Frank groaned. "I thought you had better sense than that."

"Well, you obviously don't have any other explanations for what happened to the lady."

"I think you have seen too many sci-fi movies." He scratched his stubble. "I wish a real juicy case would pop up soon. It's getting really dull around here."

"Well, I guess you don't think getting married is juicy enough," Penny said.

He leaned down to kiss her again. "Of course it is."

They concentrated their attention on flower arrangements. He grabbed his keys on the rack by the door. "I'm going to the bakery. Want anything?"

"Some danish pastries would be great!" Lois called back to him. "The ones with the cherry filling."

"You got it. I'll be right back." He headed out.

"He probably just used that as an excuse to get away from us," Maribeth said.

Penny shook her head. "No, I think he's just hungry. We ran out of eggs. And there's no cereal."

Lois and Maribeth disagreed on which flowers to select. Penny jotted down the ones that they liked. By midmorning, they settled on a half dozen flowers that they really liked. Frank returned with muffins and pastries. They showed him the ones they were thinking about, and he waved his hands. "Don't include me on this," he begged. "Whichever ones you choose will be the best ones of all."

"That is really a diplomatic way of getting out of it," Lois pointed out.

"Well, I just don't want to get blamed if it doesn't look right. Do you mind if I turn on the TV?"

"Go ahead," Penny said.

He flicked it on and grimaced at coverage of the missing woman. He watched for a couple of minutes and then turned on the History Channel.

*　*　*

At the airport, Michelle du Prix got in Trent's BMW, and a few minutes later, he pulled onto the highway. They were both silent. He concentrated on traffic, and she spent most of the time texting.

"I hate this, Trent," she said at last. "Talk to me."

His tone was cold. "Wait until we arrive at the house."

"You're treating me like a leper!"

"I'm trying not to get us into an accident."

About two hours later, he drove up the entrance road that led to Morgan House. A look of superiority flashed on her face when she eyed the sprawling house and the magnificent grounds.

She got out abruptly and marched inside. He carried her bag into the hall. He pulled out the handle and slowly lifted it upstairs. He put it in the guest room in the old section of the house and joined her in the study.

Elizabeth Ashton went to the kitchen to get them coffee and sneered when she knew Trent could not see her. Trent closed the door and sat facing Michelle.

"I think we should stop seeing each other for a while," he announced. "At least not in public."

Her eyes widened. "You drag me all the way out here to tell me this? I demand to know why."

He handed her the latest scandal sheet. "I can't take much more of this. We can't even eat in public without these fools getting in our faces."

Her eyes glazed with rage when she saw a large photograph of her coming out of Trent's Manhattan apartment building on the front page. The headline read, **"While the wife's away, mice will play."**

She seethed with anger as she read the first paragraph out loud. "While media mogul Trent Morgan's wife, Claire, has been missing, restaurant owners in Manhattan have seen him socializing with actress and model Michelle du Prix. Claire Morgan disappeared on May 26th when her 2015 Mercedes-Benz went off a country road near Lancaster, Pennsylvania…"

She shoved it back and said, "You're upset over some damned screwball paper?"

"We can do things here, where we're away from the press."

"Why can't you put them in their place?"

"I have a lot of enemies at competing papers. They love to watch me squirm."

"You just feel guilty about how miserably you treated Claire."

"That could be, but I can't take much more of this public scrutiny."

There was a knock at the door. Elizabeth stuck her head in and asked curtly, "More coffee, Miss du Prix?"

She held out the cup and smiled. "Please."

Elizabeth feigned a cheerful smile as she poured. Then she went back to the kitchen.

"It has to be this way for the time being," Trent said. "You have to understand."

Michelle jumped to her feet and shouted, "I understand, all right! Claire has always been very much a part of our relationship. Here and there! Wherever the hell she might be."

"It's not just that. I'm swamped at work right now. I'm in the process of acquiring a newspaper in Annapolis."

Michelle folded her arms and pouted. "I'm pretty busy myself. I've got to go back to New York and do another photo shoot."

"I'm glad you understand."

"No, I don't understand!" She stormed out.

She didn't feel the least bit guilty about being with Trent while his wife was "missing." She had her sights on the master bedroom, curled up beside Trent. She didn't like being relegated to the guest bedroom. Her lips curled with disgust when she looked around the cramped room. It was not at all what she was accustomed to. She was used to a lot of space. She could have cared less that Claire had decorated it with antiques from the Colonial era. Michelle wasn't one for rustic old rooms.

The furniture looked uncomfortable. She cringed when she sat on the four-poster bed. The mattress was as hard as a rock. She glanced across the room at pastel portraits of long dead ancestors hanging in domed frames. Their stern expressions gave her the creeps. They probably didn't know what the word *fun* meant.

The fan on the bureau was on full blast, and it still felt like an oven in there. She opened the window and looked out. At least there was a nice view of the yard and garden.

She marched out and decided to take a walk to blow off steam.

✻  ✻  ✻

A week later, Logan pulled next to the lawn and started toward Morgan House. Bill appeared from around the hedges. He had such an earnest look that Logan could not bear to give him the bad news. But it had to be done.

"Thank you for coming, Detective Logan," Bill said quickly. "Have you found out anything new?"

"I'm afraid not."

"But there must be something that you can do."

"As you know, there have been a lot of false reports in the newspapers and on social media. I tracked down my last lead two weeks ago. There's nothing more I can do. I'm sorry."

"Do you believe the reports?"

"Some of them are pretty farfetched. But some of them seem logical."

"What do you mean?"

"I believe she may have hooked up with someone. Maybe a wealthy businessman. She's probably wearing a disguise and using an assumed name. She obviously isn't using credit cards. She left them in her purse. If she had any other cards on her, we would have been able to do a credit check. The case has gotten people so excited, they would believe anything."

"Please keep looking."

"I'll do what I can, but I can't guarantee we'll find her. It doesn't help that your father mentioned the reward money in his press conference. Now every crackpot out there just wants to cash in on it. I'll let you know if I find out anything new." He walked down the cobblestone walkway, toward his car.

Trent popped his head out the front door and waved at him. "Good morning, Detective Logan. Please don't leave yet. I need to have a word with you."

He hurriedly descended the front steps and went up to the detective. Trent had on a white tennis shirt and tan khaki shorts.

"Have you found out anything new?"

Logan told him what he had just discussed with Bill. "I just don't see this case leading anywhere. At least not in this area. I believe she's alive somewhere and out of my jurisdiction. If I find out anything, you'll be the first to know. So long, Mr. Morgan."

He opened his car door and slid behind the wheel. He was about to turn the key when he saw Bill go over to his father and wave his hands at him. Father and son were standing practically nose to nose. Logan rolled down the window to hear what they were saying. They were so busy yelling, they didn't realize that he was still in his car.

"Are you suddenly feeling guilty?"

"This isn't the time," Trent said through clenched teeth.

"You're pathetic! Sometimes I can't believe we're related." He marched down the path leading to the backyard.

"Bill, wait!" Trent started to go after him when the front door opened and Michelle appeared on the porch with a bulky suitcase by her side.

"Let him go," she said. "He has good sense. And so do I. It's obvious we won't be able to have a romantic get-together here any time soon. I'm going back to New York."

"You just don't understand."

"You need to make a choice, Trent. Do you love Claire or me? And just so you know, you don't need to bother taking me back to the airport. I called a taxi. It will be here in a few minutes."

She laboriously pushed the suitcase down the steps. Trent rushed after her and stood on the driveway, waving his arms and pleading.

"Michelle, stay here tonight. Don't leave like this."

She stopped in her tracks and looked back at him. "I'll stay if you promise not to mention Claire or the newspaper pictures of us."

He reached for her hand and pressed hard. "All right."

"I'd better call the taxi company and cancel the order."

Logan whistled as he started the engine. Glancing at the rear view mirror, he saw Trent pulling the suitcase up the front steps and following her inside.

*　　*　　*

Frank and Gramps spent a relaxing day fishing at their favorite spot near Valley Forge. The water was like glass. A tranquil feeling came over them. It was a nice, quiet time to be together before Frank married Penny.

Gramps laughed. "So you're actually tying the knot. I never thought you'd do it."

"Well, I guess you were wrong." Frank felt a tug and reeled in a bass. He pulled it off the hook and tossed it in the bucket.

"I'm so happy for you two. You deserve it after all that you've been through to get to the altar."

"I know."

"I think Penny has really made an impact on your life."

"I know. I didn't make it easy for her. And neither did she."

"Well, I'm glad you worked everything out."

Frank concentrated on fishing. They were quiet.

"Do you have any leads on that disappearing lady?"

Frank shook his head and grunted. "It's as if she vanished from the face of the earth."

"If you ask me, I'd say the husband did it. He probably hid the body somewhere and left everything in her car that way to throw you off."

At this point, he was tired of hearing everyone's theories about what happened to the woman. He and Flosky had searched the area for two weeks and had come up with nothing. "If she is alive, she's not in our jurisdiction anyway. We've been looking, and no one has seen her. Except the Amish farmer. And he said she just walked off when he left her alone."

"So that proves her husband didn't kill her then. Maybe they met up somewhere, and he bumped her off."

"It doesn't sound likely, Gramps. She'll show up when she wants to show up. She's obviously upset that her husband is dumping her for a younger, sexier woman. It's like Trent said. She's doing it to get attention."

"Well, I'm sure you and Penny will never have that kind of problem."

"No, we won't. It took us long enough to get to this point, I'm not going to blow it this time. She has made me a different man, Gramps. She makes me happy."

Gramps wiped away tears. "I'm glad."

There was another long silence.

"Your folks would be so pleased," Gramps said at last.

Frank said nothing.

"You know, Penny's always right. Right?"

Frank nodded and grunted.

"She really has turned you around. You used to be so pig-headed. I don't know how she did it."

"I don't know either."

Conversation shifted to baseball. And then they talked about how hot it was. Gramps griped about how awful the beach traffic was. By the time they packed it up for the day, the parking lot was practically full. The drive back to Gramps's apartment in Jenkintown was bumper to bumper. It was a beautiful Saturday afternoon in June. It would only get a lot more crowded with the Fourth of July approaching.

Frank arrived back at his apartment later that night. After a long, hot shower, he snuggled with Penny on the sofa and watched the middle of a Hallmark romance with her.

# CHAPTER 8

Penny's heartbeat accelerates. She walks down the aisle with her father's hand in hers. All her friends and family beam with excitement. They walk in slow motion. They will never get there.

She takes one look at Frank at the altar, her face aglow.

She is about to take his hand. Her father pulls up the veil.

She stands next to Frank; their eyes are on the minister. He utters prayers that she cannot hear. They sound jumbled up, like he's in a washing machine.

Then it happens. Frank's smartphone goes off.

"I'm sorry, I have to take this," he says. His words make a whirring noise. She watches him rush out of the church with Joe Flosky right behind him.

Maybe he should marry Flosky!

Everyone stands in shock and horror. No one knows what to do.

She screams—

Penny awoke with a start. She had been having the same dream two weeks before the wedding. Now she knew how Frank felt when he had had nightmares shortly after moving to Townsend. Fortunately, they went away several months after his transfer.

Her current fear that Frank would ditch her at the altar was only temporary. Would he do it? In the back of her mind, she pictured his colleagues betting whether they would actually get married or whether Frank would go off to investigate a body found in a field or something. If he did, she'd be the star player in his next investigation. Maybe that would be a way that they could spend more time together.

*   *   *

Penny gazed at herself in the mirror, fussing over her makeup and shoulder-length dark hair. Her mother and sister helped put her veil on.

"You look fine," Maribeth said before Penny could complain about her appearance.

Lois grinned. "Then I guess we're good to go. Are you ready?"

"Ready as I'll ever be, I guess," Penny said.

Lois reached for her sister's hand and helped her to her feet. "Then let's get you hitched."

Before going out, Penny looked at herself from head to foot once again. The wedding dress accentuated her slender figure. They started to head toward the door when Maribeth took a moment to adjust Penny's veil. She sized it up and gave her the thumbs-up. They walked toward the church's vestibule. Her father beamed when he saw them coming toward him.

He gushed, his eyes moistening. "You look beautiful, honey."

She reached for his hands and squeezed them. "Thanks, Dad!"

"What's the latest report?" asked Lois. "Is he here or not?"

George nodded. "He was there a minute ago. I didn't see him rushing out the front door with his partner to chase after a dead body or something. Unless they tore out the back way."

"I don't hear a loud commotion going on in there," Lois said. She peeked through the double doors and saw the groom at the altar. "He's still there."

"Good, let's hope we can keep it that way."

The wedding march started playing, and an usher opened the doors. Penny held back tears of joy as they walked down the long red carpeted aisle, passing by all her friends and family, who loved and supported her. Frank looked dashing in his dress uniform. He was glowing. The groomsmen stood proudly in their dress uniforms. Sunlight shone brilliantly through the magnificent stained glass windows.

When they reached the altar, George lifted the veil, and Frank took her hand. George sat next to Maribeth, watching and waiting in anticipation.

Frank looked over at Gramps and winked. The minister said a prayer, and everyone bowed their heads. Then he spoke at great length about the value of patience and kindness.

Penny held Frank's hand. It felt clammy.

"And does anyone show cause why these two should not be married today?" asked the minister.

There were no alarms or buzzers. No urgent calls for the groom to drop everything and go look at a dead body.

Frank and Penny knelt at the altar, and he blessed them. Then they exchanged rings with their vows, and the minister blessed them with another prayer.

"I pronounce you husband and wife. You may kiss your bride."

Frank leaned in, and they kissed. Everyone clapped and whistled. The organist played the wedding march, and they proceeded out. Then they greeted all of their happy guests.

Harry and Gwen Winters shook their hands. Flosky was right behind them.

"You can pay me later," Harry told Joe.

Gwen eyed her husband mysteriously. "What are you talking about?"

"I put down a hundred bucks that Frank would dump Penny at the altar to hover over a dead body or something."

Frank slapped Joe's shoulder and roared with laughter. "You lost the bet? Them's the breaks, pal."

Penny grinned. "Your mother should have taught you not to gamble in the first place, Joe."

"True love conquers all," Joe said as he merged with the crowd.

"I wouldn't have stopped the wedding if an earthquake cut the church in half," Frank said as he leaned down to kiss her.

"That's what I love about you, honey. You're so romantic."

Frank laughed. "What can I say?"

"They should write books full of Frank Logan dating tips," Harry commented dryly as he moved through the crowd.

"It should be what not to do," Gwen added.

Frank squeezed Penny's hand. "And what to do to land the woman of your dreams."

Helen Fergussen rushed up to the happy couple. Her husband, Gus, waited patiently for his turn to talk to his downstairs neighbors.

Helen gushed. "I just knew that you would finally get hitched!"

"It took a lot of patience," Penny said. She leaned in and gave Helen a big hug.

"Thank you for all of your advice."

"I wasn't the easiest person to deal with," Frank admitted.

Gus grinned. "And I enjoyed all the ball games we watched while they were in the other room talking about your love life."

"A lot of good times," Frank agreed. "Thank you both for coming."

A few minutes later, the limousine driver drove them to the fire hall. Guests waited in anticipation as Frank and Penny entered the room for the first time as a married couple. His former colleagues in Philadelphia cheered and whistled as they walked toward them. Sergeant Avery Cox stepped toward him and grinned. He slapped him on the shoulder and said, "I never thought I'd see the day when Frank Logan finally got himself hitched."

They hugged each other. Frank laughed. "How's it going, man?"

"Not bad. The door is open if you want to come back to the big city. You can work the graveyard shift or something."

"I just love working with the dregs of society that come out at night."

"Like Weird Bob."

"Is he still raving gibberish to everybody he meets?"

"Yep."

Penny went up to them all smiles. "Are you talking shop at our wedding?"

Frank grinned back. "Guilty as charged."

"It's nice to see you again," she said. "How are you doing?"

"The same. I've been trying to whisk him back to Philly."

"And what did he tell you?"

"He likes it out in the country where he's his own boss."

"Well, I'm not exactly my own boss. I still have to answer to my superiors."

"And to me!" Penny said pointing to herself.

Avery grinned. "I can't believe you actually pulled this thing off."

Frank squeezed Penny's hand. "I think this lady here had a lot to do with it."

"He pretended not to get my hints."

"And the hints from everybody we know," Frank added.

"So what did the trick?" Avery asked.

"She finally wore me down."

"I did no such thing," Penny corrected her new husband.

Frank grinned and laughed. "It was about time, wouldn't you say?"

"Yeah, it was getting kind of old doing the dating thing," agreed Penny.

"Well, however it happened, I'm really glad for the both of you."

"Please don't say we make a beautiful couple," Frank said.

Avery winked and laughed. "You're the most beautiful groom of them all."

Penny looked warmly at her guest. "Well, if you'll excuse me, there are some other guests who are anxious to talk to me. It was sure nice seeing you again."

"Likewise," Avery said.

"Are you working on any juicy cases?" Frank asked his former colleague.

"We just cracked a nasty drug bust. Multiple arrests in an abandoned warehouse."

"It's always in an abandoned warehouse. The crooks should try more tropical locations."

"If they went to Hawaii, I'd be the first to seek them out."

"How about you?

Frank told him about the Claire Morgan case and how it had gone cold.

"It figures you'd get a case that makes national news. It's amazing that in such a small town, things happen."

"Never a dull moment. See, I told you so. Maybe you could come to my neck of the woods. We've got a sergeant who's going to retire soon. Plenty of job opportunities."

Cox grinned. "You're always thinking about other people."

They mingled with Frank's former colleagues at the Philadelphia police department.

Across the room, the Lanes sat at a large round table with Gramps. Steven smirked as he listened to his mother tell a hilarious story about his sister, the bride, when they were small children. At twenty-eight, Steven was tall and lean with shaggy dark hair and a cheerful demeanor. It was his goal in life to get Frank not to take himself so seriously. Frank could often be intense when he was concentrating on a case. Some people would say that Frank was unpleasant and irritable, especially when a case wasn't going anywhere. Steven did his best to get him to lighten up. He had as much trouble getting Frank to relax as Penny did trying to get him to marry her.

Gramps's eyes gleamed with pleasure as he watched the bride and groom flit about the room. He leaned forward. "It's a good thing she didn't listen to you. I know Frank tends to be moody and consumed with his job. But she trained him very well."

"That's for sure," Maribeth agreed.

"I bet a lot of people lost the bet," Steven Lane said. "It was fifty-fifty. It could have gone in the crapper."

"I'm glad that it didn't," Maribeth said.

"I fought the urge to call him on his cell phone just before she walked down the aisle and send in an anonymous tip or something."

"Well, I certainly am glad that you showed some restraint," Maribeth said.

"It would've been interesting to see what he would have done. A real testament to their love if he had stayed—which he did."

"There's nothing that could have prevented him from tying the knot with the woman of his dreams," Gramps said. "He has gone through so much—and she has helped heal a lot of his past wounds."

"That's what we love about Penny," Maribeth said. "She always tries to help people."

"I don't think she would have loved him when he was in junior high school. He was a total mess back then."

Steven stirred his coffee. "Weren't we all?"

Maribeth squeezed her son's hand. "Well, you got your act together. You're married, and you have two wonderful children."

"I guess we all have our crosses to bear," Steven said.

Penny and Frank rushed over to them. Penny reached for her father's hand. "I would be honored to have the first dance with my father."

George gushed. "And the honor is mine." He stood, and they headed over to the dance floor.

"May I have this dance?"

"I hope he's not asking me," Gramps said laughing.

Maribeth patted Gramps's hand and chuckled. "I think he was talking to me, dear."

Frank winked at his grandfather. "We can go fishing after the honeymoon."

"That's good enough for me."

Maribeth took Frank's hand. He escorted her to the dance floor and grinned. "Well, after all these years, your hard work finally paid off. We're hitched. I'm really glad that Penny is as pig-headed as I am and didn't listen to you two."

"So am I, so am I."

They danced next to George and Penny as Gramps watched in adoration.

# CHAPTER 9

Michelle du Prix overslept and rushed to her photo shoot. She sat on a crowded subway car, and texted Trent a quick apology about their argument. She stumbled into the dressing room, and stylists quickly applied makeup. Moments later, she bustled into the studio, all apologies.

"I'm sorry, Rolf. I didn't think the subway would ever get moving."

He kissed her cheek. "Don't be late again, Mickey. We're late as it is! The Wicked Witch of the West is breathing down my neck to produce. Hop to it, girl!"

Clunky chains wrapped around his neck. His shirt was unbuttoned enough to advertise his hairy chest. Flowing red hair hung loosely from a large bald spot at the top of his head. Sideburns extended below his ear lobes, and his goatee came to a point below his chin.

His assistant, Sabrina, wore black from head to foot. She was lanky and gaunt with magenta-dyed short hair. She wore a nose ring and didn't put on any makeup.

Gretchen and Yvonne were as emaciated as Michelle du Prix. No amount of makeup could conceal the stoned look in their eyes.

Rock music blasted from the radio. Rolf clapped and shouted, "Come on! That, a girl! Ease up a bit, Gretchen!"

Strobe lights flashed one after another as he shot the pictures.

"Make like you're giving me a big kiss!"

Gretchen moistened her lips, opening them wide.

"That's perfect, Gretchen! Beautiful! Loosen up a bit. Shake your muscles. That's it. We're having fun!"

Sabrina misted water on their hair and chests. The girls huddled together and looked up at the camera.

Rolf clapped and shouted, "Costume and makeup change! Yvonne, I'm going for a look here. Help me out! I want something mysterious but alluring."

He paraded around the set, barking out instructions. The crew snapped to it. Ten minutes later, the models returned clad in black. Their faces were streaked with lines of bright colors.

Gretchen ran her fingers through her auburn hair. Michelle puckered and gazed longingly into the lens like she was about to make love to the camera. Yvonne had her hands on her face so you could only see her hazel eyes. Her dark hair blended with the shadows.

"That's it!" Rolf exclaimed. "Beautiful! I just love it!"

When he got the shots he wanted, Sabrina spritzed them with water again. The strobe lights flashed one after another.

"That's it. Gretchen, shake your hair! That's it. Yvonne, look like you're really having fun! Loosen up, people. Move your heads around. That's it. Tease me, Michelle! That's great! You're beautiful!"

✳ ✳ ✳

Nestled on her hotel room bed in the Poconos that odd woman paged through fashion magazines. She had ventured out to purchase ones with supermodel Michelle du Prix on the covers. It was the first time she had been out in days. She did not buy them for fashion tips, however. She had her reasons.

She removed the latest cover photo of Michelle du Prix and taped it to the mirror. She drew a curly mustache with a black magic marker. For an added touch, she blacked out her front teeth. Uncontrollable laughter burst from her as she continued cutting out photos.

She had all her meals sent to the room and left generous tips. A week into her stay, the maid found fashion magazines cut up and the pieces scattered in the trash can. By now, hotel staffers were circulating rumors about their mysterious guest.

Rita leaned down to pull out clean sheets from the dryer and started to fold them. She glanced over at Milly, who was shoving dirty linen into the washing machine.

"That lady in room 55 isn't playing with a full deck, if you ask me."

"She's odd, that's for sure."

Rita went on to mention the fashion magazines in the trash can. "Who would do something like that?"

"Well, I ain't setting foot in that room!" Milly pressed the on button and loaded her cart with neatly pressed linens. She pushed it into the hall and rode the elevator to the fifth floor.

Meanwhile, Bobby Simms was setting up for the late afternoon rush that was about to bombard the hotel restaurant. He listened to the wait staff's stories about their encounters with that weird woman in room 55. Their stories twisted into something wild and tantalizing.

"The next time that crazy bat calls for room service, I won't do it!" Christine exclaimed. "She's extremely picky about what she eats. Nothing's ever good enough for her! It's either too hot or too cold."

"But we always deal with people like that," Nate reminded her.

Christine shook her head. "Not like her. She's the devil!"

"She can't be that bad."

"You should see the crazy crap that she's got in her room! She spends all day lounging around on her bed cutting out pictures from fashion magazines. That's all she does."

"How do you know that?"

"Because I've seen her doing it too!" Theresa cut in. "She's in her bathrobe at three o'clock in the afternoon."

"I wonder where she came from."

"Maybe she's a movie star in disguise."

"Or some nut job who just happened to check in here," Rob added.

"Oh, come on, you guys," Nate said. "You shouldn't talk about guests like that. Maybe she has her reasons for doing the things she's doing. She is on vacation, after all. Maybe she's just bored. Maybe she's just doing it for kicks. Who knows?"

"Well then, you handle her next room service request," Christine said. "What's she doing with those pictures anyway?"

"I saw her pasting them on the mirror!" Rob said.

"And then she ripped them off the mirror and burned them!" Theresa exclaimed. "There were ashes in the trash can. I could barely make out a few of the pretty faces on the pictures she torched. It's a wonder we didn't have to call the fire department over that crazy bitch! I told her not to do it. I should've called the hotel manager."

They finished setting up the dining room and headed into the kitchen. The chefs had their own wild stories about that woman. As the week dragged on, they came up with more juicy stories about that woman in room 55.

# CHAPTER 10

Mary Shannon poured a glass of Pinot Noir and lay on the king-size bed watching the news on a large flat-screen TV over the cabinet in the luxury suite. It was a five star hotel, but she had seen much better. But, it would do.

Pillows of varying sizes and shapes were elegantly arranged along the headboard. The quilt was a rose color. The furniture was acceptable. An abstract print of ice skaters on a pond hung over the bed. Across the room, there was a large mirror and desk. A photograph of Camelback Mountain hung to the right. From the window, there was a magnificent view of the mountains in the distance. In an adjoining room, there was a lounge with a love seat and a reclining chair. There was even a small kitchen and dining room.

She raised the volume when a photograph of Claire Morgan flashed on the screen next to the anchorman. She erupted into uncontrollable fits of laughter as she watched.

"She has been missing for two months," the anchorman announced. "Local officials in the Lancaster area called off the search for lack of evidence. Trent Morgan had this to say."

There was now a close-up of Trent sitting in his living room.

"It's unacceptable that the police aren't pursuing the case," he said. "A lot more can be done. There are areas they have not checked."

He looked into the camera lens and pleaded with the audience. "I'm offering a $25,000 reward to anyone who has information about the disappearance of my wife."

The anchorman cut to other news.

Mary fluffed the pillows and piled them high so she could sit up. She poured another glass of Pinot Noir and drank quickly.

Boredom set in, and she continued clipping newspaper articles pertaining to Claire Morgan's disappearance. Then she leafed through fashion magazines again. Every time she saw a photograph of Michelle du Prix, she cut it out and added it to her shrine.

By the end of her first week at the hotel, Mary had grown tired of room service. A few nights ago, she dined out and met the most charming gentleman named Hank something. He was a burst of energy, which was something she desperately needed right now. He promised to call that afternoon. She had been waiting for the telephone to ring for over an hour.

She did not like to be stood up. She could not handle rejection.

When the telephone rang, she scrambled to answer it. Her voice sounded like pure sunshine. "Hello?"

"Hiya, baby!"

"Hank, sweetie!"

"You'll be ready by seven?"

"I'll be ready."

"You're one in a million, Mary!"

She hung up, glanced at her green plastic digital wristwatch. It was quarter after five. She hated to get out of bed, but enough was enough. She had napped on and off that afternoon, preparing for her third late night out with Hank what's-his-face.

She removed her robe, folded it neatly on the bed, and wandered into the bathroom. It was a large room with a marble sink that had an array of shampoos and gels and body lotions. A Jacuzzi was across the room

She went over to the Plexiglas shower door that was wrapped around the stall. She turned on the jet spray spigot which produced powerful flows of water, and drew a bubble bath. She slipped in, and closed her eyes.

\* \* \*

Hank Cummings was a strapping man in his mid-forties, with a warm personality and a cheerful smile. His cheeks were hidden behind a thick mustache and beard. His attire shouted cowboy from head to foot. A large white cowboy hat covered his red hair. He had a white button-down shirt with a large Indian medallion tie clasp, a large buffalo belt buckle, blue jeans, and leather cowboy boots.

He adjusted his sunglasses and lurked in a lounge just off the lobby. There were only a couple of other people there at this hour. Every so often, he peeked out the door to see if Mary Shannon was coming. Even though he lived in Texas, he was paranoid that someone he knew would see him there. He hoped he could go unrecognized. If a friend or colleague saw him, he would have to answer a slew of questions. What are you doing here? How are the wife and kids?

He checked the time. It was five minutes after seven. He lit a cigarette and paced, glancing at his gold watch every five minutes.

At half past seven, he went into the lobby and checked to see if Mary was there. Then he went to make sure she wasn't waiting outside. She was not there, so he went back inside.

He sat in a vacant seat and hid behind a newspaper. Ten minutes later, he looked up and saw her coming down the winding brown marble staircase with the intricately carved rails. She looked magnificent in a bright-red evening dress. She was beaming. In a matter of moments, all eyes were on her as she stepped off the landing. She kissed his cheek, and he took her hand in his. People gaped as they entered the dining room. At ten o'clock, they finished a four-course meal and moved to the bar for drinks and dancing. By now, Mary had loosened up, and was ready for fun. They danced, and she was the life of the party. Her abundance of energy drove men wild. They stared longingly at her. They all wanted to be with her. It was only a matter of time before Hank was left in the dust. He just sat at the table, shaking his head in disbelief.

Now it was time for a breather. She strutted over to a table with three young unattached men looking for companionship with rich, older women. But not too old. She figured they were in their late twenties. They were obviously single. There were no marks on their ring fingers. Therefore, they had not just removed their symbols of love and married lives in exchange for anonymity with a woman they picked up in a hotel bar.

She shrieked with laughter. "Oh, that's so funny. You're so clever—what did you say your name was?"

"Robert Timko." He grinned and placed his right hand on her thigh.

She gently removed it and laughed heartily. "My, what a naughty boy you are!"

He moved closer and sneaked a peek at her package. "I'll show you just how naughty I am. So what'll it be? My room or yours?"

She laughed hysterically.

"You're an intriguing woman, Mary."

She leaned forward and patted his face. "Why, thank you, sweetie!"

Hank Cummings stomped over to them. "Come on, Mary!" He pulled her onto the dance floor, and she gyrated to the rhythm of the music.

Fifteen minutes later, she sauntered over to the bar and said, "Another beer, please."

The bartender looked at her legs, slowly moving his eyes to her bosom. He handed her the beer and gawked as she slinked back to the table. He mechanically handed customers their beers and made change, his eyes fixed on her figure. He watched as she guzzled her beer. His eyes stayed on her as she resumed her dancing. Three songs later, Hank had to rest. He pulled her over to the table and eased into a chair.

"Party pooper!"

He patted her right knee and said, "You're gonna kill me, baby! I need a breather!"

Mary planted her lips against his, and then slowly pulled away. She winked and shook her hips as she sauntered back onto the dance floor. She looked around the room, in pursuit of another handsome dance partner.

*　*　*

Bartender Don Simms was mixing drinks and watching the eleven o'clock news. He handed a customer a beer and pointed to Mary Shannon. "That woman's unbelievable."

"She's too much for me."

"I bet she's loaded."

"I'd marry her."

Another man plopped next to him and asked for Jack Daniel's. While preparing it, the bartender caught a glimpse of Claire Morgan's photograph on the news. He reached for the remote control under the counter and raised the volume.

"Authorities are asking for more information about the whereabouts of Claire Morgan, wife of media mogul Trent Morgan," the anchorman announced.

The bartender studied her features. Then he glanced over at the woman in red on the dance floor. He looked at the TV picture again. He handed the man his drink, his eyes fixed on the dance floor.

"Oh my God!" he exclaimed.

All the men gathered at the bar looked at him in alarm. "What's wrong, Don?" they asked.

He pointed to the dance floor and said, "It's her. That woman over there. I think it's her!"

They listened carefully to what the anchorman said.

"Trent Morgan is offering a $25,000 reward for anyone who has information about his wife. She was last seen wearing a violet evening dress. She may have changed her hair color. She disappeared in the early evening hours of May twenty-sixth. If you have any information, please contact—"

Don scribbled down the 800 number and dialed the police station.

"Townsend police," the dispatcher said.

"Hello, I'm a bartender at the Hill Crest Hotel in the Poconos."

"What can I do for you?"

"I think I saw that missing woman that's been on TV."

"You and thousands of others."

"I'm serious. I could swear it's her. This woman fits the picture they show on TV."

"Where?"

"She's right here!"

*　*　*

Bill Morgan cringed in disgust when he looked down at his father and Michelle locking lips on the family room sofa about 1:00 a.m. They were really going at it. Then his father pulled away, shaking his hands.

"What's wrong?" she asked.

"You have the nerve to ask? Like you don't know."

"Come on. She'll turn up."

"Claire might be dead, and you expect that I'm going to go to bed with you. You must be joking."

"But I need you!"

"We'll have plenty of time for that later."

"I thought I could—"

He grumbled and stomped out onto the patio.

"Trent, don't you dare leave me! Damn you, Trent!" She cursed and went after him.

Bill scowled and marched back to his bedroom. He went over to the shelf and reached for the hardback adventure novel he was in the middle of reading. He got back in bed and opened it to where he left off.

*　*　*

Trent and Michelle were drinking coffee in the family room about nine o'clock the next morning. Bill was reading the newspaper, trying to ignore them. Elizabeth Ashton entered the room and said, "It's the Poconos police department, Mr. Morgan. They think they know where your wife is, sir."

"Oh my God!" he exclaimed.

She handed him the portable phone and stood quietly at the door.

"This is Trent Morgan."

"I'm Detective Sam Roundtree of the Oak Ridge Police Department, up in the Poconos. A bartender at a hotel here was watching the news last night. He thinks he saw a woman matching your wife's description on the dance floor. I went to see her for myself, and I'm pretty sure that his story checks out."

"It's a miracle! What a relief. I was worried sick!"

"Right now, she's still in her hotel room. But we'll need you to come here to make a positive identification. We'll keep an eye on her so she doesn't leave the premises."

"Thank you. I'm on my way!"

He pressed the off button and was in such a hurry that he didn't say a word to Michelle. He went to the foyer, fumbled for the keys on the rack, and walked hurriedly out the front door. Bill and Michelle darted after him.

\* \* \*

About 2:00 p.m., Trent pulled into a wooded entrance that led to the Hill Crest Hotel. A couple of minutes later, they saw it coming up on their right. Ionic columns stretched across the front porch. The grounds were lush with well-manicured boxwood bushes and a row of pink roses on either side of the front steps. White wrought-iron lawn chairs were out front. It looked like the perfect setting for a murder mystery.

Trent slipped into a parking space and trekked across the lawn. Bill and Michelle followed him up the front steps and pushed through a revolving door. The lobby was expansive with a red carpet. The reception desk had the same marble pattern as the stairway. The woodwork and molding were splendidly designed by master architects. The wallpaper had a red rose floral pattern.

Trent went up to the hotel clerk and introduced himself. "A detective Roundtree said he would meet me here."

The clerk telephoned the police station. "He said he's on his way, sir. If you'll have a seat, he should be here soon."

They sat in burgundy wing chairs arranged in a semicircle around mahogany coffee tables in a lounge by the revolving door. Lamps with green shades sat on antique end tables. Kelly-green silk curtains hung on the high windows. Massive brown marble columns divided the reception area and the lounge.

Trent read the *Wall Street Journal*, until Detective Roundtree pushed through the revolving door. He was a pudgy middle-aged man with a bald spot. He went over to the reception desk and the clerk pointed in their direction. Detective Roundtree went over and introduced himself.

"Where is she?" Trent asked impatiently.

"She's still up in her room," Roundtree told him.

"Can we see her?" Bill asked.

"I'll bring her down," Roundtree said.

About fifteen minutes later, they saw a woman with auburn hair wearing a pink silk dress at the top of the staircase. At first, they weren't sure it was her. She was about fifty pounds lighter. Her hair was slicked back, not Claire's normal style. It looked much longer now. Makeup made her look ten or fifteen years younger.

The woman slowly descended the winding staircase and walked in their direction. When she got close to them, Trent took one look at her and cried, "Oh my God, it is her!"

Bill threw his arms around her and said, "Mother, we were worried sick!"

She winced and pulled away, eying him suspiciously. "Do I know you?"

Her voice sounded hoarse and unrefined. Trent leaned over to kiss her, and she slapped his face.

"Who the hell do you think you are? And why are you making me stay in my room, Detective?"

Detective Roundtree looked at Trent. "Is this your wife?" It took all his patience to deal with such a difficult woman.

Trent nodded and looked back at his wife. "You have a lot of explaining to do, Claire."

"Who the hell is Claire? I'm not Claire!"

Michelle pulled Trent aside and whispered, "She's nuts."

"She's just confused." Trent looked back at his wife and said, "It's okay. We'll get you some help, Claire."

"Stop calling me that! My name is Mary Shannon!"

Trent stood there with his hands at his sides, not knowing quite what to say.

Bill looked glumly at her and said, "Oh, Mother. It's okay. We'll get you help."

"So you're saying you don't recognize these people?" Detective Roundtree asked Mary.

"I've never seen them in my life. Get them the hell away from me! I'm just trying to have a relaxing vacation. I don't need this right now!"

"I'm your husband, Trent. We've been married for twenty-eight years."

"And I'm your son, Bill."

Mary looked blankly across the lobby at Michelle, who was glaring back at Trent. She went over to her and asked, "Are you my daughter?"

Michelle cringed and said, "No!"

Mary pointed to Bill. "Then you must be his girlfriend."

Michelle shook her head.

Bill looked over at the detective and asked, "What's going to happen to her?"

"I'm guessing that she must have hit her head or something. She probably has amnesia. I recommend that you have her examined by a physician. She should have a complete physical. We'll have a psychiatrist evaluate her."

"Can we take her with us?" Bill asked.

"Not now. I called an ambulance. They should be here soon." Just then, he saw the ambulance pull down the driveway. "They need to examine you in your room, Ms. Shannon. Come on, I'll take you upstairs." He reached for her hand, and she folded her arms.

"I can walk by myself!" she snapped.

Trent and Bill started to go after them, but Detective Roundtree told them to remain in the lobby. Their faces dropped as they watched the paramedics going upstairs with them. It was the first time in years that father and son had worked together rather than against each other.

114

Michelle stood with her hands on her hips. She seethed as she studied the sullen expression on Trent's face. He still loved Claire. There was no doubt about it.

All of Michelle's insecurities came flooding back. Trent had never loved her. She would never find true love. It was just what her father, Buddy, drilled into her head when she was a little girl. Claire would come home soon. Michelle knew she had to do something quickly.

\* \* \*

Paramedics Alex Grant and Jane Sawyer exchanged nervous glances upon entering the room. Detective Roundtree looked back at them and nodded in agreement.

The charred remains of pictures were piled in a trash can that was filled to capacity. Discarded fashion magazines were below them. Other magazines lay strewn on the king-size bed. One of them was open and a gaping hole was cut out of one of the pictures. Scissors lay on top of it.

"You're just wasting your time!" Mary screamed. "I don't know why you're doing this."

Jane Sawyer smiled and said, "It's procedure, Mrs. Morgan. It won't take long."

"For the last time! I'm Mary Shannon, for Christ's sake!"

"I'm sorry, Ms. Shannon."

A half an hour later, the paramedics finished their preliminary examination. Alex Grant outlined what was to come next. His tone was soothing. "We have to take you to the hospital, ma'am."

She folded her arms and shouted, "You can't make me go with you!"

Jane Sawyer took Mary's hand and said, "We aren't equipped to be able to give you all the help you need. Doctors can help you there."

"No! Get your filthy hands off me!"

Detective Roundtree offered assistance. Mary kicked and screamed so much that they had to restrain her.

"Let me go! I'll have your badge for this!"

Detective Roundtree held her down while Alex Grant gave her a sedative. They waited for it to take effect and escorted her downstairs. Trent and Bill watched helplessly as they put her in the ambulance. Trent insisted on going with them and climbed in back. Bill followed in his father's BMW.

☆ ☆ ☆

Bill sped to catch up with the ambulance. Michelle sat beside him, her arms folded in a frozen stance, as she stared out the window. The sun roof was open. Air blew their hair to-and-fro.

Neither of them uttered a word. They did not want to be trapped in the same car together for any length of time.

The road narrowed, and he slowed down. He maneuvered around a sharp turn and edged his way down a steep hill.

They were a mile from the nearest town when Michelle said, "I can't believe you buy her act."

"Don't you think you've caused enough trouble?"

"Oh, shut up!"

He craned his neck to face her. "What do you see in him? You can't tell me you really love him."

"Go to hell!" She kicked her heels on the dashboard and scowled.

They were arguing at the only traffic light in town. Passersby could hear everything they were saying. Townspeople watched and listened for entertainment.

"You don't want me to see your father. You're jealous."

"Dammit, Michelle, I still love you! How can you just break up with me and—and start going with him?"

"You'll never understand."

"Try me. I deserve some kind of explanation."

The light turned green, and he sped to catch up with the ambulance.

"Your father is so decent. He treats me really well. I never had that before. It's the first time in my life that I ever felt so totally connected to someone. We have a lot in common."

"That's bull!"

"He never loved your mother! They're toxic together."

"But we were good together."

"Get over it. I have. Maybe if you had listened to me—but no, you were too consumed with your career."

"I've busted my butt getting my business off the ground. You would be a nobody if it weren't for me! I made you what you are, and don't forget it!"

"Just leave me alone!"

He had his eyes off the road at the wrong moment, and the car swerved. He made a sharp turn to the left and almost hit an oncoming motorist. He slammed on the brakes, missing it by inches.

Bill and Michelle leaned back in their seats, their hearts racing. The other driver swore and shook his fist as he sped past them.

"Do you see what you almost did?"

"What I almost did? Learn to drive!" She folded her arms and remained silent.

A few minutes later, Bill followed the ambulance driver through an archway cut into a tall stone wall at the hospital entrance and down a tree-lined road for about a mile. Pine trees were kept like prisoners behind a chain-link fence. The hospital loomed in the distance. It looked like a sprawling brick Victorian mansion with bay windows at the center and individual apartments and towers with pointed roofs, like in horror movies.

A sudden feeling of uneasiness came over Michelle when she saw a patient wandering the grounds as if in a daze. A burly male staffer in a hospital uniform walked alongside him. Others sat on benches and read. Sprinklers sprayed begonias near the front steps.

Bill slipped into a parking space, and Michelle hopped out before the car stopped.

"Thank God I don't have to be around you anymore!" She stomped into the building.

# CHAPTER 11

Trent Morgan told hospital staff that his wife had a crescent-shaped birthmark on her left thigh. When a physician examined Mary Shannon, he determined that she was, in fact, Claire Morgan. The next step was to figure out why she was going by another name. Did she really believe she was Mary, or was she faking it?

Trent watched his wife through a one-way mirror. Doctors were giving her a psychological examination. They asked a series of questions and jotted notes. A black doctor named Karl Thompson seemed to be in charge. He was burly with a salt-and-pepper beard. His voice was deep and authoritative.

Two hours later, the door opened, and Dr. Thompson went over to Trent and introduced himself. "I need to talk to you, Mr. Morgan."

"What's wrong with my wife? I never dreamed she would have to be taken to a psychiatric hospital. I thought she was just confused. She was in an accident and must have hit her head."

"I understand. Let's go to my office. She might be able to hear our conversation."

They walked down a series of winding corridors and went into Dr. Thompson's spacious fifth floor office. Trent glanced at medical degrees on the wall as he walked across the room. He went over to the window behind the desk and admired the magnificent view of the mountains in the distance.

"What a beautiful view," Trent said as he eased into a red leather chair.

"Isn't it terrific? I find it peaceful."

Trent nodded in agreement. His eyes trained on a five-by-seven color snapshot of Dr. Thompson's wife and children on the desk.

"You have a lovely family."

"Thank you," the doctor said. He put on his reading glasses and reviewed his notes.

Trent looked over at an abstract watercolor painting of ballet dancers opposite the window. Then he admired the hanging plants over the desk.

When Dr. Thompson was finished, Trent asked, "What's wrong with her?"

"We can't seem to determine that at the moment.

"How long will she have to be here?"

"It could take a week or more. It depends on what we find."

"She must have hit her head so hard in the car accident that she lost her memory."

"That is a distinct possibility, Mr. Morgan. At the present, there doesn't appear to be anything physically wrong with her. But we will run some more psychological tests. I have also set up an appointment to do a CAT scan and an MRI to determine if there is an organic cause. We won't know anything until we do the tests. Does your wife have a history of mental illness in her family?"

Trent shrugged his shoulders. "I'm not really sure."

"You don't have to tell me now. Give it some thought. It could help unlock the key to her current condition. Many mental illnesses are believed to be hereditary."

"I didn't know." He was quiet for a couple of minutes. Then he said, "She had an aunt who was very high-strung. She was manic depressive."

"Do you know anything else about her aunt?"

"Let me give it some thought."

Dr. Thompson jotted another note. "Was your wife under stress?"

Trent described his current marital problems. "I asked Claire for a divorce the night she disappeared."

"So it is true what I've been reading."

"Could that be what's wrong with her?"

"In some cases, people block out unpleasant experiences. A blow to the head could trigger what is known as retrograde amnesia. Your wife might have been in a fugue state after the accident. That's when someone has amnesia and wanders off and starts a new identity."

"That would explain why she thinks she's this Mary person. Will she ever remember us?"

"In some cases, people have had so much pain, that they unintentionally choose not to remember. Maybe they don't want to remember and block it out."

"It's all my fault."

"Don't blame yourself. We don't even know that that's what the problem is."

"Maybe she's faking it to get back at me."

"That's possible."

The telephone rang, and he answered it. "Oh hello, David." He looked back at Trent and said, "I have to take this call. Talk to my receptionist, and we can schedule a meeting for next week."

Trent got up and went out to make the appointment.

☼　☼　☼

A week later, Dr. Thompson called to tell Trent that he had completed the tests on Claire, also known as Mary. They could not find anything wrong with her brain functioning.

"What does that mean?" Trent asked.

"It's hard to say. We need to keep her here a while longer for evaluation."

"How much longer?"

"As long as it takes. She has a mental block and needs extensive psychotherapy."

"I would like her to be treated at home, if that is at all possible. She would feel more comfortable there."

"Not if she doesn't know who she is. It may be a shock to her system. She will receive proper care at the hospital."

Trent mulled it over a moment. "Well, keep me posted. Thank you for calling."

He hung up and sat at the foot of the bed.

Michelle rubbed his shoulders and said, "Don't think about it."

"It's easy for you to say. I feel so bad about things." He got up and walked hurriedly toward the door. He looked back at her and said, "I'm going to stay in the guest room until she gets better. I feel so bad about what we're doing that I don't know what I'll do."

"Damn you!" she shouted after him.

\* \* \*

One morning, Mary was in bed when Dr. Thompson came by for her thirty minute session. She smiled as he entered the room.

"How are you doing today, Mary?"

She pushed hair out of her eyes and said, "Fine thanks, Doc."

"Last time, you were angry because people mistake you for someone else."

She waved her arms and said, "What can I do? That Trent Morgan character keeps calling to talk to me. And then there's his son, Bill. And that woman who's always hanging onto Mr. Morgan! At first, I thought she was his daughter or somebody. Then I thought she was going with the son. She's Mr. Morgan's girlfriend. He may be a pest, but he seems to be worried about my welfare for some reason. And I really need a man who is that caring."

Dr. Thompson's tone was slow and soothing. "They are concerned about you, Mary."

"I don't see why. Can't you just tell me who they are?"

"I can't do that. It's better that you remember on your own. Can you remember anything at all?"

"I'm afraid not. I wish I did."

"Can you remember your earliest childhood memories, Claire?"

"My name is Mary!" she snapped.

"I'm sorry." He repeated the question.

She closed her eyes, deep in thought. "I remember playing with a baby doll on a porch swing. I was singing. I think it was summer. I was waiting for my older sister to take me swimming—"

* * *

Dr. Thompson worked hard at unlocking Mary's childhood memories, but she was still blocked. He reviewed the test results and studied his notes from their sessions. There was something not quite right. He addressed the issue at their next session.

"As you know, we did a number of tests. We don't believe that there's anything, physically wrong you. The psychological tests we gave you also don't appear out of the ordinary. You answered our questions in a coherent manner. And we have just finished evaluating your handwriting analysis. It matches Claire Morgan's handwriting, Mary. A person's handwriting often shows a significant change at the onset of mental illness. Yet your handwriting remains the same. Can you tell me why that might be?"

She twisted her bangs and looked away. "I don't know."

"Let's cut to the chase, Mrs. Morgan," he blurted out. "You can quit your foolish act. We're onto you."

"I don't know what you mean."

"Your husband told me the stunts you pull to get attention. You go away for days without saying where you are. That's only the half of it."

Tears streamed down her face. "I don't know what you're talking about."

"I have treated many amnesia patients. They usually have some impaired brain functioning. In time, the injury they sustained improves, and they resume normal functioning, enough to remember who they are, for the most part. Some remain the same. You don't fit any of those categories. I believe you are a very good actress."

She waved her hands in the air and raved. "Why would I want to do that?"

"To get attention. We have been observing you for two weeks, and your behavior remains the same."

"But didn't you say it could take several months to regain lost memories?"

"That's true, but not in your case."

Her eyes were wild with rage. "I resent what you're implying! That—that I'm faking it!"

"Well, do you have any other suggestions, Mrs. Morgan?"

"I'm Mary!" she insisted. "Why won't anyone believe me?"

"All right, have it your way, Mary. Maybe we have been wrong all along. Maybe you do have amnesia. Maybe you really can't help it." He referred to notes that the paramedics wrote pertaining to their encounter with the woman in room 55. "According to paramedics Alex Grant and Jane Sawyer, you were doing some pretty odd things in your hotel room. They saw the charred remains of pictures in the trash can. Discarded fashion magazines were at the bottom. Magazines with gigantic holes cut out of the pages were spread out all over your bed. Detective Roundtree agreed that this behavior was strange. Why did you do it?"

"I was bored. It gave me something to do."

"Only a really unstable person would do a thing like that. Maybe we should do some more tests."

"I'm not unstable! I—I was just doing it to have a kick or two. You know, when you watch a beauty pageant and pick apart the contestants because they're so gorgeous. No one could ever look as good as they do. Everybody does it."

"I have never done it. It's demeaning. You have serious self-esteem issues that we need to work on. How long have you had these feelings of low self-esteem?"

When the woman's thirty minutes were up, a frustrated Dr. Thompson left in a hurry.

# CHAPTER 12

Everyone whistled and cheered when a well-tanned Frank Logan strode toward his desk.

Flosky grinned and said, "Welcome back, pal. The place hasn't been the same without you."

"I didn't miss it for a minute." Logan sat down and sorted through a pile of mail. Then he attacked a mountainous stack of paperwork. He groaned and said, "That's not something I want to have to deal with when I come back from my honeymoon. Did anything exciting happen while I was gone? Any shootings or stabbings?"

Flosky shook his head. "The lady that disappeared was spotted at a swanky hotel in the Poconos."

Logan whistled. "No kidding. You go away for a couple of weeks and things happen. I guess her family is relieved to have her back safely at home."

Flosky told him that Claire Morgan was in a Poconos psychiatric hospital. "Right now, Trent Morgan says she's under observation. The shrinks think she has amnesia or something. If you ask me, I think she's faking it."

"Only time will tell, my friend. Well, at least they found her."

"The really good news is that the hotel bartender is a lot richer now. He's the one who spotted her. He called the police."

"Well, good for him." Logan concentrated his attention on the paperwork. "Now we won't have to deal with Trent and Bill Morgan bugging us every other minute."

"Really." Flosky went back to his own pile of paperwork. "I'm glad you're back."

"Thanks. It's good to see you too. You really do need to get some sun. You look kind of pale."

☼   ☼   ☼

Maribeth Lane gushed at the beautiful sunset pictures in Penny's photo album. Penny flipped a page and her mother burst out laughing at the sight of Frank in scuba-diving getup.

"It's so beautiful under the sea," Penny said. "There are so many interesting fish down there, and we don't even know it."

Maribeth grinned when she saw a picture of Frank riding on a dolphin. "They're so cute together!"

"It was totally amazing. You and Dad should try it."

"I don't think he's up to something like that. We'll just have to admire the pictures. I would like to frame one for a Christmas present—hint, hint."

Penny flipped a page and pointed to images of the palm trees on the pristine beach. On the next page, there were pictures of them dressed in formal attire for the captain's dinner in the ship's restaurant. There were ones with Frank and Penny goofing around with the waiter from Turkey, and ones with their fellow passengers at the dinner table. She went on to talk about how interesting they were.

"I bet they were really excited when they found out that Frank is a detective," Maribeth said.

"Well, you know how he is. He's usually pretty tight-lipped about a case he's working on. But he wasn't in his own neck of the woods. He sort of went overboard when everybody asked him if he'd investigated any juicy cases."

"I bet you couldn't get him to shut up."

"It was a challenge, to say the least."

"They were eating it up. Or he was."

"Well, there were a lot of things he couldn't really talk about when we were eating, if you know what I mean. I'm sure he chatted them up at the pool or at the gym when I wasn't there."

Maribeth flipped the page and laughed at a photo of Penny on a pool chair in her bikini and straw hat and sunglasses. She was drinking one of those drinks with an umbrella. The glass was humongous. She had a big dumb grin. There was another picture of Frank in the swimming pool. There were others of them in the Jacuzzi with tropical drinks in their hands. Penny flipped another page and pointed to the pastel-colored buildings on one of the islands they visited.

Frank came in carrying grocery bags and put them on the kitchen counter. He went over to Maribeth and leaned down to hug her.

"Is she talking about me again?"

"I'm afraid so," Maribeth said.

"We have to break her of that habit."

"Well, you pass the husband category with flying colors."

"Well, good. I don't want to have to go to sensitivity classes or something."

"It looks like you had a wonderful trip."

"It beats hovering over a dead body." He went into the kitchen and put the groceries away.

Penny and Maribeth continued looking at the pictures.

"There's a job opening at an ad agency near Townsend," Penny said. "I'm thinking of applying for it."

# CHAPTER 13

Claire/Mary was in the day room, reading the morning news-paper, when she heard her name mentioned. She looked at the monitor desk down the hall and saw a man in a leather jacket talking to the nurse. He had on a red paisley button-down shirt and baggy Dockers.

"She isn't receiving visitors," the nurse told him.

"It's vitally important that I speak to her."

Claire saw him lean forward and slip her a card.

"No members of the press! Mrs. Morgan left strict orders not to be disturbed."

Claire/Mary could smell his cologne as she approached the monitor desk. At closer inspection, he appeared to be an unsavory type. His eyes were cold and shifty. He had a swarthy complexion. Dark stubble covered his face.

She grinned and said, "That's okay, Sherry. I don't get many visitors. What's your name, sir?"

He smiled and introduced himself as Jerry Hawke of the *National Inquisitor Magazine*. He had a thick Brooklyn accent. She glanced down at his beer belly and wondered how much gel he used to slick back his hair. It looked thick and greasy.

He handed her a business card and said, "I've been trying to get in here to talk to you, ma'am."

Her eyes lit up at the realization that millions of Americans were that interested in reading about her *disappearance*. Maybe it was time to end her adventure. At least for Bill's sake.

She grinned. "I'm flattered."

He signed in and followed Claire/Mary to her room. It was a modest room with a single bed, a small desk and mirror, and a couple of chairs. It was clearly not what she was accustomed to.

He pulled a chair close to her and asked, "How are you feeling?"

"Frustrated," she admitted. "I'm so isolated here. It's in the middle of nowhere. Just take a look outside and you'll see why."

He looked down at the spacious grounds. Patients were sitting on lawn chairs near a pond. Others were wandering along a wooded trail. A chain-link fence was in the distance, making escape virtually impossible.

He leaned forward and said, "Americans are dying to know, Mrs. Morgan. How did you pull it off? Where did you go?"

"Visiting hours are over in two hours. It will take a long time."

"I've got plenty of time, Mrs. Morgan. We might not be finished in one sitting, if you don't mind."

She smiled a beguiling smile and cocked her head. "It's perfectly okay, Jerry. Where shall I begin?"

"Did you really get into an argument with your husband before you 'disappeared'?"

"It was brutal." Then she told him about the fight in every detail.

"What happened next?"

"I packed my suitcase. Then I went to a special little box I keep in my closet for emergencies. I keep a healthy amount of cash in it, you see."

There was a glint in his eyes. "How much?" he asked eagerly.

"I would rather not say."

"Oh, come on. You're willing to talk to me. Just average it out."

"It was about $50,000. A little more or a little less."

He looked at her in stunned silence, his mouth agape. "Do you really expect me to believe that?"

"It's true! I came up with many clever ways to conceal it in my clothes and in the bag I was carrying."

"How come you had so much cash lying around?"

Her eyes watered. She reached for a Kleenex and wiped away the tears. "I knew my husband was going to drop the bomb on me. I wanted to be prepared. Surely, you can understand that."

He nodded. "Did your husband know about your stash?"

"I don't think so. I took out a little bit at a time for several months so it wouldn't be noticeable. Trent was so busy, he wouldn't have known anyway."

"So you had wads of cash on you. Then what happened?"

"I drove off. Trent was talking to that bitch Michelle du Prix on his smartphone. I knew I had to get out of there, or I'd kill him! That was when I orchestrated my plan. I had been formulating it on and off for months, but I was only going to use it if and when the circumstance arose. And it did.

"The roads in that area are windy and treacherous. There is a large pond in the middle of a meadow, about ten minutes from our home. It's lovely! We used to picnic there. But anyway, I drove the car into a tree near the pond. The front window shattered, so I took a sliver in my fingers and cut them to draw blood."

Hawke gasped. "You don't say?"

"Then I smeared some blood on the car seat and left my pearl necklace on the floor. Then I wandered up to the road until I heard a horse and buggy. You see, there are a lot of Amish farmers in that area. They drive their damn buggies up and down the road and drive everyone crazy. Sometimes I wonder how many motorists are killed because of those damned horse and buggies!

"Anyway, a nice young Amish man picked me up—" She paused and giggled at her odd choice of words. "He was nice enough to give me a ride to his farm."

She told Hawke that she slipped out when he went to put his horse in the stable. Hawke wrote feverishly and continually asked her to repeat things.

"Where did you go after that?"

"I walked to a town that isn't too far from there. I fixed myself up in a gorgeous veil so that no one would recognize me and took a train to Syracuse. From there, I began living off my money. I stayed in Syracuse until I got bored. Then I moved to other towns."

"But weren't you worried that the police would find you? Your face was plastered all over the place."

She leaned in and tapped his left arm. "That's what made it even more thrilling! All I knew was that I was getting back at Trent big time! When he said he wanted the divorce that was the straw that broke the camel's back. I wanted to get out of there. So that's what I did. And I was thoroughly enjoying my travels—spending money like there was no tomorrow—living in luxury at five-star hotels."

"But weren't you worried that people would recognize you?"

"I used disguises. I wore veils and large hats over my head and put on sunglasses. It was a lot of fun! But then the money supply started to dwindle."

"What did you do then? How did you survive?"

She winked and leaned close to him. "Through the kindness of strangers. I impressed people that I met at social gatherings so much that they often paid for meals. Businessmen especially took a fancy to me."

Hawke grinned and said, "You didn't—whore to get money, did you?"

"Good heavens, no!"

"I'm sorry."

She grinned. "Don't worry about it, Jerry! These men fell in love the moment they laid eyes on me. They offered to pay for meals, rooms, you name it. I went with them on trips and offered to be their secretaries. Is that the proper term these days? And we went on trips all over the country. I even went to Rio!"

"I find that hard to believe," Hawke commented dryly. "And so will my readers. How did you get out of the country without a passport? You would have needed one to go to Rio. And you didn't want to reveal your true identity."

She grinned and winked. "Now just ask yourself how farfetched the whole thing sounds anyway. Imagine a wealthy woman staging her own car accident and cutting her fingers with broken glass to get away from her husband!"

He chuckled at the thought. "That's true. But you were just trying to scare him, weren't you?"

She tilted her head and giggled. "You can use your imagination there, honey."

"Your picture was all over the TV and internet and newspapers and magazines. I find it hard to believe that the people you hung out with didn't recognize you."

"Well, they didn't!"

"So you're telling me that they had no clue who you were. Your husband offered a $25,000 reward, for God's sake."

"It's true, just ask my friend Hank—Hank—something. Why, he was staying at the hotel where I was staying until my unfortunate arrival here. Oh, he probably won't want to talk to you, seeing how he's married and all. Sure, I knew that they were married. But it's not as if I would have actually gone to bed with them! But I suppose it's still cheating, even if we didn't do anything. I just needed the companionship. I don't enjoy being alone. What's wrong with harmless drinking and dancing and a little harmless flirting? A girl's got to have a good time once in a while. You could talk to that bartender at the hotel. He's the one who recognized me. I really hope he enjoys the reward money."

Jerry rolled his eyes. "Is there any truth to the rumors of your sightings across the country?"

She laughed and patted his hand. "That's another story! You see, I wanted people to notice me. I would walk into public places long enough to be seen. Then I'd leave in a hurry. I'd post comments on social media on the hotel laptop. Then I'd go back to my room, type press releases, and send them to local newspapers. That's one thing you never forget about being a reporter."

"That's right, you were once a reporter," Hawke said.

"That's right. I was a stringer in high school. Then I did some more freelance work in college. The *Tribune*'s editor hired me as a full-time general assignment reporter right out of college. We got a lot of crank press releases. Sometimes we reported on them, sometimes we didn't. It just depended on how desperate for extra stories we were. We had to fill holes."

Hawke nodded in recognition. "I get it. Did you meet Trent when you worked there?"

Her eyes sparkled as she remembered. "Yes, he was a city editor. The publisher really liked him. So when he died, he left Trent in charge of the paper. That was the beginning. We fell in love and got married. I did it to get back at my parents. They loathed him. Perhaps that's what drew me to him in the first place. At any rate, Trent did so well in his second year, that he borrowed money from my parents' inheritance to start another newspaper. And the rest is history."

"You must really hate Trent to do a thing like this."

"I wanted to get his attention, that's all."

"And it worked. They were all worried sick."

"I'm only sorry that I worried my son and my housekeeper."

"What would you say to Trent right now?

"I don't know," she said after a long silence.

"Don't get shy on me now. You've been talking up a storm. What would you say to him?"

Her voice shook. "That Michelle will never make him happy. I'm the only one who knows him."

"Don't you think that there is a double-standard thing going on here? You did all this to get back at him for cheating on you with Ms. du Prix, and yet you just admitted to hanging out with a lot of men on your wild adventures."

"I never slept with them. We were just having a good time. There's nothing wrong with that."

"Are you sorry that you did it?"

"No, I can't say that I am. He deserved it."

Hawke thanked her and rushed out of the room. He was giddy. His body tingled. He felt like a child on Christmas day.

# CHAPTER 14

The magazine article was printed at rapid speed and hit the newspaper stands two days later. A photograph pictured Claire sitting on a lawn chair with the hospital in the background. In bold type, the headline read, "**Claire Morgan admits her disappearance was a hoax.**"

Trent read the story and shouted, "Damn!"

Elizabeth Ashton took one look at him and hurried into the kitchen. Bill chose the safety of his bedroom.

A few minutes later, Trent finished reading the article and tossed the magazine across the room.

"That witch!" he shouted. "I'll kill her!"

Bill gathered the courage to go to him. He put his hand on his shoulder and asked, "Are you okay, Dad?"

Trent pointed to the magazine on the beige rug and shouted, "No, I'm not! Did you see what she did?"

Bill nodded.

"We were worried sick, and she was gallivanting around!"

"She had her reasons. She wasn't happy. You were making her miserable. She just did it to get your attention."

"She sure as hell did that." Trent pounded the stairs and marched into his bedroom. He reached for his smartphone on the bedside table and dialed Michelle's number. She was in her penthouse in New York City.

"Did you see it?" he asked, out of breath.

"Yes! That lying witch!"

"Something must be done."

"I've been telling you that all along, Trent. You just weren't listening."

"I won't let her get away with it."

"What do you have in mind?"

"Come to Townsend. I really need you. I'm sorry I didn't listen. You kept telling me that she was just trying to get attention, and I shoved you aside. Please forgive me. Just come as soon as possible."

"I have a photo shoot in Baltimore in a couple of days. I can rent a car and drive out to see you."

"Do it. Maybe you can help me figure out a way to convince Claire to sign the divorce papers."

✳    ✳    ✳

Dr. Thompson seethed with anger when he read the magazine article online. A few minutes later, his session with Claire Morgan turned chilly.

"There are a lot of people who are desperate to have your hospital bed, Mrs. Morgan. So I'm not going to continue to indulge your charade."

She got up and paced. Tears trickled down her cheeks. She wiped them with her palms, her arms flailing. Her hair was unruly. Her bangs fell into her eyes.

"It's horrible!" she squeaked. "If you discharge me, I don't know what I'll do!"

He observed her body language and jotted, "Shows signs of agitation."

"Trent is a louse! I'll kill him! I'm afraid I wouldn't have much choice after all the things he's done to me."

"All right. You have just threatened to murder your husband. You have to work out your anger issues, Mrs. Morgan."

She folded her arms and pouted. "You just don't understand!"

"Try me. Let's start off with your faked amnesia. Why did you do it?"

She ran her hands through her hair and looked at him cockeyed. "It was my last shot. I thought I could win him back. I think it worked. He's so worried about me it will only be a matter of time before he leaves Michelle."

"But what if he doesn't?"

"I don't know what I'll do!"

"You're setting yourself up for a fall. He's obviously madly in love with his girlfriend."

"What would you do if your wife left you for another man?"

"I don't know. I would be upset. But I would handle it in a nonviolent manner."

His eyes seemed to probe her every movement. She turned around and looked out the window.

"How long have you had these feelings of low self-worth?"

"It all started when Trent got wrapped up with his career. I knocked myself silly to make him happy—to be more appealing—then he started seeing Michelle and..."

Twenty minutes later, Dr. Thompson glanced at the brass clock on his desk and said, "I'm afraid there's nothing more that I can do for you, Mrs. Morgan. As I said before, there are a lot of patients who really need your bed. I spoke to your husband a little while ago. We both think it's in your best interest to be treated at home. You can talk to a therapist on an outpatient basis."

When the session ended, he shook her hand and wished her luck. Then he headed out.

\* \* \*

Trent was so angry that he refused to pick up Claire from the hospital. Bill had to go get her. The ride home was chilly. Neither of them uttered a word. When they arrived home, Bill dragged her suitcase into her bedroom and cringed when he saw women's lingerie on the floor. On his way out, he saw Michelle standing at the bathroom door.

He glared at her and said, "You have some nerve. You just left that here out of spite."

"You have a nerve barging in here unannounced."

"My mother has been through enough, Michelle, especially the way you both treated her. Don't get me wrong. I'm furious about everything she's done. But I really don't blame her. If it hadn't been for you, she wouldn't have done what she did."

Michelle scoffed. "She brought it on herself."

"I really don't want to hear this. I'm warning you. Start packing and get the hell out or—"

"Is that a threat?"

"You can take it any way you want." He slammed the door and marched down the hall. He stood quietly with his hands at his sides and looked down at his parents in the family room. They were arguing again.

"You son of a bitch!" she shouted. "How dare you! How can you leave me for that tramp?"

"Easy. One might ask how a sane man could stand living with an egomaniacal woman like you. You're selfish. The very idea that you staged your disappearance and made us think you were dead all that time! And to top it off, you pretended not to know us when you were finally tracked down. You have a lot of nerve, Claire, and I refuse to take it anymore! I've had enough of your childish games!"

"The hell with you!" She stomped out the French doors and took a long walk to blow off steam.

Trent looked up at his son leaning on the rail. Bill glared at him and walked hurriedly to his bedroom.

# CHAPTER 15

By late August, tension mounted with the soaring temperature. Michelle was unrelenting in her desire to be free from Claire's clutches.

She and Claire were having tea on the patio about 9:30 a.m. They were not there for a friendly chat, though. Michelle was the last person Claire wanted to spend time alone with. She had accepted Michelle's invitation with trepidation, realizing that something had to be done to remedy the situation.

Michelle had a mean streak, and she was very good at getting people to do what she wanted. If Claire wouldn't listen to Trent, Michelle was bound and determined for her to finally get the message. She was not prepared for Claire's ammunition, however.

"Why don't we be honest with each other, Claire? You don't want to be here, and I certainly don't want to be here. We hate each other."

"Why don't you tell me why you really wanted to talk to me?"

"All right, I will. If you don't sign the divorce papers, I'll marry Trent anyway."

Claire laughed. "Come now, do you really expect I won't put up a good fight? Bigamy. I wonder how long a prison sentence Trent will receive. I'll visit him every other weekend. I hope he'll be able to fight off the horny inmates. Do Mormon men in Utah still have multiple wives?"

"You're a cruel, vindictive woman! If I were Trent, I could think of ways to get rid of you."

"And I could think of some ways to get rid of you too, dearie." Claire opened a large canvas bag that was on the table and shoved a manila envelope toward her rival. "Merry Christmas. Go ahead, open it."

Michelle peeled off the seal and shook the contents out onto the table. She cupped her hands over her face and gasped at the eight-by-ten color glossies. She was in her birthday suit.

"How did—how did you get these?"

"I hired a private detective to do some digging. He knows a lot of sleazy photographers in New York City. He paid him a pretty penny for these porno shots."

Michelle shook the photos at her and shouted, "You witch!"

"Are you going to leave my husband, or do I have to hand these beauties to the press?"

"That's blackmail!"

"You hit the nail on the head, dearie. Trent won't think so highly of you after he sees these. Make your choice. You can go back to him or see yourself in girly magazines around the world. Take your pick."

"Go ahead. See if I care. Maybe I'll get a *Playboy* spread. Or maybe even a movie deal. It would be a great career opportunity."

Claire burst into uncontrollable laughter. "You must be delusional. You can't act. And you're too skinny. Men wouldn't pay to look at you. Hollywood starlets lose roles at about thirty-five. So that doesn't give you much time, sweetie. It could also be detrimental to your career. That means your career could be destroyed."

"I know what it means!"

"You could get a movie deal out of it, but I'm afraid Trent will look at you as a cheap whore! He's old fashioned, but he's human. He gave into temptation. That's the only explanation for why he would go with someone like you. I still can't understand what he sees in you."

"Damn you!"

"He's a powerful man. Don't underestimate him. He has the power to make or break people."

"He loves me!"

"If you think that, you really are delusional."

"He'll stand by me!"

"Not after he sees these photos. If they go to press, he'll destroy you."

Michelle was quiet. "I didn't think of it that way."

"That's the idea, dearie. All I have to do is post them online, and they'll go viral."

"It won't matter. I'll just tell him I was desperate for money then. I was just a kid. He'll understand."

"No, he won't."

Michelle stared at her in astonishment. She couldn't believe she had fallen into Claire's snare. "You lying bitch! You treat Trent like dog meat! You don't deserve him!"

Claire's tone softened. "I'll cut you some slack. After all, you were so kind to him during my absence. I'll give you one week to tell him you're leaving him. If you're still here after that, I'll post these photos online. And then poof! Do you understand?"

"Yes," Michelle croaked. Tears streamed down her cheeks. She rose and stomped down the patio steps.

Michelle mulled over her situation. She knew Trent loved her. They were really good together. If Claire leaked the photos to the press, he would probably stand by her. But she had nagging doubts. In the back of her mind, she worried how he would react. He was so overcome with guilt about the whole mess. He always had to do the right thing.

What if he didn't understand? He was a powerful man with connections. It could hurt her modeling career. She was not willing to sacrifice everything she had worked so hard to achieve. She did not want to wind up strung out on drugs like her little sister Amanda. She could still have a loving husband and successful career. To do that, she had to find a way to silence Claire.

With deadline day fast approaching, Michelle scrambled to formulate a plan. She had lost patience and was prepared to give Trent an ultimatum. They went out to the garden to speak privately. Trent promised that he would talk to Claire soon, but Michelle didn't believe him. She accused him of letting Claire walk all over him. They argued, and she stomped across the lawn.

*　*　*

Later that morning, Trent and Michelle sat by the weeping willow tree that overlooked the pond and gazed into each other's eyes. It was the only place they could talk without being overheard. He told her that Claire still refused to divorce him. Michelle got so angry that she called him a wimp and scrambled to her feet. He walked hurriedly after her and pulled her right arm toward him.

"Let go. You're hurting me!"

"Listen to me! Give me some more time!"

She pulled free and clenched her teeth. "I've given you plenty of time, and she won't divorce you! The selfish cow! I can only wait so long."

"There has to be a way."

"I can think of some things."

"Like what?"

She smiled. "Maybe you should just kill her."

"Think of a logical solution, Michelle."

"Okay, take her to court. You can sue her for mental cruelty. She made you think she was dead for months. Call her bluff. See if she'll want to fork over a pretty penny in legal fees."

"She wouldn't care. The added attention would make people feel sorry for her. Then they would think I'm a louse. I'm afraid that's her one flaw—vanity."

"Do you have any other solutions?"

"I'm afraid not."

They saw Bill coming toward them and slipped into the greenhouse. Trent checked to see if Marty was there. He did not see him, so they continued their chat.

"Maybe you should kill her," Michelle said. "I'm not kidding."

"I don't believe we're having this conversation."

"I can. I've had just about enough of hearing Claire's complaints. We can make it look like an accident. That's it!"

"But how?"

"The poor thing was so depressed when she found out you were divorcing her that she committed suicide."

"How on earth would we pull it off?"

"We could slip something in her drink."

He looked at her incredulously. "But how do we do that?"

"Don't worry. Leave that to me. I'm sure there are a lot of garden supplies in the shed that are poisonous. All we have to do is slip something in her drink when she isn't looking. We'll need to create a diversion. I'll distract her, and you can slip it into her drink."

"Why do I have to do it? You're the one who dreamed the whole thing up."

"We can decide that later. This is the only way to get rid of her."

He took a deep breath and said, "If you say so. I can't believe you're involving me in something this absurd."

She grabbed his hand and pulled him along with her. "Come on, let's make a plan!"

They went outside and walked hurriedly toward the house.

Marty Brown stepped out of the forsythia bushes, three rows down. He had been taking a break from spraying weed killer and had heard everything they said.

\*　　\*　　\*

Elizabeth handed Marty a glass of water. He drank heartily and held out his hand for more. She went over to the faucet, refilled the glass, and handed it back to him.

"Ahhhh, that hit the spot!"

"You look beat, Marty."

"I'd just love to be in air conditioning. Especially today. It was already ninety-five degrees at ten this morning."

"I don't know how you do it."

"You're lucky waiting on the Morgans hand and foot—in air conditioning."

"At least you can work in the great outdoors."

He grunted. "What's the latest gossip?"

She told him about last night's argument between Claire and Trent. "She won't give him the divorce, and he's upset. He wants to marry Miss du Prix."

He leaned forward and lowered his voice, "Hey listen, speaking of Miss du Prix. They went into the greenhouse this morning and were talking about Mrs. Morgan. I could hear everything they were saying. They didn't even know I was there."

"It isn't good to eavesdrop, Marty. I try not to when I'm in the kitchen, but it's hard not to."

His eyes crossed. "I think Mrs. Morgan is in some kind of danger."

She looked at him skeptically. "What do you mean?"

He told her how angry Michelle got when she found out that Claire still refused to divorce Trent. "She said the only way to get rid of Mrs. Morgan is to poison her!"

Elizabeth's eyes widened. "What?"

"They want to kill her! I think they're gonna put poison in her drink!"

"Have you been drinking again?"

"I'm serious!"

"I think the sun is making you silly, Marty."

"I know what I heard!"

"Maybe they were kidding."

"I don't think so. I think they were serious."

"Maybe you heard it wrong. You know how people can get things all wrong if they hear part of a conversation?"

"I was there from the beginning!"

She studied his earnest expression and knew he was telling the truth. She could usually tell when someone was telling the truth or lying.

"Hmm, that is a troublesome thought."

"I just thought you should know."

"Thanks for telling me, Marty."

He finished taking his lunch break and went back outside to continue the yard work.

\* \* \*

Claire was sunning herself on the patio. Elizabeth poured tea in her cup and said, "Fine day, isn't it, Claire?"

"That's for sure."

Elizabeth started to go into the house but went back over to Claire instead. "As you know, I'm not one to hold things back."

Claire looked warmly at her dear friend and said, "By all means, unload your problems."

Elizabeth pulled a chair next to her and whispered, "It's not safe here."

"What do you mean?"

"Marty overheard some things."

"I don't understand."

"He overheard your husband and Miss du Prix talking."

Claire smiled and said, "What were they doing—plotting to get rid of me?"

Elizabeth nodded.

Claire batted her eyelashes. "Oh, really? How are they going to do it?"

Elizabeth was emphatic. She put her hand on Claire's and said, "I'm serious. You must listen to me. Marty said they were talking about how if you wouldn't give him the divorce, they'd have to kill you. They're going to put poison in your drink. Just be careful."

"Are you sure Marty wasn't drinking?"

"I'm certain that he wasn't. They're planning something."

Claire smiled wryly, considering it for a moment. "Thank you for telling me, Liz."

"Just be careful. I think they're serious." Elizabeth stood and went back inside.

Claire leaned back in the deck chair and doused herself with sunblock. She closed her eyes and let the hot sun do its magic.

"Trent would have to be really desperate to try and bump me off," she muttered.

Bill emerged around the high bushes where his mother was lying and slipped into the house. He could not believe what he had just heard. He knew his parents could not stand being around each other, but he did not expect his father to plot to get rid of her that way.

# CHAPTER 16

About five thirty, Bill watched his father pour a glass of wine at the bar. Michelle went over to him, and he handed it to her. She went over to the French doors and sneered at Claire, who was still lying on a lawn chair with earbuds on.

About an hour later, Elizabeth rang the bell and began serving the meal. Trent sat at the head of the table, with Michelle across from him. Claire had to get dressed and arrived twenty minutes late. They were in the middle of eating. She and Michelle exchanged artificial smiles.

"That's my chair, dearie," Claire said.

"You were late."

"Cut it out!" Bill cried. "You're acting like three-year-olds."

Claire sat across from her son and glared at Michelle. "Who forgot to put the trash out?"

Michelle shot Trent an irritated look. "Are you going to let her talk to me that way?"

"No, honey." He turned his attention to his soon to be ex-wife. "Claire, you have no right treating people the way you do. One of these days, someone is going to put you in your place."

"Is that a threat?"

"It's only a piece of advice."

They quieted down when Elizabeth entered the room. "Is there anything I can do for you?"

"Would you get a bottle of wine, please?" Michelle asked.

Elizabeth went into the family room and came back carrying a bottle of Cabernet Sauvignon. She eyed Michelle suspiciously and poured her drink. Then she poured wine for Trent and Bill. She went over to Claire and asked, "Would you like some more wine, Mrs. Morgan?"

Claire held out her glass and said, "Please."

She poured the drink and headed out of the room. After Elizabeth had gone, they finished eating. Trent asked Bill and Michelle to go into the family room so he could speak privately to Claire. As Michelle left, Claire looked at her and said, "I'll send out press releases first thing tomorrow morning. And Twitter is just a click away."

Michelle gave her the evil eye as she walked out.

Trent looked incredulously at his wife. "What the devil was that about?"

"Oh nothing," Claire answered coolly.

Trent reached in his jacket pocket and slid an envelope toward Claire. "Ned Leiberman has drawn up the divorce papers, and I signed a copy. It's up to you now. I mean it this time. We can do this cordially, or we can battle it out in court. I don't want to do that."

"Don't be ridiculous." Claire reached for her glass and swallowed hard. "We've been through this before. I won't give you the divorce."

"Be reasonable."

"You don't love her. You only think you do."

"I do so! She makes me happy."

"She doesn't deserve you. She's just a whore."

"She's not a whore."

"Perhaps that was a bit harsh. But she certainly doesn't meet our social standards."

"Just the way I didn't meet your parents' approval. It comes to that, does it?"

"But that was different. We really loved each other."

"If you can call it that."

"You have the nerve to divorce me. You wouldn't be anywhere without my parents' inheritance. It certainly bought a couple of newspapers, didn't it?"

"That's true."

"If we get a divorce, sole ownership of the newspapers will revert to me. And I shall simply sell them. How do you like that?"

"I don't care about the money. Michelle and I are good together."

"That's debatable."

Trent pressured her to sign the divorce papers, and they shouted at each other. She got up and yanked the tablecloth. Glassware shattered, thousands of pieces scattering across the floor. Elizabeth Ashton rushed in to see what was wrong. She saw Claire standing over Trent, screaming bloody murder. Her eyes were wild. She was a mad-woman.

Trent wiped his mouth with a napkin and said, "I never want to see your lying face around here again! I'm sure we can work out a reasonable alimony arrangement."

"I don't want your damned alimony!" Claire wailed. "You aren't leaving me! I refuse to give you the divorce!" She brushed past Elizabeth and stormed off.

Trent shook his head in disbelief. Elizabeth began cleaning up the mess. Then she busied herself with kitchen chores in a vain attempt to block out that ugly scene.

She had always cleaned up after them. It was too bad she couldn't clean up the mess of their broken marriage.

\* \* \*

Bill sat on the sofa in the family room and texted. He blocked out his parents' screaming. He pretended Michelle wasn't sitting at the bar. They both looked up in horror when they heard the sound of breaking glass but then went back to what they were doing.

Claire stood in the entryway and scowled at Michelle, who had no idea she was there. Claire watched her sprinkle powder into her wine and stir it with a swizzle stick.

Claire marched into the room and went over to the bar to pour her own drink. She eyed Michelle icily as she set it on the end table next to the sofa. She went over to the telephone on the desk and watched Michelle's reaction as she picked up the receiver.

Trent burst into the room and shouted, "I've had just about enough of this roller-coaster ride we're on, Claire!"

Claire turned to face him and waved her hands in the air. They were now standing practically nose to nose with each other. "As far as I'm concerned, you caused the problem when you started sneaking around with that bitch!"

"Shut the hell up!" Michelle cried. She went over to the end table and switched glasses while they were arguing. Out of the corner of her eye, Claire saw what she did.

Bill rushed over to his parents and said, "Leave her alone, Dad!"

"I won't leave her alone! She's being unreasonable."

"He belongs with me!" Michelle laid her drink on the coffee table and put her arms around him. She kissed him full on the lips, her eyes on Claire. Bill cringed and looked away.

Claire started dialing the *Main Line Chronicle.* "Hello, this is Claire Morgan. Is Todd Stevens there?"

Michelle went over to her and said, "Go ahead and call him. See if I care."

Bill stared at them in astonishment. "What are you talking about?"

"It is none of your concern, Bill," Claire said. "This is between Michelle and me."

Trent threw up his arms and yelled, "Oh, for Christ's sake!" He yanked the receiver out of her hands and told Todd to disregard the call. Then he hung up.

"You don't know what you're doing," Claire said. "I have dirt on your girlfriend here." She opened her purse and waved the private detective's business card around. "Wouldn't you just love to know what Wally Baker found out about her? I'm sure millions of people worldwide would be curious, too."

"You bitch!" Michelle screeched. Then she started hitting Claire.

Bill went over and stood in between them to break them up. "Come on, you two!"

Michelle shoved him so hard that he fell and hit his head on the end table. Trent pushed Claire out of the way and tried to console Michelle. She hurled profanities at Claire. Bill jumped up and slapped his father's back. Then they began hitting each other. Michelle stood there screaming.

Claire got her drink and went over to the coffee table. While they were distracted, she switched glasses.

The fight was over in less than five minutes. It just seemed longer. Trent stormed onto the patio in a fury. Bill went up to his room to get away from them.

Michelle reached for her glass on the coffee table and forced the wine down quickly. Elizabeth quietly entered the room, figuring it was safe to go in there now that she didn't hear any arguing, and started collecting dirty glasses.

Michelle went back to the bar and put the empty glass down. She reached for a bottle of wine and was about to pour another drink when Elizabeth picked up the dirty glass for her and quietly exited the room. Michelle poured wine into another glass and drank quickly to calm her nerves. She glared at Claire.

Claire cast a cold eye on Michelle and said, "You and I are going to have a little chat. Now!"

"Why the hell should I?"

"Believe me you definitely want to hear what I have to say."

"Fine, make it quick."

"So we are at an impasse," Claire said. "How shall it be? Will you leave my husband? Or will I call Todd back?"

"Call him back, see if I care. I'll give the press a sob story about how I made a mistake when I was a kid. I'll say I was desperate for money and cry a little bit. It's true. My fans will eat it up. Maybe I'll get a movie deal out of it."

"I'm sure you'll do just fine, if you could only learn to act. Some actresses have it, others don't."

"I've been given bad reviews, and I can take it."

"You didn't take Mac Yeager's review so well. I got a perfect view of your brawl from my bedroom window. We could have sold tickets to it."

"He had it coming."

"I think you get more bad reviews than good ones. From what I understand, you got excellent reviews in some other flicks."

"What are you talking about?"

"I didn't think there was much acting involved in those X-rated films."

Michelle's eyes flashed with horror. "What does that mean?"

"I think you know what I mean. My detective friend did some more digging and found out that you did some porno flicks. Don't deny it. I have you on film. I finally have you where I want you. Trent won't understand. If you leave tonight, this never has to leave the room. You can go back to doing what you do best. Think it over."

Michelle stared at her in astonishment. Surely, the poison should be taking effect by now.

"But you're supposed to be—" Michelle started choking and clutched her throat.

"What's wrong with you? Don't play sick on me."

Michelle gasped for breath. "You bitch—" she managed to blurt out.

"What the hell is wrong with you?"

"I—I can't breathe!" She leaned on the desk and looked back at Claire. "What—what did you do to me?" Then it suddenly dawned on her. She looked down at the wine glass and then at Claire. "You did this to me!"

"What on earth are you talking about?"

"The drinks—"

"I guess there was a glitch in your plan to poison me. I'm sorry about that. I know how much you wanted to be with my husband. You'll never have him now."

Michelle tried to talk, but her speech sounded strangled. She staggered toward the French doors, waving to get Trent's attention. His back was turned, and he didn't see her.

She tried to bang on the door but didn't have strength to bang loud enough for him to hear it.

She dropped to her knees and lay on the beige carpet, thrashing about like a wild animal. Her entire body started shaking. Her face twitched horribly. She was having convulsions. Her body rocked to and fro. She was wheezing uncontrollably. She was sobbing like a mad woman, her screaming strangled.

"What's wrong?" Claire asked, faking concern.

"You—you did this to me." Michelle choked one last time, and then her body suddenly was very still.

Claire screamed in faked horror as she stood helplessly over Michelle's lifeless body on the beige carpet. Michelle's body lay in a twisted heap like something from a nightmare, her eyes staring up at her nemesis.

# CHAPTER 17

After Criminologist Lynne Tulley photographed Michelle du Prix's twisted body on the family room floor, Coroner Stan Green leaned down to examine the corpse. At fifty-five, he was heavyset with a large, round face. He had a short, gray mustache and a bald spot. He had worked on numerous corpses during his career. He felt that he was making a difference. His fine investigative techniques helped put many criminals behind bars. He helped victims' families find closure and deal with the tragedy of losing their loved ones.

Logan and Flosky took extensive notes. Lieutenant Winters sketched how Michelle du Prix looked lying on the floor.

Trent sat at the bar staring blankly at the chaos around him. His eyes were wide with horror.

Logan went over to him and said, "Tell me what happened. Take your time."

"We were at dinner. She seemed fine all evening—but then she spoke privately to Claire. I was out on the patio and heard a loud scream. I ran back in, and saw Michelle lying dead on the floor. It was just awful!"

"Did Claire tell you how it happened?"

"Yes. She said Michelle started choking and couldn't breathe. And then—and then she just lay on the floor shaking uncontrollably." He bowed his head and said, "I can't believe this happened. I can't believe she's dead! She was too young! She had so much to live for."

"You look a bit shaken up. Maybe you should get some rest, Mr. Morgan. If I have any more questions I can talk to you later."

"I can't believe it!" Trent cried.

❊   ❊   ❊

Claire and Bill were sitting on patio chairs. Bill rubbed her hand to help calm her shattered nerves. There was a large Band-Aid on his forehead.

Logan went over to them and waved at Bill. Then he looked at her and said, "So you're the infamous Claire Morgan. Now we finally meet in person."

"It's nice to meet you, Detective Logan. I'm sorry we aren't meeting in better circumstances."

Logan looked grim. "I never usually meet people in happy circumstances. I usually have to calm them down after something tragic like this happens."

"I'm sorry I caused so much trouble. But I just had to do it. I wanted people to know what Trent did to me."

"I'm not here to discuss your marital problems, Mrs. Morgan. I just have a few questions to ask about what happened to Michelle du Prix. I understand that you were the last person to see her alive. Can you tell me what happened?"

It took all of Logan's skills as a trained detective to decipher what Claire was trying to tell him about the horrible chain of events that led to Michelle du Prix's horrifying death that night. Claire was so upset that she couldn't calm down, despite all of Bill's efforts.

"We got into an argument, and Michelle started hyperventilating," Claire said. "And then—and then she started choking and couldn't breathe. And then—and then she just fell on the floor shaking uncontrollably. It was truly the most frightening thing I've ever witnessed in my life. It was just horrible!"

"Did she appear sick before that?"

Claire shook her head. "She was fine. We were all eating dinner. And after that, we drank wine in the family room."

"Did you notice anything off about her tonight?"

"Not that I can recall."

"They got into a nasty argument," Bill cut in. "It got so bad that I fell and hit my head on the coffee table." He did not want to admit that Michelle had pushed him.

"That would explain the bandage on your forehead," Logan observed. "What was the argument about?"

He waved his right hand and said, "The usual. You didn't tell Detective Logan the whole story, Mother."

Logan looked at Claire and asked, "And what is that?"

She said that Trent had asked Bill and Michelle to go into the family room so they could talk privately. When he told her that he had signed divorce papers, they got into an argument.

"They took the fight into the den a few minutes later," Bill said. "Only it was between Michelle and my mother then. It was a knock-down, drag-out fight that involved all of us."

Logan's eyebrows arched. "You don't say."

"I got so irritated that I went up to my room to get away from them. My father went to the patio."

"What were you arguing about?" Logan asked Claire.

"What do you think? Trent, of course."

"Did you hurt Michelle in any way?"

"Of course not!" she snapped. "She was fine all night, like I said. And then—and then she fell on the floor shaking all over. It was horrible! I can't believe it."

Logan thanked them and told them to call him if they remembered anything else. Then he went back into the family room to talk with his colleagues.

*   *   *

Logan went over to the morgue the next morning. Before going in, he put on a plastic suit, latex gloves, and a mask. He braced himself as he went into the room, not knowing what awaited him this time. Over the years, he had seen some pretty nasty things in that room. He had seen a lot of corpses with their guts splayed open on the stainless-steel autopsy table, their body fluids draining in the holes. He had observed his fair share of gunshot wounds and stabbings. All the signs of death were all over the autopsy room. He often saw body parts being weighed on a scale. As scientific as it was, he knew that Stan was trying to discover answers to help grieving family members find closure so they could pick up the broken pieces of their shattered lives.

Stan was leaning over Michelle du Prix's body on the autopsy table. He had put a protective hood over the corpse. Logan stared at the gaping hole that extended from Michelle's chest and neck to her naval. He cringed when Stan reached his hands in, removed her liver, and placed it on a scale to take measurements.

Maintaining a safe distance, Logan asked, "What's up?"

"She won't bite. Come on, Frank. Don't be a baby." He motioned for him to come closer.

Logan went over to him and cringed when he looked down at the greenish flesh of her face. "What did you find?"

"Do you see anything unusual about her blood?"

"No."

"It's a dead giveaway. Excuse the pun. It has a cherry red color."

"No kidding! So what are you saying?"

"Think about it."

"She didn't die a natural death, that's for sure."

"No, she didn't. Her blood and tissues are a cherry red color. There's a distinct almond odor. Take a whiff."

"No thanks. I'll take your word for it."

"It has to be cyanide. Someone poisoned her. Or she did it to herself."

"She just finished eating dinner and had a glass of wine about eight o'clock. Shortly after that, she started choking and wound up having the convulsions on the floor."

"Effects of cyanide are instantaneous. A maximum of about ten to twenty minutes. I suspect that someone in the room with her must have put the poison in her drink at some time after dinner, when no one was looking." Stan stuck his hands in the gaping hole and removed Michelle's heart. Then he placed it on the scale and weighed it. Then he wrote down the measurements.

"What kind of product would have contained the cyanide?"

Stan shrugged his shoulders. "It could have been from a household cleaning product. Insecticides and pesticides also contain cyanide. A little bit of it could have somehow been slipped into her drink. I'll have to run some tests to know for sure."

"How long until you find out?"

"It will take as long as it takes. I'll let you know when I find out something."

"Thanks." Logan walked hurriedly out of the room, removed his protective gear, and made a beeline for the locker room. He washed up with disinfectant soap and headed back to Morgan House.

It was pushing one hundred degrees. Logan dabbed his face with a damp cloth and whistled as he wandered to the backyard patio. He saw Trent Morgan sitting at a white wrought-iron table, laboring over paperwork.

Trent looked up to see the detective coming toward him and asked, "What can I do for you, Detective?"

"I was wondering if you could clear up something for me, Mr. Morgan."

Trent cleared off a spot at the table and motioned for him to sit down. Logan eased into the chair and looked over at the garden.

"I just wanted to ask some more questions about Michelle du Prix. We just found out that she was poisoned."

Trent gaped at him in disbelief. "Poisoned?"

"The coroner found cyanide in her system, Mr. Morgan."

"I don't believe it!"

"Tell me everything that happened last night."

Trent tapped his pen and was eerily silent. A couple of minutes later, he said, "Michelle went into the den just before five."

"How was she acting?"

"She was a bit nervous. That's perfectly understandable, coming to dinner to be with her boyfriend's wife."

"Then what happened?"

Once again, Trent mentioned the argument he and Claire got into over dinner when he presented her with the divorce papers that he had signed. "You must think all we do is get into fights around this place."

"It's perfectly natural for people to get into arguments once in a while. But it isn't so great if they do it all the time. And it sounds like that was your pattern, arguing a lot."

"I have to admit, there has been a lot of tension around here. But Claire gives as good as she gets."

"Did Michelle seem nervous or upset during dinner?"

"The atmosphere was chilly, to say the least. She and Claire were giving each other dirty looks like high school girls fighting over a boyfriend."

"Then what happened?"

"Claire got so angry she yanked the tablecloth. Glass smashed all over the place, and Elizabeth had to come in to take care of it."

Logan shook his head in disbelief.

"When I went to the family room, they were all in there."

"What time was that?"

"About seven thirty."

"How did Michelle feel at that time?"

"Her nerves were shot to hell. I think we were all on edge after the incident. She fixed me a drink to help calm my nerves."

"Where was your wife?"

"I think she was sitting at the bar drinking a glass of wine."

"How about Bill?"

"He was on the sofa, texting someone. He was probably just trying to ignore us."

"Then what happened?"

Trent told him about the events leading up to the next argument.

"Why did Claire call your newspaper editor?"

"I don't know. I think she must have had something on Michelle. That was the only thing I could figure. Maybe it was just one of her cheap melodramatic ploys to get back at me. She waved a business card around and said, 'Wouldn't you just love to know what Wally Baker found out about her? I'm sure millions of people worldwide would be curious, too.'"

"Who is Wally Baker?"

"The private detective Claire hired to dig up dirt on Michelle."

"Do you know what she meant?"

"I'm afraid not. Michelle flew into a rage and started hitting Claire."

"Hmmm. Then what happened?"

Trent described in graphic detail the brawl that ensued.

"Did you find out why they were mad at each other?"

"No. I got so angry that I went out on the patio. And Bill went up to his bedroom."

"Do you have any idea what they were talking about?"

Trent shook his head. "Not a clue. Claire wouldn't say."

"What time was that?"

"About seven thirty."

"And then what happened?"

"I heard Claire screaming and rushed in to see what was happening. And that's when—and that's when I saw Michelle lying on the floor."

"Is your wife here?"

"I think she's taking a nap."

"Thanks. I didn't mean to upset you."

Trent's face twitched as he watched Logan pull open the French doors and go inside. He spread out his papers and resumed work on renovation plans for his newly acquired newspaper in Annapolis, Maryland. The resumes of tech-savvy college graduates lay in a neat pile next to his paperwork.

*　*　*

Logan smelled pine oil as he watched Elizabeth Ashton tidying up. Nothing appeared ruffled or out of place. She handed him a mug of coffee, and he asked her some questions before Claire came downstairs. She told him that she had overheard Trent and Claire arguing about getting a divorce again. She couldn't hear what the argument in the family room was about.

She looked across the room, and her jaw dropped when she saw Claire coming downstairs. She was now a strawberry blonde. She had put on too much makeup and looked gaudy. She had on a red silk robe that clashed with her new hair color.

Elizabeth lowered her voice and said, "I really can't talk now. Talk to me in the kitchen." She quietly exited.

"May I help you?" Claire asked all smiles.

Logan smiled politely at her and said, "I need to ask you some more questions about Michelle du Prix. I just found out that she was poisoned."

Claire gasped. "Oh my God! That's horrible. Are you sure?"

He nodded and looked intently at her. "I believe that someone in this house did it."

"Did it ever occur to you that they were trying to do away with me?"

"Who was trying to do away with you, ma'am?"

She leaned forward and lowered her voice. "Elizabeth heard some things."

169

"What did she hear, ma'am?"

"Some pretty damaging things from my husband."

"What do you mean?"

"Well, she didn't actually hear it. But Marty did. You know him. He's our gardener."

"What did he hear?"

She revealed everything Elizabeth had told her. "I was shocked when I first heard about it."

"Uh-huh. And you actually expect me to believe your theatrics?"

"It's true. Ask Elizabeth if you don't believe me."

"Why should I believe anything you tell me? You admitted faking your disappearance to that magazine reporter. When you came home, you saw Michelle du Prix still hanging around your husband. Maybe you slipped some cyanide in her drink to get her out of the picture."

"I would never do such a thing! I don't even know where one would get cyanide. They were out to get me. Trent did this! Arrest him before he kills me for real!"

"Then tell me what happened. Who hated Michelle du Prix enough to slip cyanide in her drink? She was an obvious threat to you Mrs. Morgan."

"I may have played a little joke on my husband, but I would never resort to murder."

"She was a threat, and she wasn't going away. You had motive."

She pushed hair out of her eyes and said, "They had just enough reason to want me out of the way. Did you ever think about that, Frank?"

"Let's think about that in a moment. Tell me everything that happened last night."

"Trent told me I had better give him the divorce, and I asked, 'Is that a threat?' But he didn't say anything. Then we started shouting at each other, as usual."

"Then what happened?"

"I found him at the bar in the den," she lied. "It's his way. He always has a drink to calm his nerves."

"Where were Bill and Michelle?"

"She was at the bar drinking her wine. And Bill was on the sofa texting someone. He does that too much. It's habit-forming, isn't it?"

Logan nodded. "How long were they in the family room while you and Trent argued?"

"I don't know."

"Were they there the whole time?"

"You'll have to ask Bill."

"What happened after you went into the family room?"

She told him about the brawl that soon followed but neglected to mention the private detective she hired to dig up dirt on Michelle. She also failed to mention switching the wine glasses.

"When things calmed down, Michelle insisted on talking to me. She wanted to iron out some problems."

"What time was that?"

"About a quarter to eight."

"How long did you talk to her?"

"About ten minutes. She was acting odd. She wasn't feeling well." She went on to describe the horrible chain of events that followed.

"So you were you the last one to see her alive, right?"

She nodded.

"When you were at the bar, did anybody pour you a drink?"

"Trent poured another glass of wine for me as a peace offering, I suppose," she lied. "He told me it would help calm me down."

He smiled and said, "Thank you for your help, Mrs. Morgan."

"You must believe me. They were trying to kill me! You should be looking into that."

He promised he would and started to go into the kitchen when Bill passed him in the hallway. They went into the porch and sat down.

"What nonsense is my mother telling you?"

"She claims that your father and Michelle were plotting to kill her. Is that true?"

Bill looked into Logan's dark eyes and said, "She'll say anything. I really thought she was gone. You don't know how used I felt when she gabbed to that hack magazine writer. We worried for nothing. You were right all along."

Logan grunted. "I'm afraid so." He told him that Michelle had been poisoned and wanted to know what Bill had done after he left his parents alone in the dining room.

"I had another glass of wine. And then Michelle arrived!"

"You don't sound too fond of her."

"I couldn't stand her!" He watched Logan jotting notes and hoped that he hadn't included his last statement. "I didn't mean it that way—it's not as if I would have wanted to do her in."

"You must have resented your father for going with a woman who could have passed for your sister—or your girlfriend."

Bill's facial muscles twitched.

"I struck a nerve, didn't I?"

"I don't know what you're getting at."

"You were dating her, weren't you?"

"You're off base!"

"It's true. I have excellent instincts. When I was here a few weeks ago, I noticed how you acted around Michelle and your father. I sensed a lot of tension in the room. I didn't ask you if you had dated Michelle because I didn't think it was relevant at the time. But it was. We were on the patio when you offered to pay me to find your mother. Do you remember?"

"Yeah, so what?"

"I said I didn't know how I would feel if my girlfriend left me for another man. Then you said, 'It feels like a knife twisting in your guts.' And when I asked what you meant, you said you didn't want to talk about it. You were talking about Michelle, weren't you?"

Bill nodded reluctantly. "I loved her very much. I thought she loved me. But it never would have worked out."

"Why not?"

"We were always arguing about inane things."

"It must have really upset you when she started seeing your father."

"I was furious!" he snapped. Then he carefully chose his next words. "I was angry at her, but I wouldn't hurt her. I wouldn't hurt anyone."

Logan asked how long he and Michelle were in the family room. He wasn't sure because he had to go upstairs to make a phone call. When he came downstairs, he saw Michelle at the bar. He poured another glass of wine, and they sat in silence, listening to his parents arguing in the dining room.

"How long were you gone?"

"About five or ten minutes. I had to talk to a client."

"I understand that your parents continued their argument when you came back downstairs. What was it about?"

Bill groaned and told him about it in graphic detail. His parents hadn't gotten it out of their system.

"My mother got angry and waved a business card in Michelle's face."

"Do you know why your mother did it?"

"I don't know why she does anything. I know that Michelle wasn't happy about it. Maybe she had dirt on her. She was going to call the editor at my father's newspaper in Philly."

"So you have no idea why your mother wanted to call the newspaper?"

Bill shook his head. He relayed the horrible chain of events that led to hitting his head on the coffee table. He lied and told Logan that it was his father who shoved him.

Logan checked his notes and said, "That will be all. Thank you for being so patient."

"You can think what you like, but I didn't do this horrible thing to her." He went out the porch door and descended the steps. Logan watched him disappear from view around the bushes.

"Hmmm, he has a lot of hidden anger."

He went back into the family room, but Claire was not there now. He looked around and mumbled, "Nothing's out of place. Maids always have to destroy evidence."

"We are only doing our jobs."

He looked over at Elizabeth Ashton who was standing in the doorway.

"I'm sorry, I didn't—"

She smiled wryly and said, "I'm always cleaning up behind them."

"Did you clean this room the night that Michelle du Prix was poisoned?"

She nodded.

"Was anything out of the ordinary?"

"Well, there were a few wine glasses here and there. I just put them in the dishwasher."

"So what you're telling me is that you basically destroyed the evidence?"

She gasped and looked wild-eyed at him. "I didn't mean to. I—I was just tidying up, that's all. A force of habit."

He jotted it in his notepad and looked harshly at her. He huffed and said, "When did you pick up the dirty glasses?"

"About five or ten minutes before Miss du Prix collapsed on the floor. Oh, it was horrible. I knew Mrs. Morgan was upset. They both were before it happened. I went to get the dirty glasses and could sense the tension. It was just terrible. That was before—before they got into the argument."

"Did you hear what they were saying?"

She shook her head. "I had turned on the dishwasher at that point. I couldn't hear anything over all that racket."

"A few minutes ago, you told me that Claire refused to sign the divorce papers, and they got into an argument over it."

"I can't talk about it here. They might hear."

"Can we go somewhere else?"

She led him into the kitchen and sat across from him.

She told him that she heard a loud noise in the dining room about quarter after seven. She rushed into the room to find broken glass smashed all over the place. Claire had apparently yanked the tablecloth. They were screaming at each other. It took her forever to clean the mess. Later on, she started the dishwasher and heard muffled screams coming from the family room. She couldn't hear what they were saying though. About five minutes later, it died down for a little while.

"About quarter of eight, I heard a loud shrieking noise, and I rushed into the family room to see what was happening. And that's when—and that's when I saw her lying on the floor like that. It was God awful! Her face was a funny color, and she was clutching her throat like she was choking."

"I know I'm asking a lot of questions, and I appreciate your patience. But this is very important. Did you tell Claire that Trent and Michelle were plotting to kill her?"

She nodded and said, "Marty told me."

"What did he say?"

"I could lose my job for this," she said in a hushed tone. "I'd rather not say."

"It could be very important," Logan urged.

"Ask him yourself. I don't want to say the wrong thing."

"I can understand your reluctance to tell me, Mrs. Ashton. But I need to hear your side of the story."

She told him that Marty was taking a break when he mentioned overhearing Michelle and Trent discussing ways to get rid of Claire. "I thought he was drunk at first. But he was cold sober. He swore to me it was true and they weren't joking. But you better ask him the rest yourself. And you never heard it from me."

Logan thanked her and went outside to look for Marty. He heard the rider lawn mower in the distance, and waved at the old man as he turned toward him.

"I guess I'll have to talk to him tomorrow morning," Logan muttered as he headed back to his car.

✼   ✼   ✼

A few minutes later, Marty Brown drove the riding lawnmower into the shed and turned off the engine. He reached for a rag and wiped sweat from his face. He headed toward the patio and saw Trent hovering over paperwork at the table. He waved at him, and Trent returned the gesture.

Marty went over to him and said, "I know why that detective wanted to talk to you."

Trent rubbed his eyes and looked at him. "What was that, Marty?"

He repeated his comment, and Trent looked back at his paperwork. "It's just a lot of red tape. Nothing that would concern you."

"Did they find out she was poisoned yet?"

Trent dropped what he was doing and leaned on the rail. "What did you say?"

"I think you know what I said. Sometimes I think you can hear every conversation on these grounds. If you open your ears."

"What are you talking about? You're not making any sense."

"I see people coming and going here. You might not have known I was working in the greenhouse the other day. But I was there."

Trent hurried down the steps and led him away from the house. When they were out of earshot, he grabbed the old man by the collar and said, "What are you talking about?"

"You told Miss du Prix that Mrs. Morgan wasn't going to give you the divorce. Then she got upset and said, 'Maybe we should kill the old bat.' So then you planned a way to get rid of her."

Trent shoved him. Marty started to fall back but caught himself. "You were just imagining it, old man. You heard part of the conversation. We were just joking."

"I don't suppose pesticide from the shed would be a bit suspicious. It's poisonous, you know."

"What do you mean?"

"Miss du Prix said she'd take care of it. And now she's dead. I think she slipped the stuff in your wife's drink and got it by mistake."

"You're out of your mind!" Then reality sank in. Trent put his right hand over his mouth and gasped, "Oh my God."

Marty grinned, his eyes sparkling. His remaining teeth glinted in the sunlight. "Detective Logan knows you wanted a divorce. You didn't tell him the whole story. It won't take long for him to figure—"

"Okay, what do you want? This is blackmail, isn't it?"

Marty wiped dirt off his hands and nodded. "I think a cool five hundred thousand clams should set me for life."

"If I give you the money, you'll shut your mouth?"

"Uh-huh." He laughed heartily.

"I'll give you an additional $5,000 if you'll get out of the country."

"I've always wanted to go to the Bahamas. Or maybe Europe."

"I don't care where you go, just get out of here!"

"If you don't come up with the money before the bank closes today, I'll start talking."

"I can't get it that quickly. It will look suspicious if I withdraw that much."

"You'll think of a way."

Trent reached in his jacket pocket and wiped his forehead with his handkerchief. "All right," he said at last.

"Drop the money off at my apartment."

"No, I can't do that. I don't want anybody to see me."

"All right, meet me in the shed at midnight."

"Okay."

"If you're a few thousand short, I'll tell Detective Logan everything."

Trent looked over his shoulder to see if anyone was watching. Marty whistled gleefully as he watched him walk hurriedly across the lawn.

*　*　*

Marty was beaming when he entered the kitchen and sat down at the table about two o'clock. He looked exhausted from a hard day's work out in the blistering sun. Elizabeth handed him a glass of water and sat across from him. He gulped it down and asked for a refill.

"You really have to quit working out in the hot sun so much," she admonished. "Just take a look at your face. It's all red! You'll drop over from heatstroke one of these days if you're not careful."

"I don't got to worry about that no more." He reached for a paper towel and wiped perspiration off his face.

She eyed him suspiciously. "What do you mean?"

"Mr. Morgan just canned me."

She gasped. "Did he catch you drinking again?"

"Well, it had something to do with it."

She tapped his hand. "Oh, Marty, I'm so sorry to see you go. I'll miss our little talks."

He grinned. "Me too."

"You don't look that shook up over it," she observed.

"Maybe I'm just sick of busting my butt out there every day and not being appreciated."

"Don't put yourself down. The Morgans love your work."

"Maybe she does. He's a pain in the ass. I'm glad to be out of here."

"Do you know where you'll go?"

There was a glint in his eyes. "I've got lots of options. My cash cow just hit me lucky."

She stared at him in astonishment. "What's that supposed to mean?"

He wouldn't say. He finished his drink in one gulp and wiped his moist mouth with his right hand. "Well, I just had to come to say good-bye. Sometimes I took more breaks than I probably should have—just to chat with you."

"I thought so. Well, I'm glad you told me. You'll keep in touch?"

He grinned. "If I'm in town, I'll take you to the finest restaurant in town."

"The diner it is then."

"No, it has to be better than that. Fancy food with fancy napkins like the Morgans got."

"You couldn't afford something like that."

"Maybe I just might."

"Marty, what have you done?"

He got up without answering and limped out of the room. Elizabeth shook her head in disbelief.

☆  ☆  ☆

About quarter of six, Logan poured coffee into his mug and sat at his desk. He reviewed his notes and then reached for his digital recorder. He pressed record and started comprising a suspect list for the Michelle du Prix murder investigation.

"For once, nothing seems too complicated about this case. The suspect list seems to just involve five people at the Morgan residence. They are:

"Trent Morgan: Was having an affair with Michelle. His wife, Claire, refused to get a divorce when he pressured her to do so. The gardener, Martin Brown, allegedly overheard Trent and Michelle plotting to poison Claire. I'll have to talk to Brown in the morning. Motive: Unclear.

"Claire Morgan: Trent's put-upon wife. She was so angry that Trent was cheating on her with Michelle, that she became incensed when he told her he wanted a divorce. They got into an argument and she mysteriously vanished for several weeks. She resurfaced at a hotel in the Poconos and was taken to a mental hospital. Tension between the three of them escalated when she came back home. Elizabeth Ashton told Claire about the alleged plot to poison her a few hours before Michelle drank the wine with the cyanide in it.

Is Claire to be believed? She admitted faking her disappearance to a magazine writer. According to her husband and son, she has done things like that before. If she had prior knowledge of the plot to murder her, could she have switched the drinks during the argument? Claire definitely wanted Michelle out of the way.

At some point after dinner, Trent and Bill both heard Michelle say to Claire, 'Go ahead, call him. See if I care.' Or something like that. Did Claire have something on Michelle? Would that have been reason enough for Michelle to want her out of the way? Claire certainly had sufficient reason to want Michelle gone.

Motive: Revenge; jealousy.

"William Morgan: Claire and Trent's son. He is Michelle's jealous ex-boyfriend. He's angry that his father started dating her. He was alone in the family room with Michelle for several minutes while his parents were arguing in the dining room that night. Maybe he slipped the poison into Michelle's drink while she wasn't looking. Maybe he found out about the plot to poison Claire and turned the tables on them. Motive: jealousy.

"Elizabeth Ashton: the Morgans' housekeeper and cook. The gardener told her about Trent and Michelle's alleged plot to poison Claire. She was serving everyone drinks at dinner. At some point, Bill went upstairs to take a call while his parents were arguing in the dining room. Michelle isn't here to say what happened when she was alone in the family room. Maybe Elizabeth put the poison in Michelle's drink. The major clinker in the case is that Mrs. Ashton washed the dishes, washing away the evidence. Maybe she was just doing her job. Maybe she was trying to protect someone or herself. Motive: Unclear.

"Martin Brown: the Morgans' gardener. He apparently overheard Trent and Michelle plotting to murder Claire. He told Elizabeth what he overheard, and she told Claire hours before Michelle dropped dead from cyanide poisoning. Brown has been caught drinking on the job. And he is known for telling tall tales. Two people were warned in advance, whether it was actually true or not. It gave Claire or Elizabeth plenty of time to put poison in Michelle's wine. I doubt that Elizabeth had any reason to do it, but it's worth checking into.

"Brown was cutting the grass when I went to talk to him. I need to talk to him tomorrow morning. Maybe I can figure out if he was actually telling the truth about the murder plot."

Logan pressed the off button and put the digital recorder in his desk drawer. Then he headed back to his apartment.

# CHAPTER 18

L ogan unfolded the *Lancaster Tribune* and read the lead story.

"Model Poisoned at Morgan House
by Rob Wilcox
Lancaster, Pa.

Up—and—coming actress and model Michelle du Prix, 26, was poisoned Tuesday night at the home of her long-time friend Trent Morgan, owner of the *Main Line Chronicle*.

"The family had just finished eating dinner and were having drinks in their family room, when Ms. du Prix started hyperventilating and collapsed on the floor," said lead detective Frank Logan of the Townsend Police Department. "Death was instantaneous."

Medical Examiner Stanley J. Green discovered cyanide in Ms. du Prix's bloodstream. Neither Green nor Detective Logan would make further comments.

Du Prix was a successful fashion model..."

Logan tossed the newspaper in the trash can and shouted, "I didn't tell Wilcox that Michelle was poisoned. How did he find out about it?"

"He was snooping around here yesterday," Flosky said. "He must've overheard you talking to Stan on the phone. He's a slippery character. He was in and out in a flash. He's like a dog running with a bone when he gets a lead."

Logan grumbled and fumed while reviewing yesterday's notes.

At nine o'clock, he headed out to Morgan House to talk to Marty Brown. He pulled up the driveway and parked on the lawn. He looked around but didn't see the old man. He went up to the front steps and rang the bell. The door opened, and Elizabeth Ashton looked at him sternly.

"Good morning, Detective Logan. What can I do for you?"

"I'm here to see Marty. Have you seen him?"

"He doesn't work here anymore."

"What do you mean?"

"I'm sorry. I can't talk about it."

She started to close the door, but he shoved his foot in the jamb. "But you told me to come back this morning. Did he quit?"

"His services were no longer needed."

"That's odd. Yesterday, you gave no indication that he would be terminated."

"I didn't know."

"Do you know how I can get in contact with him?"

"Well, a little while ago I looked out the back window and saw his pickup truck by the shed. Maybe he came back to get his things."

Logan thanked her and headed for the shed. He saw a rusty tan pickup truck parked under an oak tree in front of the shed.

The smell of stale cigarette butts permeated his nostrils as he entered the building. He shook his head in disbelief when he saw beer cans strewn across the dusty floor. Rakes and shovels were hanging on hooks. Cans and bottles of varying sizes and shapes lined the shelves next to it. He glanced over at neatly coiled ropes lying in a large wooden box. Oil and gas cans sat next to a John Deere rider lawnmower. Mulch bags were stacked on top of each other across the room. At the right, there was a well-worn workbench with gardening equipment overflowing from the drawers.

There was no sign of Marty Brown, so Logan went into the greenhouse. As soon as he stepped foot inside, he felt dwarfed by the hanging baskets that dangled from the ceiling. Rafters stretched across the length of the building. When he reached the end of the row, he saw potted plants on shelves to his left. To his right, marigolds and geraniums were growing in large clay pots.

He moved into the next room and wiped perspiration from his forehead as he proceeded down the row. It certainly was a hothouse.

"Marty!" he yelled. "It's Detective Logan. I need to talk to you."

He listened carefully, but there was no response. He went into the next room and whistled when he saw the cactus display. One of them was about ten feet tall. When he reached the end of the row, he saw pruning tools on a metal table to the right.

He continued down the path. A ficus and other large leafy bushes stuck out from both sides of the row. Palm trees reached to the ceiling. He turned to his right and went in the opposite direction. When he reached the end of the path, he looked down and saw a piece of broken clay pot. Part of a white flower petal was strewn across his path.

He heard his voice rise as he called out Marty's name again. He reached for his weapon and proceeded with more caution.

"Mr. Brown!"

He was just about to round the corner when he saw soil scattered across the cement floor. He pushed palm tree branches out of the way and elbowed his way across. When he got a clear view, he saw a chair lying on its side. He looked up and saw Marty Brown hanging from a support beam.

# CHAPTER 19

Logan sketched the grisly scene and took notes. When criminologist Lynne Tulley finished photographing the hanging man, Lieutenant Winters and Detective Flosky helped take down his body. Tulley dusted for prints on the ladder and then on the chair that had been knocked over.

"That's interesting," she said.

Logan went over to her and asked, "What's that?"

"There are fingerprints on the ladder but not on the chair."

"That is strange. If he hanged himself, he would have touched the chair to position it under the rope."

"You're right. I suspect the prints on the ladder will be from Marty Brown. He could have used the ladder with or without gloves. But the chair is another story."

Winters and Flosky laid Brown's body on a white sheet and looked him over carefully.

"So what do you think?" Winters asked Logan.

"Isn't it obvious?" He pointed to the back of Marty Brown's neck. "You see the bruise?"

"It looks like somebody came up from behind and choked him first. Look at the rope marks."

"If he hanged himself, wouldn't the rope have made an upside-down V-shaped bruise? There's just a straight line where the killer exerted pressure. And his fingerprints aren't on the chair or the ladder. He was murdered."

Winters nodded in agreement. "It had to be somebody strong enough to hoist him up there. But we'd better wait for Stan's autopsy report."

Logan looked down and noticed that a couple of yellow orchids had been stomped on. Their stems were broken. He knelt down to get a closer look and discovered a man's shoe print embedded in the dirt. The toe end was pointing toward the exit.

"Harry, come here. I found a footprint."

Lieutenant Winters went over to take a look. "That doesn't prove anything. It could have been there for days."

"Or it could convict a murderer."

Lynne went over to take a look and said, "They're still fresh. They're not dried up, which proves that the footprint is recent."

Logan looked at Winters and said, "Which throws your theory about it being here for days right out the window. The killer tore out of here in a hurry and probably stepped on the flowers in the process."

"That would explain why the plant stems are broken. The killer was in a real hurry to get out of here and didn't realize that he'd stepped on the flowers."

"He probably thought he could get away with it. But we'll get him."

Lynne leaned down and photographed the footprint and flowers that had been stepped on. Then she sprayed the footprint with a fixative and placed a wooden frame around it. She stirred plaster and water in a bucket while they continued looking for clues.

"It's interesting," Logan said. "I was going to talk to him. And then he wound up with a noose around his neck."

"You don't suppose what Brown told the housekeeper is true?" Winters asked.

"I'm starting to believe it."

Flosky emerged from behind a cactus display and said, "Take a look at this. I think I found something."

They went over to him, and he pointed to a dark blue piece of material about the size of a dime that was caught on a branch. It was gathered into evidence.

Logan went to take a look for clues in the shed. He held his breath so he didn't have to smell the cigarette butts again. He leaned down and picked up a discarded beer can from the floor. It was half empty. He reached for another one. It was empty. He shoved them into plastic baggies and stuck evidence stickers on them. He wrote down the pertinent information, signed, and dated them. At this point, he wasn't sure if more than one person had been drinking from them. He jotted notes in his pad and drew a thumbnail sketch of the room. His eyes were drawn to a pesticide can on the shelf. He could tell by looking at dust rings that it had been moved recently and hadn't been put back in the same spot. He collected it into an evidence baggie, labeled, dated, and initialed it.

He went over to the work bench and rummaged through drawers. In one, he found grimy gloves and various gardening tools. He picked them up at random and examined them. They were rusty and had caked-in dirt. A block and tackle was shoved in another drawer.

He went back over to his colleagues, who were searching for clues outside the greenhouse. He reached for a handkerchief in his jacket pocket and wiped perspiration off his face. It was too hot to be wandering around outside all day. And it had been a lot hotter in the greenhouse.

Flosky leaned down and pointed at the grass. There was a large section that had been flattened. A trail of displaced blades pointed toward the greenhouse. Lieutenant Winters went back inside to tell Lynne Tulley to take a picture of it after she finished making the plaster mold of the footprint.

The Morgans were standing behind the cordoned-off area. Logan went over to offer his condolences and quietly took note of their attire. Trent had on a long-sleeved button-down shirt with no missing buttons or loose threads. Perspiration dripped from his face. Armpit stains moistened his shirt.

Bill wore a tennis shirt and shorts, which was the sensible thing to wear in ninety-five degree weather. He had blue terrycloth bands around his wrists. There were no cuts or bruises on his arms or legs.

Claire wore a large straw hat and a peach-colored sundress.

Elizabeth Ashton was blubbering. Her eyes were red and puffy. Hair was sticking up on the back of her head. She had an apron over a gray blouse and dress. Claire rubbed her shoulder and spoke to her softly. Logan looked down at Elizabeth's apron. There was a brown stain on it.

Trent was stone-faced. "It's a tragedy," he said without emotion.

There was a blank expression on Elizabeth's face. "Why did he do it? He had so much to live for."

"I don't know, ma'am," Logan said. "Who knows why people do what they do?" He turned to face Trent and asked, "When did you last see him, Mr. Morgan?"

"About one o'clock yesterday afternoon. I confronted him about his drinking and told him to leave the premises immediately. I gave him until this morning to pick up his belongings."

"How did he take it?"

"Not well, I'm afraid. I felt bad for him, but there was nothing else I could do. If only he could have cleaned himself up. But something had to be done. I gave him a second chance, but he didn't listen. I gave him a lot of chances. I should have fired him a long time ago."

"He always did his work!" Elizabeth bawled. "You just had it in for him!" She walked hurriedly across the lawn.

Claire frowned. "She isn't taking it well. None of us are. My nerves are shot. I need a brandy." She went after Elizabeth.

Bill told the detective that he had last seen the gardener cutting the grass about two o'clock that afternoon. "I was on my way to a meeting in Philadelphia. I got back about nine o'clock last night."

"How did he seem?"

"He looked happy. That's why it came as a complete shock when we heard the bad news."

Logan thanked him and went into the house. Claire was sharing a brandy with Elizabeth. By now, the housekeeper had calmed down a bit. Logan learned that Elizabeth last saw Marty about two o'clock. She fed him lunch, as usual. Though he was hot and sweaty, he remained in good spirits for a man who had just been fired. He told her he was about to come into some money and was thinking about making plans for the future. But he would not elaborate on what those plans entailed or where the money was coming from.

Marty was still cutting the grass when Claire took a walk after lunch. Two hours later, she heard him arguing with Trent by the pond. She wiped away tears with a handkerchief and said, "Poor Marty. It must have been about the time Trent fired him. Trent didn't mention it when he came in the house. If only I had known, I would have begged him to give Marty another chance."

Logan thanked them and went back to his colleagues outside the greenhouse.

*　*　*

Three hours later, Logan and Flosky went to Marty Brown's apartment. It was a run-down building in a seedy section of town. There were about a dozen cars parked out in front. They broke the bad news to tenants who were sitting on the front steps. Logan did all the talking.

"Oh my God!" they shouted over top of each other.

A young mother burst into tears. "Oh no, not Marty! You're wrong!"

"I'm sorry, but it's true," Logan said.

An old man shouted, "It can't be! Marty? Why would he do such a thing?"

"That's what I'm trying to find out," Logan said gravely. "Did any of you see him last night?"

A young black woman stepped forward and said, "I did."

"What time did you see him?"

"I was just coming back from the IGA store down the street. It must've been about nine. That's when they close. He saw that I was having trouble with one of the bags. It had a hole in it and was starting to fall apart when I got here. He offered to help me carry it to my place. I thanked him, and we talked for a bit."

"Did he seem upset?"

"No, he was just as cheerful as usual."

"I thought he was really chipper," added the old man. "We were out here playing cards and shooting the shit. He kept talking about how he was on top of the world. I can't believe he's gone!"

"Did he say anything to you?"

"He kept talking about how he was coming into dough and was making plans to leave town and do some things he'd never done before. I just figured he got lucky with the lottery or something."

"Did he say where he was going?"

"No."

"Did you ever hear him say anything to make you think he was unhappy?"

The old man scratched his head and said, "Marty? The guy was full of life. It don't add up. It's not like him to do something like that, and I can't believe somebody would want to kill him."

"When was the last time you saw him?" Logan asked the black girl.

"It must've been quarter to ten. I remember because I was expecting a call at ten—and the phone rang right after I came in."

"He came back to the front porch right about then," the old man said. "We were just playing cards and talking."

"Did he mention that he'd lost his job?"

The old man gawked in disbelief. "No, he didn't say anything about it."

"I believe somebody tried to make it look like he hanged himself. Do you know who might have wanted to kill him?"

They couldn't believe anyone would have killed him. Marty was kind and gentle. He always helped them when they were in need.

"When was the last time you saw him?"

"We played on close to eleven. Then we went to our rooms."

"Which is your room?"

"I live on the floor under him," replied the old man.

"Did you hear him leave?"

"No, I couldn't hear a thing. I was a bit irritated about the noise, though. He always has his TV on too loud. I always said he couldn't hear. Well, I watched TV a bit and had a couple more beers. And then I turned in."

"What time was that?"

"I'd say it was about eleven thirty—quarter of twelve. And I didn't see or hear anything unusual."

"I live across from the attic door, and I didn't hear footsteps in the hall," the young black woman added.

Further questioning proved futile, so they went inside. They checked out the mail boxes in the hall. Flosky pointed to one with Marty's name and apartment number on it.

They tracked down the landlord and asked for the keys to Marty's apartment. Logan unlocked the door, and it opened up on a flight of rickety-looking wooden steps leading to Marty's attic apartment. They went upstairs and stepped over beer cans scattered on the floor as they navigated their way across the living room. They bent over so they wouldn't hit their heads on the low slanted ceiling to the left and right. A card table and folding chairs substituted for kitchen furniture. Five feet away, there was a tiny refrigerator. Next to it, there was a toaster oven on the counter.

They walked down a narrow hallway beyond the kitchen and noticed the bathroom door was open. At the end of the hall, a door was ajar. Logan pushed it open, and they went inside. Next to the window, there was a bed and a small end table. A bureau drawer was half open. Shirts were hanging out. Travel brochures were scattered on top.

"It looks like he was planning a trip," Flosky said.

"It ties in with something his friend was saying. It sounds like he was planning on skipping town."

"This apartment must be dirt cheap. How could he afford a trip like this?"

"Maybe he had a bundle saved up. But I doubt it. I think you're onto something, Joe."

They looked around for a few more minutes but did not find anything out of the ordinary. On their way out, they spotted a heavyset Hispanic woman in the hallway. She remembered seeing Marty Brown leaving about eleven thirty the previous evening. They thanked her and headed back to the office.

☆ ☆ ☆

The next morning, Stan Green dropped by the police station and handed Logan the lab report. "You were right, Frank. It looks like Martin Brown was strangled. You were right about the bruise on the back of his neck. The bruise marks don't correlate with a suicide. Somebody came up from behind and strangled him. And then the murderer made it look like he hanged himself."

"Only the person responsible didn't take into account that there were no fingerprints on the chair and rope. Criminals always think they can get away with it."

Stan nodded. "They always forget something and wind up in prison."

"Did you figure out what time he died?"

"Between one and two in the morning. He had been drinking alcohol prior to his murder."

"Could you tell when he had his last drink?"

"About one in the morning."

"What about Michelle's poisoning? Did you find out anything from the lab tests?"

"I ran a test on the pesticide that you found in the shed, and it was a positive match. The murderer must have scooped some powder out of the can and poured it into the wine glass."

"But we'll never know for sure because the housekeeper washed away the evidence."

"It's a shame."

"But at least we know how she was poisoned. Trying to prove it will be a lot harder though. Thanks, Stan."

"If you have any questions, you know where I'll be."

✳ ✳ ✳

Chief Jack Ward grumbled as he did paperwork. He scratched his short red hair and reached for his glass of tea. At forty-eight, he had earned a reputation for being a shrewd police officer. He earned numerous awards for his sharp instincts and bravery. He had been on the force for nearly twenty-five years before he made chief and was assigned to the Townsend Police Department.

He went over to ask Logan if he had found out anything new about the Martin Brown case.

Logan looked up at his large, round face and said, "The plaster mold of the shoe print turned out to be a size twelve. According to the forensic report, the blue fabric we found on the branch came from a nylon jogging jacket. And dirt scuff marks found on the back of Marty Brown's shoes matched the streak marks found on the grass leading from the shed to the greenhouse."

The chief grunted. "Interesting. Anything else?"

"I've been studying prints that Lynne Tulley lifted from the beer bottles from the shed. Marty Brown's fingerprints are on one of the bottles. A different set are on other ones. It looks like Marty had a guest that night, but I'm not having any luck identifying whose prints they belong to. I'm betting that they're Trent Morgan's. But I just need to make sure the prints are Trent's before I can move further on it."

"Well, you'll figure it out. Keep me posted."

# CHAPTER 20

The next morning, Elizabeth Ashton frowned at Logan from the front door. "Good morning, Detective. May I help you?"

"I have a few more questions about Marty Brown. Is it all right if I come in?"

She unlocked the door and led him into the kitchen. They sat facing each other once again.

"You told me that Marty seemed happy when he told you he'd been fired. It seems pretty strange, doesn't it?"

She nodded her agreement.

"Can you remember everything he said or did when he came in to talk with you?"

"Hmm, let me see. I was cleaning up from lunch when he came in for his break. He was quite fond of me. I liked him too. It's been lonely since Horace died—that's my late husband, bless him. Marty and I kept each other company. Especially when the Morgans go to New York. They were kind enough to let us stay on to take care of things. Well, at any rate, Marty didn't have much money.

He worked with his hands all his life. We often sat here dreaming about what we'd do if we struck it rich on the lotteries. He played the numbers every week. I think he finally found a way of making his dreams come true."

"Was he blackmailing Trent?"

She shook her head.

"Surely, Marty must've told you. Come on, we're talking about your friend. Somebody tried to make it look like Marty hanged himself. He must have said or done something. Did he tell you anything else or not?"

She shook her head. "We were just talking and then out of the blue, he says Trent fired him! He was acting odd for a man who had just been canned."

"In what way?"

"He was smiling and happy. Not the way most people would be acting after they just got fired."

"I agree. That is strange. Can you think of anything else?"

Elizabeth shook her head. "He acted like he was going to be coming into money soon. But he didn't say how."

"Really?"

"It doesn't look too good for Mr. Morgan, does it?"

"I'm not sure yet," Logan admitted.

"I could lose my job for this."

"Mrs. Morgan depends on you. And I don't think she wants to find a replacement anytime soon. You did the right thing. Thanks again."

He went into the dining room and saw Claire Morgan sitting at the table. She looked up and her face beamed.

"Good morning, Detective Logan. Have you found out why Marty did it? The poor, sweet old man."

"We're still investigating."

She sighed and said, "It's so very sad."

Logan nodded in agreement. "The other day, you told me Mrs. Ashton warned you that your life was in danger. Then Marty Brown wound up dead. Do you know anyone who might have wanted to murder him?"

She gasped. "But he hanged himself. You mean, you think Marty was murdered?"

"I'm afraid so, ma'am."

"Oh my God! How much more of this can I take?"

"Where were you between one and two that morning?"

Her eyes widened in horror. "You think that I killed him?"

"I'm sorry, Mrs. Morgan. I just have to ask."

"I was tossing and turning in bed! This whole mess with Michelle has thrown me for a loop. It's a tragedy! She was so young. I don't think I'll ever quite recover."

Logan rolled his eyes and grunted. "Do you expect me to believe that? It was no secret that you hated the woman."

"That's true, but I didn't want that to happen."

"Where was your son?"

"How would I know? I suppose he was in bed. Surely, you don't think he did it? He had no reason—"

"He used to date Michelle du Prix, correct?"

"Why yes, but that was years ago. I can assure you that they worked out their differences a long time before Trent made his moves on her."

"Maybe he was jealous his father was going to marry her. Maybe he overheard them plotting to do away with you. The walls appear to be paper thin around here. He was alone with her when you were arguing with Trent. Maybe he put poison in her drink when you and Trent were arguing in the dining room."

"He wouldn't do such a thing!" she squeaked.

"Well, it's just a theory." He checked his notes. After a long, uncomfortable silence, he asked, "Where was Trent between one and two that morning?"

"I don't know! I awoke about twelve thirty, and he wasn't there next to me. He has this habit of just getting up and wandering around the grounds when he has trouble sleeping. I can't really blame him for his insomnia with all that's been going on lately. I'm afraid I brought it on myself. But what was I to do?"

"Were you alone the whole hour and a half?"

"Yes, well, I think I might have drifted off here and there. I think I finally went back to sleep about one thirty. When I was lying in bed awake, he wasn't there. He was beside me about six o'clock. I know that for sure."

"Is Trent here?"

"He had business in New York."

"How convenient."

"You don't think he did it, do you?"

"I'd rather not discuss what I think at the moment. Thank you for your help, Mrs. Morgan." He showed himself out.

He started down the front steps when he saw Bill appear from around the hedges.

"Good morning, Detective Logan. Have you heard anything new?"

Logan shook his head.

"It's such a horrible tragedy," Bill continued.

"Where were you between one and two that morning?"

"I couldn't sleep, so I came downstairs to read in the den."

"Did you see anybody wandering around out back?"

Bill mulled it over in his head and said, "Well, I think I saw my father wandering around the backyard about—ten thirty or so."

"Did you see which direction he was headed?"

Logan detected a moment of recognition, like he was about to say something.

"I wasn't really paying too much attention, I guess."

"Did you go to the greenhouse later that night?"

"If you think I bumped off poor old Marty, you're crazy!" Bill shouted. "I was back in bed way before then!"

He brushed past the detective and bounded up the steps.

⁕　⁕　⁕

"Can you believe Detective Logan had the nerve to accuse you of murdering Marty?"

"You get too uptight, Mother," Bill said. "Come sit down. You're making me nervous with all your pacing." He fixed her a tumbler of Scotch on the rocks and said, "Have a drink. It will calm your nerves."

She waved her arms in the air and raved. "How can you be calm at a time like this? Two people are dead! The police are in and out of here, searching for clues, asking personal questions and—and thinking you killed Marty!"

"He's just doing his job."

"How can you say that? Aren't you nervous? What will people think?"

"Don't worry about what people think. I'm okay, you're okay. Dad is at a meeting. Marty hanged himself because he was upset about losing his job."

"That isn't true!" Elizabeth interrupted. "He was on top of the world, and you know it!"

"Marty lived in a bad neighborhood," Bill corrected her. "He was a drunk. And he was depressed. I don't care what the police say."

Elizabeth glared at him. "I think we all know what really happened. Why isn't your father here?"

"He's at a meeting!" Bill snapped.

"Isn't it convenient how he just left town?"

"Please!" Claire implored. "I can't take much more! Just leave me alone, both of you!" She sat on the sofa and put her hands over her face.

"All right, but if I hear anymore lip from you, Liz, you're out of here," he warned.

"You aren't my boss!" Elizabeth shot back.

He glared at her with an evil intensity. "Don't cross me! If you're smart, you'll shut your mouth."

"Fine!"

\* \* \*

Trent Morgan came back at 2:00 a.m. and went straight to bed. He awoke at ten o'clock and took a long hot shower. He slipped into a navy-blue nylon jogging outfit and darted across the lawn. About an hour later, he wiped his sweat soaked face with a towel, and eased into a patio chair. Elizabeth went over to him and smiled flatly as she poured coffee. She went back to the kitchen and dialed the police station.

"Hello, I'd like to speak to Detective Logan, please."

A minute later, he said, "This is Detective Logan."

"Hello, this is Elizabeth Ashton. Mr. Morgan is out on the patio having coffee. I just thought that you might want to know."

"Thanks."

Elizabeth delayed serving Trent his breakfast for as long as she could. Trent was half finished eating an omelet, when she took Logan out back. She already had a coffee mug waiting for him.

Trent hid his face behind the newspaper and grunted while Logan made small talk. Then the chitchat turned ugly.

"Where were you between one and two o'clock Tuesday morning?"

Trent looked up from the newspaper and stared at him in astonishment. "What do you mean by that?"

"Your wife said you weren't in bed then."

Trent's right eyebrow arched. "Oh, did she? I don't see what that has to do with anything." He looked back at the paper and continued reading.

"I'm just trying to get at the facts, Mr. Morgan," Logan said coolly. "Where were you?"

He rolled his eyes and said, "I was reading in the study."

"Do you know why somebody would have wanted to kill Marty?"

"I thought he hanged himself."

"That's what someone wants us to think. But there's strong evidence that supports the murder theory. The killer wanted to make us think he was depressed after you fired him. But everyone I talked to says he was on top of the world. It makes you wonder, doesn't it?"

"I suppose so."

"I mean, he was fired. Why would he have been so happy after he lost his job?"

"I don't know. Maybe he was pretending to be happy. People are funny that way."

"His friend thought he had won the lottery or something. I just don't get why he hanged himself. He was planning a trip to Greece. I saw travel brochures at his apartment."

"Really?"

"Yeah. It's amazing he had a change of plans."

Trent grunted and continued reading the newspaper. "Yeah."

"It's amazing he was able to afford a trip like that on his salary."

"That's none of your business!" Trent snapped.

"If a man has been murdered, it is my business. I just think the timing is suspicious. Suddenly he can afford a trip like that."

"I paid him quite handsomely over the years," Trent grumbled. "Maybe he had been saving up."

"That's not true, Mr. Morgan. I checked his bank account. He was broke."

"I can't help it if he squandered his money on alcohol. He was a good worker—when he wanted to be. I don't have time to deal with problem workers. I don't feel the least bit guilty firing him. He blew it."

"I understand."

"You try to help a person and look what happens. You get slapped in the face. He promised that he would never drink on the job again, and he did. I was more than patient with him. I would have fired him a very long time ago, but Claire insisted that I give him another chance. But enough was enough. I had to let him go. It's plain and simple."

"Maybe you're right. But I just think the timing is odd, don't you?"

"I never thought about it. But we're talking about Marty here. He always dreamed about things that were beyond his reach. Maybe he got the brochures so he could look at the pictures of pretty women. I don't see what this has to do with anything."

"Perhaps you're right, Mr. Morgan. I suppose we'll find some more clues soon. Half of the time, I'm going on a tangent."

"Is there anything else I can help you with, Detective? I'm busy."

"Friends and neighbors said he spent most of the night with them. Why did he come back here?"

"How would I know? Maybe he was so despondent that I fired him, he didn't know what he was doing. Maybe he was out of his head drunk. I'm not a heartless man, Detective Logan. It's too bad he couldn't get himself straightened out."

"I don't think he was drinking alone. I think he had company. Where were you again?"

"When I can't sleep, I read in the study. Are you accusing me of something?"

"No, I'm just trying to determine where everyone was at the time Marty was murdered. How long were you in there?"

A spasm of irritation flashed on Trent's face. "About an hour."

"What time did you get back in bed?"

"About twelve thirty."

"Your wife was lying awake in bed at that time. She said you weren't there."

"Well, she's mistaken. Maybe she was asleep."

"That could be. But she was reading. Unless there's something wrong with your clock. She said you were by her side at about six o'clock."

"I think you're wasting your time."

"That could be. But I have to ask these questions. Especially when somebody dies under mysterious circumstances. We found a footprint near Marty's hanging body. And it didn't match his shoe size. Our criminologist made a plaster mold of it, and guess what?"

"What?" Trent asked angrily.

"It matches your shoe size and style."

"So what does that prove?"

"It proves that you were in the greenhouse."

Trent rolled his eyes in disgust. "I can't believe you expect me to sit here and listen to this drivel when I have things to do. It doesn't prove a thing. I own this property. I have every right to go in the greenhouse. The footprint could have been there from a week ago!"

"That could be, but I don't think so," Logan continued undaunted. "It was near the chair that was lying on the floor. There was a broken pot a few feet from Marty Brown's hanging body. I believe you knocked over the pot when you were dragging him into the greenhouse. You thought you had cleaned up behind yourself, but you didn't realize you stepped on flowers near the crime scene. In the process of dragging him into the greenhouse, you ripped your jacket sleeve. Maybe you did it when you were exiting the building. We found a piece of your blue jacket caught on a branch."

"So what? I could have done that week's ago!"

"It doesn't really matter."

"Then why the hell are you wasting my time with all of this?"

"Because I'm trying to get at the truth, Mr. Morgan." Logan eyed him intently until Trent looked away. "Your footprint was found in the dirt near the chair. You also managed to step on a couple of flower stems."

Trent stared at him incredulously a moment. "It still doesn't prove anything. I could've done it days ago."

"The plants were still fresh—not dried up. It links you to the crime."

Trent leaned forward and knocked over his coffee mug. It fell on the patio floor and broke. He jumped up, all apologies. "I'm sorry, Detective. Are you all right? Let me get Elizabeth. She'll take care of it."

"It's okay."

Trent went over to the door and shouted, "Elizabeth, come here please!"

A moment later, she stuck her head out the French doors and saw what the problem was.

"I'll take care of it, sir." She returned carrying a cloth and a dustpan.

"I've been under so much stress after what happened to Michelle and now Marty's suicide," Trent said.

Elizabeth finished mopping the table and went back into the house. Logan waited for Trent to calm down and then went in for the kill.

"I think Marty overheard you and Michelle plotting to poison your wife. Maybe he was going to tell me everything he knew. Unless you gave him enough money."

"He was just angry that I fired him."

"I find it interesting that he seemed so chipper when he said good-bye to Elizabeth. Did you offer him hush money to keep him quiet?"

Trent rubbed a wet cloth on his coffee-stained shirt and said, "Marty was a blowhard! He blathered and made up stories left and right to cover up his incompetence! I must change my shirt. I don't want the stain to set." He went inside and slammed the French doors.

"He's really nervous," Logan murmured.

He reached into his jacket pocket for a rubber glove. He got on his hands and knees and searched for the handle of the broken mug that Elizabeth had not scooped up in the dustpan. He stuffed it into an evidence bag and wrote, "Trent Morgan's prints." He initialed and dated it. Then he walked hurriedly to his car.

# CHAPTER 21

Logan went back to the police station and reviewed his notes. Then he pressed record and spoke into his digital recorder.

"An update. Gardener Martin Brown was discovered hanging from a support beam in the greenhouse on the Morgan property. Stan Green's report confirms what we suspected—that the rope marks on Brown's neck are not consistent with a suicide. Someone made it look like he hanged himself. Brown's fingerprints were not found on the chair. The ladder had his prints on it, but he was always using it.

"Other evidence includes the following: A man's shoe print was discovered in the greenhouse. It matches Trent Morgan's shoe size and style. He stepped on flower stems in the process. They were not all dried up, which indicates that the footprint was fairly recent. Part of a broken clay pot was found near Marty's hanging body. A crushed flower that was in it was near the body. It turned out to be an orchid. The blue fabric we discovered on a tree branch in the greenhouse came from a nylon jogging jacket like the one I have seen Trent Morgan wearing. A blood spot was found on a thorn bush. A DNA test was done, and Trent was a perfect match. In addition, we discovered a trail of displaced grass leading from the shed to the greenhouse. Philadelphia crime lab technicians were able to match dirt scuff marks on the back of Mr. Brown's shoes to the displaced grass patterns.

"Detective Flosky and I searched Brown's apartment and found travel brochures for the Greek islands. Maybe he planned on traveling there, which raises another question. How could a man on Brown's limited budget be able to afford to travel somewhere that's so expensive?

"Trent Morgan: Right now, he's the primary suspect. Though it probably can't be proved that he plotted to murder his wife without the gardener's statement, evidence suggests that he murdered Marty Brown. On the night that Marty died, Trent was spotted wandering in the vicinity of the greenhouse by both Claire and William. They reported different times he was taking his walk though. I need to check it. I just collected prints from his coffee mug and will try to match it to the ones we found at the crime scene.

"Motive: he needed to get rid of Brown in a hurry before he squealed?

"Claire Morgan: She is an admitted liar, so nothing she says should be believed. She told me that she awoke at 12:30 a.m. and Trent wasn't in bed. She thinks she went back to sleep about an hour later. He wasn't there the whole time she lay in bed reading. Motive: unclear.

"William Morgan: He saw his father wandering around in back of the house about 10:30 p.m. His parents both reported different times. Motive: unclear.

"Elizabeth Ashton: She was Marty's longtime friend. They spent a lot of time talking to each other. The number one question is if he told her he was blackmailing Trent about the plot to murder Claire. Mrs. Ashton said that Brown seemed pretty chipper right after Trent Morgan fired him. Was he expecting to get money out of Trent? Maybe he really did overhear Trent and Michelle plot to poison Claire. It's the only explanation for why Marty would have been so cheerful after being fired. Maybe he was blackmailing Trent. Now that Marty is dead, I can't prove it. She would have had no reason to murder her old friend.

"Elizabeth washed the glass that Michelle du Prix drank out of destroying the evidence. Did Mrs. Ashton just tidy up out of habit? Or did she do it to protect the Morgans? Motive: Unclear."

Logan pressed the off button and packed up for the day.

*　*　*

Penny showed Gwen Winters their trip pictures while their husbands discussed the Michelle du Prix and Marty Brown murder investigations over beers at Barney's.

"We'll probably never be able to prove who poisoned her thanks to the maid washing away the evidence," Frank said.

"And we can't go by what Claire Morgan or Elizabeth Ashton said, either," Joe Flosky added. "How do we know that Marty Brown was telling the truth in the first place? He could've just said he heard Trent and Michelle plotting to poison Claire."

"That's what I think too. If Trent had anything to do with it, he'll get off on a technicality. Any lawyer worth his salt will harp on the lack of evidence."

"That washed away in the dishwasher," Harry Winters said.

"And now that Marty Brown is out of the picture, we'll never know the truth, will we?" Frank guzzled his beer down and wiped froth off his lips with a napkin.

"Marty must've been blackmailing Trent," Joe suggested. "The maid said he was pretty cheerful for a guy that just got canned."

Frank nodded and grunted. "Really."

"Well, it's damn certain that Marty was murdered," Harry Winters added. "No prints on the chair. The marks on his neck. Trent's footprint isn't enough to prove that he did it. Well hopefully, the forensics techs will find something that'll link Trent to the crime."

"I hope so," Frank said. "You won't want to be around me if he walks."

"Trust me, pal, we know!" Joe cried.

"Don't bore her with the pictures, honey," Frank told Penny. "People don't really care that much about other people's trip pictures."

"Oh, stop. I think they're great." Gwen looked at her husband and said, "You're overdue for a vacation, Harry."

"You won't let me forget it. Thanks."

"You gotta go," Frank urged. "You won't believe how blue the water is. You can stand there in the ocean and see your feet in some places. It's unbelievable!"

# CHAPTER 22

A week later, Logan headed back to Morgan House to pay Trent a surprise visit. He rang the bell, but there was no answer. The door finally opened, and Claire stuck her head out.

She smiled and said, "Detective Logan. May I help you?"

"I need to talk to your husband again."

"This is a bad time. He's having a meeting with staff from the *Main Line Chronicle*."

"It's urgent. I really must talk to him."

"All right, if you insist. I'll see what I can do."

She went into the family room and smiled at Trent's associates, who were sitting around the room, clipboards in hand. Piles of budget reports and financial statements covered the coffee table. Competing newspapers lay next to them. A smartphone was on the table. The speaker phone was on and voices were talking over each other on the other end.

"Trent, Detective Logan is here to see you."

"Tell him I'm in a meeting!"

"I did. He says it's urgent."

"Tell him I'll be with him in a few minutes."

"I'm afraid I can't do that," Logan said from the entryway.

"I'm sorry, Trent."

"That's all right, Claire." He looked over at his colleagues and said, "Please excuse the interruption. I'll be right back." He rose and briskly led Logan toward the backyard patio.

"What do you want? Can't you see I'm busy here?"

"You were very careless, Mr. Morgan."

"What are you talking about?"

"People think they can outsmart the police. But not this time. You thought you were really clever. I suppose you wore gloves when you strangled Marty Brown. We didn't think we'd be able to get any prints in the shed, but we did."

"Are you out of your mind? How dare you accuse me of murder!"

"The Philadelphia crime lab technicians are top notch," Logan went on. "I assume you must have wiped your prints off the beer bottle you drank from. But you neglected to wipe off the prints you made around the rim of the bottle. People always do. I really enjoyed our little chat the other day. I'm sorry I upset you. I didn't mean for you to jump out of your skin. It's too bad the mug broke. It's also too bad Mrs. Ashton didn't pick up all the pieces. I managed to get a real good copy of your prints and guess what? It's a perfect match for the one we lifted from the shed."

"You'll never be able to prove it. My lawyer can discredit witnesses left and right. It's still my shed. It doesn't prove anything. I can go in there any time I want to have a drink or two."

"The evidence we gathered corresponds with everything Elizabeth told Claire. The coroner found cyanide in Michelle's bloodstream. I believe Michelle slipped it into your wife's drink— or maybe you did. There's probably no way to prove that now. You got into a fight with your son—and in the struggle, things got muddled. Michelle and Claire tried to break you up. And when it was over, Michelle mistakenly took the wrong glass. The one with the poison."

"It's true that Michelle and I talked about trying to get Claire to sign the divorce papers, but Marty only heard part of the conversation. And there's no way to prove it now because he hanged himself."

"That's what you wanted everyone to think. You didn't want to take any chances and you thought you could get away with it. No one would be the wiser. Here's what happened. He was blackmailing you. You went to the shed with the money. You both had some beers. You waited till you knew he was inebriated, slipped gloves on, came up from behind, and snapped the rope around his neck. Then you dragged him into the greenhouse. We discovered displaced blades of grass pointing toward the greenhouse. Not to mention the footprint in the dirt and the flower stems that had been stepped on near the chair. Then you tied the noose and strung him from the support beam and kicked the chair away to make it look like he did himself in. We found a strand of hair on the floor that matched Marty's."

Trent clapped and said, "Bravo! A very good story. You should be a fiction writer."

"I believe that's how it happened."

"That doesn't prove anything.

"Oh, yes it does."

Trent eyed him suspiciously. "What—what are you talking about?"

"Remember the ripped jacket? Well, I failed to mention that in the process of either entering or exiting the greenhouse, you scratched your arm on a thorn bush. It's really painful. I can't tell you how many times I've done that when I go on walks in the woods. A dot of blood was found on the branch. And guess what? We did a DNA test. And you're a perfect match. It places you at the scene of the crime."

"It's still my greenhouse. It doesn't prove that I did it!"

"Oh, yes, it does." He whipped out handcuffs and slapped them around Trent's wrists. "Trent Morgan. You're under arrest for the murder of Marty Brown. You have the right to remain silent..."

When the detective had finished reading Trent his rights, Trent's coworkers stood in stunned silence as they watched Logan push him out the front door. Claire beamed as she watched Trent being whisked away in Logan's police car.

# CHAPTER 23

At fifty-eight, G. Walter Ackroyd was an intimidating foe with a reputation for being a ruthless defense attorney. Dishonesty came easily for him. He would lie, cheat, or steal if need be. He would resort to every trick in the book to get his clients off. He had no conscience. He never exercised, and it showed. He was stocky with thick-set eyes and horn-rimmed glasses. His hair was unnaturally black. It looked like he went swimming in hair dye. He spent too much time with his nose in legal books.

A guard escorted Trent Morgan into the interrogation room and left them alone.

"Talk to me," Ackroyd said. "How did this happen?"

"Detective Logan actually believes I murdered two people. It's absurd."

"Start from the beginning."

"It's all because of Claire. Our marriage was over, and she just wouldn't accept it. She had us worried for months when she pulled her disappearing act. It was just a ploy to make me feel sorry for her.

And it worked. How could I have been so ignorant?" He slammed his hand on the table and stared back at the attorney. "I stopped feeling sorry for her after she did that damned magazine story. She made a laughing stock out of me and I wasn't going to let her get away with it."

He told him how angry he got when Claire refused to sign the divorce papers.

"Damn her! Michelle didn't want to sneak around either. So one day we were walking in the woods and got to talking about the situation. We ended up in the greenhouse and didn't think anybody was around. Jokingly, she said maybe we should just get rid of her."

"Be careful what you say. A prosecutor will tear you apart if you say something like that. It sounds like a threat."

"We didn't mean it. I thought she was just kidding. My gardener overheard our conversation and talked to my housekeeper. And the housekeeper told Claire."

"When did that happen?"

"The day before Michelle drank the poisoned wine."

"Try to tell me everything you remember about the night she died."

Trent relayed the whole ugly chain of events that led up to Michelle's gruesome death.

Ackroyd asked the same questions Logan had: Were Bill and Michelle in the family room the whole time? Did they have drinks? Did Elizabeth serve them, or did they get their own drinks? Who served Michelle's drink?

"Those are stupid questions," Trent said. "Why does everyone want to know what we were drinking?"

"We need to establish who had the means and opportunity to slip the poison into Michelle's glass."

"How would I know what Bill and Michelle were doing? You know damn well that Claire and I were arguing in the dining room. They could have been in and out several times before we went back in there."

"These are points we need to determine, Trent. Why were Claire and Michelle angry with each other?"

"I was having an affair for God's sake, Walter!"

Ackroyd leaned back in his seat and said, "I think there's more to it. Did she have something on Michelle du Prix?"

Trent shrugged his shoulders. "I don't know. Michelle told her to go ahead and make the call, and then, I'm not sure what was said that made Bill and me go at it. He just started slapping me on the back. And then we're hitting each other. Michelle and Claire had to break us up, and in the confusion, I guess Michelle got the wrong glass—the one intended for Claire."

"It won't look good. You just admitted your guilt."

"But I never touched Claire's glass! I thought Michelle was just joking."

"Are you telling me the whole truth?"

"Yes."

"If I find out you aren't being one hundred percent truthful, it could spell big trouble, Trent."

Trent leaned forward and shook his right index finger at his lawyer. "Listen, Walter. I didn't murder Michelle! And I didn't intend to murder my wife. And I certainly didn't murder Marty!"

Ackroyd folded his hands and listened intently.

"Michelle said that there were all kinds of poisons in the shed, but I didn't think she would go that far. You can't prove that she and I were in cahoots. Marty was the only one who knew anything about it—and he's dead. It's my word against that of a dead man. A known drunk, I might add."

"According to Mrs. Ashton, Marty heard you agree to poison Claire."

"There's no proof! Marty Brown is dead. He hanged himself because I had to let him go. He was a drunken fool! You're just basing everything on what she said."

"We're going to have a mighty difficult task getting jurors to believe your story."

"But it's true! Marty was a blowhard. Everybody knows he was a drunk. Maybe Michelle acted alone. So what if we joked about getting rid of Claire? How was I supposed to know that she'd actually go through with it? And they can't prove that I was working with her."

"You could be charged as an accessory to murder."

"So what if we talked about it? I can't be held responsible for something she did without my knowledge."

"You could have stopped her from doing it."

"If I testified, I could say that I didn't know what Michelle was trying to do."

"That's true, but it still doesn't dismiss the fact that you left behind mountains of incriminating evidence at the scene of Marty Brown's murder. Logan made detective very young. He came from Philadelphia. He's sharp. And he knows his stuff."

"People can't make mistakes?"

"Not in this case. He matched the prints found on the beer bottle with those you left on the coffee mug."

"So what are our options?"

Ackroyd discussed strategies to discredit prosecution witnesses, and then skimmed Elizabeth's sworn statement. "Mrs. Ashton said this the same day Marty Brown died. She said, and I quote, 'Marty told me he told Mr. Morgan that he overheard him talking to Miss du Prix the day before she was poisoned. A few days later, Marty came to tell me that Mr. Morgan had fired him. I thought it was strange the way he was acting. He seemed happy—not at all the way somebody would act if they were fired. He acted like he was going to be coming into some money soon but didn't say how. The next day, we were all shocked when Detective Logan found him hanging in the greenhouse.' End quote." Ackroyd looked back at his client and said, "I'll be honest, Trent. I don't see how I can help you. Logan has evidence linking you to Marty's murder."

"But you have to get me out of this mess!"

"The evidence is stacked against you. I believe that our only strategy is your word against that of Mr. Brown's. And he isn't around to tell his side of the story, which also doesn't help you. Your prints were traced. I can try to prove that Logan obtained them illegally when he lifted them from the mug. That might be a help. It's a known fact that Marty Brown had a drinking problem. Maybe he did just hear part of the conversation. Maybe he imagined it. That's our only defense."

"Then work with it," Trent urged.

"Michelle hated Claire enough to want her out of the way. And unless you're not telling me everything I need to know, Michelle was the one who put the poison in Claire's glass. And Michelle drank it by mistake. There's no way to prove that you put poison in the drinks because Elizabeth Ashton destroyed the evidence when she washed the dishes. But Logan does have a good case against you with Marty Brown's hanging. Your footprint in the dirt near Marty's body. The blue threads found on the branch. But it is your property.

It wouldn't be unusual that your fingerprints should be on beer bottles in the shed. And so what if your footprint was found in the greenhouse? The plants that you stepped on weren't dried up. They were still fresh, which means that you could have been there several hours before Marty was hanged. And the same can be said about the piece of your jacket that they found in the branch. It could have been there for days. But your DNA matches the blood spot found on the thorn bush. I could try to prove that they couldn't determine how long the blood stain was. It seems like a lot of circumstantial evidence. But putting it all together, it makes a pretty damaging case against you. We've got our work cut out for us."

"What do you think?"

"I think the best bet is to somehow find a way to discredit Logan." Ackroyd leafed through reports filed three months before the murder. "It has to get worse!" he exclaimed. "I'm looking at statements made during your wife's 'disappearance.' Your son said that you had a party the afternoon before her car was found abandoned in the field. 'My father got into a fight with Mac Yeager, a critic for one of his newspapers. They were hitting each other and cursing. It was ugly.'" Ackroyd adjusted his glasses and looked back at Trent. "Oh boy! It doesn't look good for you."

At that moment, there was a knock at the door.

"We're busy!" Ackroyd shouted.

A woman stuck her head in the door and apologized for the interruption. She went over to Trent and handed him a manila envelope. "I'm a process server for Blaine Simmons. You've been served."

She closed the door on her way out. Trent had a bad feeling about what the contents contained. His worst fear was confirmed when he opened the package. Divorce papers. He flipped the pages, his eyes automatically trained on Claire's signature. He lost color in his cheeks.

"She got me!" he cried. "Now she can testify against me."

Ackroyd groaned and said, "It doesn't look good for you, my friend."

# CHAPTER 24

Claire Morgan braced herself as she faced the elements. The brisk February air chilled her to the bones. Snowflakes danced around her face as she inched her way down the icy sidewalk. She stopped long enough to tighten her scarf and looked down all the way to the courthouse so she wouldn't slip on patches of ice. She lost her balance and threw her arms in the air. Bill came up from behind and reached for her hand in the nick of time.

The front entrance to the courthouse was blocked off. Construction workers were on scaffolding behind the pillars. There was a sign in large red letters that read: ENTRANCE CLOSED. PLEASE USE SIDE ENTRANCE AT TOWN CIRCLE. SORRY FOR THE INCONVENIENCE.

They walked slowly down the block and went inside. She stood there a moment, rubbing her hands and shivering.

"Come on, Mother. We'll be late."

They went up a winding marble staircase and waited outside the courtroom with reporters and spectators. A bailiff was standing five feet away. Claire's eyes were automatically drawn to his name tag. Charlie Biggs. He was stocky and going bald. He was probably in his late fifties—Trent's age. They were from different walks of life. If she had brought him home to meet her parents, they would have been displeased. She would have enjoyed watching them squirm.

In the beginning, Trent was kind and compassionate. She wondered when it all went wrong. Had she done something to trigger his infidelity? If she had married someone like Charlie, maybe none of this would be happening now. Her life would be so different. Would she be happier?

She huffed in indignation. "What's taking so long?"

"Jury selection," Biggs told her.

"How long will that take?"

"It's anybody's guess." Biggs wandered the hallway, his walkie-talkie practically attached to his lips.

Claire sat on a wooden bench next to the window. TV and newspaper reporters swarmed to get close to her. Bill pushed them away and shouted, "Leave us alone! No comment!"

"How does it feel having a murderer for an ex-husband?" they shouted over each other.

"No comment! Get the hell away from here!" Bill went over to Charlie Biggs and asked if they could be taken to a private room. Biggs led them to the bailiff's office.

"You might as well read a magazine or something," Biggs advised. "This could take all morning."

Her eyes were wild with rage. "Why on earth should it?"

"If you want your ex-husband to get a fair trial, you better hope the jurors will be on his side," Charlie said.

"I didn't think of it that way. Thank you, Charlie."

Bill patted her shoulder and said, "It'll be all right. Just relax."

"It's easy for you to say." She complained bitterly about having to wait so long for the trial to start. Bill did his best to calm her nerves.

About an hour later, he went to find out what was happening. By now, more reporters and photographers had congregated outside the courtroom. Someone spotted him, and reporters swarmed around him. He jostled to push through the crowd. He hurriedly descended the stairs and they tore after him. He went into the prothonotary office to find out what was happening. A clerk told him that they were still working on jury selection and would probably be finished in the afternoon. Bill thanked the woman and went back to keep his mother company. He broke the bad news, and she did not take it well. Her complaints grew louder. Bill eyed the clock. Time was dragging.

Jury selection dragged on until noon. Bill got sandwiches at a deli down the street and continued the difficult task of calming his mother's nerves over lunch. Thirty minutes later, he tossed the paper wrap in a trash can and went back out to the hall. Charlie Biggs brushed by, walkie-talkie close to his mouth. When he finished talking, Bill asked for an update.

"The lawyers are in chambers with Judge Robinson," he said. His walkie-talkie beeped, and he pressed the send button. Then he punched it off and announced, "The trial will start in about thirty minutes. You can all go inside. But it's more comfortable out here."

Bill went back to tell his mother the news. Then a female bailiff went over to them and said, "You can come in now. They're almost ready."

The crowd bustled into the courtroom behind them. A guard was sitting on a stool on the other side of a metal detector and instructed everyone to walk through it one at a time. Claire went through, and the alarm sounded. She opened her pocketbook and removed a key chain. He told her to go back through again. This time, she did not trigger the alarm. Bill met her on the other side, and they found seats in the visitor's row.

It was a large room with a vaulted ceiling with intricately carved woodwork. A gold chandelier stretched down from it. Oil portraits of long dead judges hung on dark-paneled walls. Morning sunlight shone through the high windows. The judge's bench was an imposing sight. It sat at the top of red carpeted steps. A portrait of George Washington on his white horse was behind it. An American flag was at the left. A Pennsylvania flag was at the right.

Bill watched police officers wandering in and out of side doors. His attention rested on the blond man in a pinstriped suit conferring with colleagues at the prosecution table. He was definitely in charge, as he barked orders to his young paralegals. They exited the courtroom, one after another. Then Mr. Big-Shot Attorney talked to his fellow lawyers. Through the course of the conversation, Bill heard a woman mention the man by name.

Bill had heard of John T. Harkens but did not know what he looked like. He had a ruddy complexion and menacing blue eyes. Small reading glasses hung off a pointy nose. At fifty-five, Harkens had gained a reputation for being brutal. In his twenty years as a trial attorney, he had won more cases than he lost.

A sudden stab of anxiety overtook Claire when she saw a female bailiff escort Trent through a door to the left of the judge's bench.

Bill held her hand and said quietly, "It's all right, Mother. Walter Ackroyd is an excellent lawyer. He knows what he's doing."

For once, she remained silent.

Everyone rose when Judge Samuel Robinson entered the room. He was a formidable African American with a reputation for being a no-nonsense judge. He was fifty-four, with bushy gray hair and eyebrows. He went over to his bench and sat down.

"You may be seated," Judge Robinson announced. Then he began the proceedings.

*Lancaster Times* reporter Rob Watkins scurried through the metal detector and found a vacant seat in back. He whipped out his pad and listened intently to the attorneys making their opening statements. He turned on his digital recorder and took avid notes as prosecutor John T. Harkens spoke. Charlie Biggs went over to him and threatened to confiscate the digital recorder. Rob turned it off and put it in his jacket pocket.

Townsend's *Times-Sentinel* reporter Kim Weston scowled at him from across the crowded room. He was like a bug that she just couldn't get rid of. She didn't need him stealing her scoop! It had been months since there had been a juicy news story like this that captured so much media attention. Now she had to deal with this little brat who was practically in her own backyard. During a break, she had to have a talk with Watkins.

"And in conclusion, ladies and gentlemen of the jury, I believe you will have no trouble finding the defendant, Trent Morgan, guilty of murder."

It was now G. Walter Ackroyd's turn. He smiled politely at the jurors and contradicted what John Harkens said. About half an hour later, he began winding down.

"And in closing, I am sure that you will find my client, Trent Morgan, not guilty. Thank you very much."

Judge Robinson ordered a short recess. Claire and Bill were taken to the witness waiting room. The trial resumed fifteen minutes later.

"Very well," Judge Robinson said. "Mr. Harkens, call your first witness."

# CHAPTER 25

Elizabeth Ashton entered the courtroom and approached the witness stand. She had on a maroon jacket and a flower-print dress. She wore a necklace with dark blue beads. Trent thought she really looked good with a little makeup and a decent hairstyle.

When she was sworn in, Harkens started with cheerful conversation. "Good morning, Mrs. Ashton. How are you this afternoon?"

"I'm fine."

"Did you work for the defendant, Trent Morgan?"

"Yes sir."

"What was your job?"

"I was housekeeper at the Morgans' home in Townsend, Pennsylvania."

"How long did you work there?"

"About fifteen years."

"Were the Morgans good employers, Mrs. Ashton?"

"Yes."

"In what way?"

"They always treated me with respect. I had good benefits and shouldn't have to worry about anything when I retire."

"Why don't you work there now?"

"My services were no longer needed."

"Why were you terminated?"

"Due to his current problems, he had no other choice."

"Why did Trent Morgan fire you, Mrs. Ashton?"

"He thought I tipped off Detective Logan."

"Why is that, Mrs. Ashton?"

"Detective Logan came by the house the morning of Mr. Morgan's arrest. I told him he was having a meeting with his newspaper staff from Philadelphia."

Harkens asked her similar questions, and then got to the point. "While you worked there, did you ever see Trent Morgan display violent behavior?"

Elizabeth swallowed hard and said, "He has a temper, but—"

"He has a temper. Did you ever hear him arguing with his wife?"

She hesitated a moment and said, "Yes."

"Was this a frequent occurrence?"

"They got into fights, sure. But it's about like any married couple, I suppose."

"What did they fight about?"

"Financial problems, for the most part," she said slowly. "I didn't mean to eavesdrop but—"

"Can you elaborate, Mrs. Ashton?"

"They disagreed about business deals. She didn't want him to purchase some newspaper companies. But he did it anyway."

"Did you stay at the Townsend home year round?"

"Yes."

"How often did they stay there?"

"Usually from March to November. Occasionally they would stay on one or two weekends during the winter."

"Did they ever fight about people with whom Mr. Morgan worked?"

She shook her head and said, "I don't know."

"Did you ever see Michelle du Prix in his bed?"

She shook her head and said, "No, but I did see her coming out of his room—partially clothed."

Loud murmurs reverberated around the courtroom.

"Was she a regular there?"

"Yes."

"Did you ever hear her talk about marrying Trent Morgan?"

"Yes."

"Did the Morgans fight about Ms. du Prix?"

"All of the time."

"Can you tell us about the nature of these fights?"

"It wasn't my place to stick my nose into things."

"When you were working in the kitchen, could you hear them arguing when they were eating dinner?"

"Yes."

"What did they usually argue about?"

"I'd hear them shouting Miss du Prix's name."

"What did Claire Morgan say about Michelle du Prix?"

"She would call her a bitch. Then I'd hear glasses break, and I'd have to go in and clean up the mess. It was usually expensive things that got broken, like china. Mr. and Mrs. Morgan would be yelling at each other."

"Did he hit her?"

She shook her head. "No. He'd yell, but he'd never hit her. He'd usually just leave the room."

"On Monday, May twenty-sixth of last year, did you hear Trent Morgan ask his wife for a divorce?"

She cringed and said, "Yes, they were at dinner, and I heard him say he wanted a divorce. That was right before she left."

"That's right, she did disappear. And she did it quite often, didn't she?"

"She just wanted to get away from him. She just wanted to get his attention, but I guess it just made things worse."

"He got really angry when she disappeared, didn't he?"

"He was fit to be tied!" Elizabeth exclaimed.

"His anger came out at a party the day before her last 'disappearance,' didn't it?"

"Yes."

"What happened?"

"I was in and out. I don't know for sure."

"Tell the jurors everything you witnessed."

Elizabeth recalled in vivid detail the argument between Michelle, Mac, and Trent the afternoon of the party on Memorial Day weekend. Mac was hurling insults at Michelle, and Trent rushed to her defense. She was so angry about Mac's stage review, that she demanded Trent print a retraction. Trent promised her he'd try to do something about it.

"I heard Mac Yeager say, 'It's a fine day in journalism when a newspaper owner gives in to the whims of his mistress.' I heard Mr. Morgan yell, 'You bastard! You're fired!'"

She went on to describe the brawl that followed. "They had to be broken up."

"Did you hear the Morgans talk about their marriage after the party?"

"The next evening. I was in the kitchen and heard them talking about Miss du Prix again. Mrs. Morgan was upset."

"And then what happened?"

"Mrs. Morgan left that night."

"How did Trent Morgan act during her absence?"

"He was really worried. She was gone for weeks. We all thought she was dead. He blamed himself and felt really guilty for how he treated her."

"At that time, he offered a $25,000 reward for her whereabouts, correct?"

"Yes."

"How did he react when he found out that she had staged her disappearance?"

"He got really angry."

"Where was Michelle du Prix while Claire Morgan was 'missing'?"

"At Morgan House. When she wasn't doing photo shoots."

"How did Michelle du Prix react when she found out that Claire Morgan was actually alive and well?"

"She didn't say anything, but I could sense that she was upset."

"What did Trent Morgan do when Claire came back home?"

"He doted on her. I overheard conversations like they were planning to work on their marriage."

"But that all changed when he read about how she staged her disappearance in a national magazine, correct?"

"Yes."

"Was he upset?"

"Yes."

"Was he angry?"

"Yes."

"Was he violent?"

"I wouldn't say he was violent. I just don't think I've ever seen him that upset before."

"Were you frightened?"

She bowed her head and said, "Yes."

There were loud murmurs around the courtroom.

"How did Michelle du Prix react to Claire Morgan's confession to the magazine reporter?"

"She was furious."

"Did you see Trent Morgan and Michelle du Prix at any time after the magazine article came out?"

"Yes."

"Where were they?"

"I looked out the window and saw them walking toward the greenhouse."

"Martin Brown, the gardener, often worked there, did he not?"

"Yes."

"You were very fond of Mr. Brown, weren't you?"

"Yes, he would always come into the kitchen on breaks, and we'd sit and chat. He was a sweet man."

"Did he mention overhearing a conversation Trent Morgan and Michelle du Prix had on the afternoon of August eighteenth?"

"Yes."

"What did he tell you?"

"He said he overheard Miss du Prix and Mr. Morgan talking about doing away with Mrs. Morgan."

"Why is that?"

"Because Mrs. Morgan wouldn't agree to divorce her husband."

She went on to say that Marty overheard Michelle tell Trent that there were a lot of pesticides in the shed that were poisonous that could be used to murder Claire.

Spectators leaned forward, anxious to hear more. Jurors listened carefully.

"Tell us what happened the night Michelle du Prix was poisoned."

Elizabeth testified that she heard Trent Morgan tell his wife that he was leaving her. Bill and Michelle left them alone so they could talk privately. Claire got really upset when Trent ordered her to sign the divorce papers.

"Would Claire Morgan sign them?" Harkens asked.

Elizabeth frowned and said, "No, I stayed in the kitchen because I knew a fight was brewing. I heard Mrs. Morgan screeching at the top of her lungs, and then she yanked off the tablecloth, and glass shattered everywhere. It was a real mess! I had to go in to clean it up."

"What were they arguing about?"

"I only heard bits and pieces. I heard something about divorce papers. All I know is that Mrs. Morgan got really upset."

"Then what happened?"

"They left the dining room, and I finished cleaning up the broken glass. It quieted down a bit, and then I heard more shouting coming from the family room a few minutes later."

"Could you hear what they were saying?"

"I heard Mrs. Morgan hurling insults at Miss du Prix. Then I heard Mr. Morgan and Bill cursing at each other. It sounded like they were hitting each other—that's when I went into the kitchen. I couldn't take much more. I started the dishwasher and could only hear muffled screaming. The dishwasher was making too much racket. A few minutes later, I heard a scream coming from the family room and rushed in to see what was happening."

"What happened?"

"Miss du Prix was lying on the floor, thrashing about."

"What was wrong with her?"

"I didn't know at the time. But it was—it was from the poison. It was a reaction from it."

"On August twenty-fifth, did you talk to Detective Frank Logan?"

"Yes."

"Did he talk to the Morgans?"

"Yes."

"Did he talk to Mr. Brown?"

She held her hand over her mouth and said, "No."

"Why is that, Mrs. Ashton?"

"He hung himself," she said flatly.

"Did he seem depressed?"

She shook her head. "He was always so full of life—happy –go-lucky. He wouldn't have done such a thing."

"Did he ever talk to you about financial problems?"

"All of the time. I always had to lend him some money. But that day, he said he didn't have to ever worry about money problems again."

"Why is that, Mrs. Ashton?"

"He said he was going to come into some money soon."

"Did he have a rich relative?"

"No, he said he just had some good luck."

"Did he tell you how that came to be?"

"No."

"Was he blackmailing Trent Morgan?"

She shrugged her shoulders. "I don't know."

"Did you think it was unusual that he seemed so happy after Trent Morgan fired him?"

"Yes."

"Did you ever wonder why such a happy man would hang himself?"

"Yes, but—but he had just been fired."

"But you thought it was odd, right?"

"Yes. He seemed happy like usual."

"Do you think it's possible that Marty Brown was blackmailing Trent Morgan?"

"Well, yes. I think it's possible, but—Marty was an honest, hardworking man. He never would have done such a thing."

"Do you think that Trent Morgan was capable of murdering Mr. Brown?"

There was a long, uncomfortable silence. "Yes."

"Nothing further."

# CHAPTER 26

G. Walter Ackroyd stared down at Elizabeth Ashton a moment before beginning cross-examination. At first, he asked her nonthreatening questions, and then got to the point.

"You testified that you have been a loyal employee of the Morgans for fifteen years, correct?"

"Yes."

"Why did Trent Morgan fire you, Mrs. Ashton?"

"He thought I tipped off Detective Logan."

"Why is that, Mrs. Ashton?"

"He came by the house the morning of Mr. Morgan's arrest. I told him that Mr. Morgan was having a meeting with his newspaper staff from Philadelphia."

"Did Detective Logan ask you questions?"

"Yes."

"What did you tell him?"

"What Marty told me."

"And what was that, Mrs. Ashton?"

"That he would be coming into money soon."

"Where was he going to get the money from?"

"He didn't say."

"When did he tell you this?"

"Right after Mr. Morgan fired him."

"Did Trent Morgan blame you for talking to Detective Logan?"

"He didn't say anything, but I sensed he was upset. I told Detective Logan I could lose my job for telling him, and he said it would be all right."

"Do you have a grudge against Mr. Morgan for firing you?"

"No, I respected his decision. It was time for me to move on anyway. After all that happened, I needed to go somewhere else. Too many bad things happened."

"I think you were angry that he fired you after all your years of loyal service. You resented Trent Morgan, didn't you, Mrs. Ashton?"

Her lips trembled. "I was upset, but under the circumstances, I knew it was time to move on."

"Were you close friends with Marty Brown, the gardener?"

"Yes, we were fond of each other."

"Did you tip off Detective Logan to get back at your employer for allegedly murdering Marty?"

"No!"

"As a housekeeper, did you have access to every room?"

"Yes. I had keys to the bedrooms and Mr. Morgan's study."

"I bet you heard a lot of juicy tidbits while working—coming and going like you did."

"I tried not to listen."

"Did you ever just half hear something that was said, when you were wandering in and out? Maybe you heard conversations out of context."

"I heard bits and pieces. I could figure things out."

"Even with the dishwasher on?"

"I could never hear anything with it on."

"You must have been a busy beaver the day of the party on Sunday, May twenty-fifth, correct?"

"It was hectic," she acknowledged. "There were about fifty people there. The Morgans hired caterers to help out. We were on our feet all day. We didn't have time to sit and rest."

"A few minutes ago, you testified that you were in the family room and heard Trent Morgan arguing with a couple of people on the patio, correct?"

"Yes."

"Did you hear it from the beginning?"

"No."

"What was the first thing you heard?"

"I think Miss du Prix was yelling about the bad review, and she was cursing at Mr. Yeager."

"Would it be safe to say that you heard the conversation out of context?"

"I guess so."

"Yes or no, Mrs. Ashton."

"Yes."

"Did the Morgans have loud music playing in the house?"

"No, it was soft. I barely noticed it."

"At what point did you realize that Trent Morgan was on the patio with Michelle du Prix and Mac Yeager?"

"When I heard them yelling."

"But you didn't see them go out there, did you?"

"No, after I was in the family room, I went back to the kitchen to get some more snack trays."

"Would it be fair to say that you missed the beginning of the talk out on the patio?"

"Yes."

"So you don't know what they were really talking about do you? They could have been talking about space travel for all you know, correct?"

"I suppose so."

"Who threw the first punch, Trent Morgan or Mac Yeager?"

"I don't know."

"So you never actually saw Trent Morgan throw the first punch the day of the party on May twenty-fifth, did you?"

"No not really."

"Was the air conditioning on that day?"

"Yes."

"It's hard to hear anything with that thing making such a racket, wouldn't you say?"

"I suppose so."

"Could you hear guests talking over the air conditioning?"

"No."

"You said you spent a great deal of time talking to Marty Brown. What did you usually talk about?"

"We always imagined what our lives would be like if we weren't doing what we were doing. He always talked about striking it rich with the lottery someday. He always went to the newsstand to get his ticket. But he never won."

"Did he ever boast or fabricate stories?"

"I don't know. Sometimes his stories seemed farfetched, but I usually always believed them."

"So you aren't sure if he was truthful?"

"I took what he said with a grain of salt."

"Do you believe everything people tell you?"

"Sometimes."

"Did you believe him when he said he overheard Trent and Michelle plotting to kill Claire Morgan?"

She contemplated his last question carefully in her mind. "I asked him if he'd been drinking, and he swore he hadn't. I didn't smell liquor on his breath. I thought maybe he had just imagined it. I even asked him if he was sure he hadn't just misunderstood or come in from the middle."

"Ah, so you didn't believe him at first. What changed your mind?"

"He seemed insistent on it—the details he gave. I knew the Morgans were always fighting. I also knew that Mr. Morgan was furious when he found out that his wife faked her disappearance. I knew there'd be trouble the first time I laid eyes on that magazine article—the one with Mrs. Morgan's interview. I heard him on the phone talking to Miss du Prix. He was livid!"

"What did he say?"

"He said she was right all along, and something had to be done."

"Is that why you believed Marty Brown?"

"Yes, his details seemed for real."

"What did he say?"

"He talked about how they planned to slip the poison into Mrs. Morgan's drink and distract her. Then they'd switch glasses."

"Did you warn Mrs. Morgan?"

"Yes, I told her everything."

"How did she react?"

"I think she was frightened. But it's hard to tell with her. She can often be high-strung—melodramatic. You can never tell if she's just putting on an act."

"So you had no way of knowing if Mr. Brown just heard part of their conversation?"

She hesitated before answering. "No sir."

Ackroyd asked her questions regarding the night Michelle du Prix died. Elizabeth repeated what she had been saying for months. The Morgans continued their argument when they went into the family room. This time, Bill and Michelle were involved.

"You just said you were only in the family room a minimum of five minutes after dinner, correct?"

"Yes."

"So you have no way of knowing if Trent Morgan slipped poison into the glass his wife was drinking?"

"No."

"And you didn't see the glass get switched, did you?"

"No."

"I think you only half hear things. When people overhear conversations—parts of conversations I should say—they often take things out of context. The conversation is distorted. You have no way of knowing if Marty Brown was telling the truth."

"That's because he's dead!" Elizabeth shrieked.

"He was a bumbling drunkard. Is it true that Trent Morgan caught him drinking alcohol on a number of occasions?"

"Yes!" she shouted through tears.

"He did it on more than one occasion, did he not?"

She nodded and said, "Yes."

"Did Trent Morgan tell Marty Brown he'd fire him if he caught him drinking?"

"Yes!"

"Marty Brown was obviously a very unhappy man. A week before he hanged himself, Trent Morgan caught him drinking in the greenhouse, did he not?"

She reached for a Kleenex and blew her nose. "Yes."

"As an employer, Trent Morgan has every right to discipline his staff, does he not?"

"Yes!" she wailed.

"So he fired him."

"Yes!"

"Mr. Brown was so angry at that point, he finished cleaning up and left for the day. That night, he played cards and had a few drinks with a friend at his apartment building. In a fit of drunken despair, he went back to the Morgans' estate late that night. He got rope and hanged himself in the greenhouse. Can you tell me with one hundred percent certainty that Marty heard Trent and Michelle's conversation?"

"No."

"Can you be one hundred percent certain that he blackmailed Trent Morgan?"

She rubbed her eyes and said, "No."

"Nothing further."

"You may step down, Mrs. Ashton," Judge Robinson instructed.

Without looking at Trent, she got up and exited the court-room. Judge Robinson adjourned for the afternoon.

# CHAPTER 27

Mac Yeager was the first witness to be sworn in the next morning. John Harkens started off asking background questions and then asked, "You have quite a reputation for panning plays and films, don't you?"

Yeager smirked and said, "Yeah, that's true."

"Did you pan a play that Michelle du Prix was in last spring?"

"Yeah. It was a lousy performance. I just call it like I see it."

"What happened when she read your review?"

He testified about their altercation on the patio at the Morgan home on Memorial Day weekend. "She was hitting my chest and raving hysterically. She was irrational."

"Was Trent Morgan with you?"

"Yes."

"What did you tell her?"

"I told her she gave a lousy performance, and she slapped my face. Then she yelled and said, 'You arrogant son of a bitch. I'll get you for this.'"

"Did Trent Morgan try to break you two up?"

"Yes, he wanted us to shut up and work out the problem in the morning. But then she demanded a retraction, and Trent said he'd see what he could do about it."

"Did you hit Trent Morgan?"

"No, he hit me."

"How did it happen?"

"Michelle and I said some ugly things to each other, and he slugged me."

"Did you say anything to provoke him?"

"I said he was giving in to the whims of his mistress, or something like that."

"How did he react?"

"He shoved me, and I fell on the patio floor."

"What did you do?"

"I pushed him back, and he landed in the bushes. We started hitting each other, and guests had to break us up. Michelle hit me on the head with a potted plant."

"Were you punished for this incident?"

Mac looked over at the jurors and said, "Yes, Trent Morgan fired me! Michelle told him to. He can't think on his own. That's one of the things she was yelling when we were on the patio."

"Had you ever seen Trent Morgan display violent tendencies in the ten years you worked with him?"

"He has a temper. He gets hyper when he's under stress. A couple of his newspapers are in financial turmoil. So he'd been on edge."

"Did you ever see him drink alcohol to calm his nerves?"

"Quite, frequently."

"Have you ever seen him intoxicated?"

"Yes."

"Was he drinking at the party last May twenty-fifth?"

"Yes."

"Has he ever displayed a violent temper when he's been drinking?"

"Yes."

"Can you elaborate?"

"He got really angry at an employee at an office Christmas party five years ago. I thought he was going to punch the guy."

"Nothing further," Harkens said.

It was Ackroyd's turn. He went over to the podium and said, "Would it be fair to say that the fight was really between you and Michelle du Prix?"

"Yes."

"In fact, wouldn't it be fair to say that you instigated the fight, Mr. Yeager?"

"No."

"Did you say anything to provoke her?"

"No."

"Come now, Mr. Yeager. You made derogatory remarks to her, did you not?"

"Yes, but she was equally vulgar."

"You testified that Trent Morgan shoved you after you made comments about his 'mistress,' did you not?"

"Yes."

"Wouldn't you hit somebody for insulting your wife or girl-friend—or boyfriend?"

Yeager scowled back at him and said, "I resent that comment. I'd do a lot of yelling, but I wouldn't hit the person. That's not my style."

"Why should I believe anything you have to say? You're a disgruntled employee. Maybe you just have it in for Trent

Morgan. He fired you. Maybe we should disregard everything you say."

"That's not true!" Yeager shot back. "I was unhappy doing entertainment reviews. I wanted to change jobs. Trent Morgan refused to listen."

"You went to work for a competing newspaper, did you not?"

"Yes."

"Did you tell your new employers about your drinking problem?"

His jaw dropped. "But that was years ago! How did you—"

"Did you tell them?"

He looked down and said, "No."

"You spent time drying out in rehab, did you not?"

"Yes, but that was almost twenty years ago. I'm sober now. What does that have to do with anything?"

"Nothing further."

The judge called a twenty minute recess, and visitors filed out of the courtroom.

＊　＊　＊

In the waiting room, Claire looked at herself in the mirror and adjusted the dove brooch on her pink dress. Bill came up from behind and told her she looked fine. She straightened his tie and centered it neatly on his blue button-down shirt. She started pacing. Every so often, she eyed the clock and chewed her nails.

"What's taking so long?" she said.

"Trials take a long time."

"It doesn't look good for your father! I don't want you to testify."

He pressed her hand and said, "I'll be okay."

"It's a nightmare!" she squeaked.

"Relax. It can't be as long as the O.J. trial."

"I don't know what I'll do if—"

"Try to think positively. Read a magazine to take your mind off it."

☆  ☆  ☆

Rob Watkins whipped out his smartphone and called his newspaper editor, Jeff Vernon. "It's a little slow now, but I expect things will pick up when the Morgans testify."

"Stick with it," Vernon said. "Keep me posted."

Rob hung up and walked hurriedly down the hallway leading to the courtroom and practically tackled a short wiry woman with blond hair.

"Look where you're going!" she snapped.

It didn't take long for him to realize that he had nearly knocked over his competitor, Kim Weston of the *Times-Sentinel* in Townsend.

"I'm sorry about that, Kim."

"Just get your head out of the clouds and watch where you're going next time," she said quickly. She was practically out of breath with excitement.

"What did you think about Mac Yeager's testimony?"

"It's too early to tell." She remained tight-lipped about everything that had happened so far. She seemed to be in a hurry.

"It will really be interesting when Claire Morgan testifies."

She smiled thinly. "I'm picturing fireworks."

"It'll be the biggest news story in weeks!"

She leaned in close to him and said, "Just don't get in my way!" And then she walked hurriedly into the courtroom. Rob raced after her.

John Harkens had already begun questioning Todd Stevens of the *Main Line Chronicle.*

"Bill Morgan and I had to break them up," Todd testified. "They were really going at it."

"Have you ever seen Trent Morgan display a violent temper, Mr. Stevens?"

"He has a temper," Todd admitted, "but the newspaper business is stressful. I've been around some owners who can be really miserable."

Harkens asked him some more questions. Then it was Ackroyd's turn.

"Where were you when the fight started, Mr. Stevens?"

"I was talking to coworkers in the den."

"Did you hear them yelling?"

"Yes. They were out on the patio. It's just off the den."

"Could you hear everything that was said?"

"For the most part." He repeated what Mac Yeager said earlier. "Then Bill Morgan and I had to break them up and drag them back into the house."

"Did Mac Yeager make lewd comments about Michelle du Prix?"

"Yes. He referred to her as Trent Morgan's mistress and made crude remarks."

Cross-examination lasted about ten more minutes. Judge Robinson called a two hour recess for lunch.

* * *

"We all knew about my father's relationship with Michelle," Bill testified. "Maybe if he had paid attention to my mother, she wouldn't have run off."

"Objection!" Ackroyd snapped. "Hearsay."

"Sustained," Judge Robinson said.

"How did your father act at the party on May twenty-fifth?" Harkens asked.

"He was nervous. Michelle was coming. He was afraid she'd seen Mac Yeager's review."

"Did she see it?"

"Yes."

"How did she react?"

"She was furious." He repeated what the others had said. She got angry. He heard them arguing and went to break up his father and Yeager. "I heard people making jokes about their relationship all afternoon. It really made me angry."

"Had you ever seen your father display violent tendencies before?"

He looked down. "Yes."

"What have you seen?"

"My parents would always argue when we ate dinner."

"Was your father drinking alcohol at those times?"

"Sometimes."

"What were the fights about?"

"It started out over little things--money, finances, and it ended up being about other things."

"What other things?"

"My mother is very insecure about her appearance. Either he was going through a midlife crisis—or she was."

"Your mother didn't like Michelle du Prix much, correct?"

"Nobody did. She was pushy and arrogant and only thought about herself. She was always trying to get my father to do things for her."

"Did he?"

"Yes."

"Would that include convincing him to poison your mother?"

"Objection!" Ackroyd shouted. "That calls for speculation."

Judge Robinson agreed and asked the court reporter to strike it. He told the jurors to disregard John Harkens's previous question.

"How would you describe the relationship between Michelle du Prix and your mother?" Harkens asked.

"It was ugly," Bill replied angrily.

"What about the relationship between your parents?"

"It was like walking on eggshells. They were always arguing."

"How did your father react when he found out that your mother staged her disappearance?"

"He was angry. And so was I. We felt used. But I really couldn't blame her. If he hadn't treated her like dirt, she wouldn't have done it in the first place. She just wanted him to notice her."

"Strike the last two sentences," Judge Robinson commanded. "This trial is not about Claire Morgan's actions. Continue Mr. Harkens."

Harkens asked him about the night that Michelle du Prix was poisoned. Once again, Bill had to endure a slew of questions about who served the drinks, and who drank what, and so on. Then Harkens moved on to other topics.

"Did your parents discuss getting a divorce over dinner that night?"

Bill testified that he and Michelle left the dining room so his parents could have a private conversation. "I heard them yelling about divorce papers. My father got angry because she refused to sign them. Michelle and I could hear every unkind word they spewed at each other."

Harkens bombarded him with more inane questions about how long he and Michelle had been the family room. Were they there the whole time? Did they serve their own drinks? And so on. Then he asked how the fight started in the family room after dinner.

"My mother went over to the phone and called Todd Stevens. Michelle said, 'Go ahead and make the call. See if I care.'"

"What did she mean by that?"

"I don't know. I didn't ask."

"Then what happened?"

Bill testified that they all got into a nasty shouting match. His father went out on the patio, and he went up to his bedroom to get away from them. About ten minutes later, he heard a scream and rushed back into the room to find Michelle lying dead on the floor.

"It must have been a horrible thing to witness."

"We were all in shock, especially when we found out that she had been poisoned!"

Harkens's questions eventually led to Marty Brown. "When was the last time you saw Mr. Brown?"

"The day before Detective Logan discovered his body. Marty was cutting the grass that afternoon."

"Did you see him earlier that day?"

"Yes."

"Did he act sad or depressed?"

"Quite the opposite. He was full of life. He was joking and laughing."

"How did your father act that day?"

Bill thought carefully before responding. "I don't know. He seemed about the same to me."

"Was he nervous or upset?"

"No more than usual. I mean, we were all pretty shocked by Michelle's murder."

"Did you see your father that night?"

"He was doing a crossword puzzle in the den."

"What time was that?"

"About eight thirty—quarter of nine."

"Were you with him the whole time?"

"No, about five minutes to nine, I went up to take a shower."

"Did you go back downstairs?"

"Yes. I had to get some financial papers I left in the family room."

"Was your father there?"

"No."

"Did you see him anywhere else in the house?"

"No."

"Did you stay in that room?"

"No, I took the papers and went back to my room."

"Did you go back downstairs at any time after that?"

"Yes. I went back down to watch TV in the den before I went to bed."

"Did you see anyone wandering on the backyard then?"

"Yes."

"Could you make out who it was?"

Bill glanced at Trent, his Adam's apple bulging. "Yes."

"Who did you see?"

There was a long, uncomfortable silence.

"Who did you see?" Harkens repeated.

"My father," he said at last.

"What time was that?"

"About eleven thirty."

"Did you see him after that?"

"No, I fell asleep at my desk."

"Nothing further."

# CHAPTER 28

G. Walter Ackroyd skimmed his notes before beginning his cross-examination of Bill Morgan. Then he went to the podium and asked background questions to make him feel at ease. Bill carefully thought out every word he said. He had been warned not to be too comfortable with Ackroyd or else he might make a fatal slip of the tongue.

"When did your father meet Michelle du Prix?" Ackroyd asked.

"About five years ago."

"Were you dating her at the time she met your father?"

"Yes."

"So you were dating her. Was it serious?"

"I would say so. We were engaged."

"But that all changed, did it not?"

"Yes."

"What happened?"

"She was consumed with her career, and we seemed to be drifting apart. When she started canceling dates and making excuses,

I knew there was something wrong. Then she said we should stop seeing each other."

"Did she give you a reason?"

"She told me she had met someone else."

"Did she tell you who her new boyfriend was?"

"Not at the time."

"But you eventually found out who her new boyfriend was, did you not?"

"That is correct."

"Who was the new man in her life?"

"My father."

There were loud whispers around the room. People leaned forward, anxiously waiting for what was to come next. They could not get enough of the twisted drama that was unfolding before their eyes.

"How did that make you feel?"

"I was furious. I felt betrayed by the love of my life. And I felt betrayed by my father—the man who was supposed to set an example. I really felt bad for my mother."

"Did she know about Michelle du Prix?"

"Not at the time. He was sneaking around. I couldn't tell her, but I think she knew."

"When did he start dating Michelle du Prix?"

"Two years ago."

"Was she dating him at the same time she was going out with you?"

Bill gnashed his teeth and said, "Yes."

"Did she tell you she was also seeing your father?"

"Not right away."

"When did you find out?"

"About four months later."

"How did you find out?"

"She kept canceling on me, so I decided to follow her."

"Did she go to a restaurant called the Garden Terrace?"

"Yes."

"Was she alone?

"No."

"Who was she there with?"

"My father."

"What were they doing?"

"They were holding hands!"

"Were you jealous of their relationship?"

Bill carefully thought about his answer. He spotted a trick and did not want to say the wrong thing. "I was upset. I felt wounded—like they had stabbed me in the back."

"Would it be fair to say that you hated Michelle du Prix for planning to marry your father?"

"I got over it. I had more important things to worry about."

"Such as?"

"Well, I was concerned about my mother's welfare. I was worried how she would react when he told her. They kept their relationship a secret for two years. But I knew. And I wasn't going to say anything to her. But I think she always knew."

"How did she act?"

"She started crying out for attention. She'd leave without saying where she was going. Sometimes she would leave for a day or two. It got to a point where we didn't let it bother us. We knew she'd be back."

"Did your mother drive off last Memorial Day, the twenty-sixth of May?"

"Yes, but it was different that time. She disappeared for a couple of months, and we were all worried."

"Did your father date Michelle during your mother's absence?"

"They saw each other in New York City, but they took themselves to our house in Townsend to keep it a secret."

"Deep down, you resented Michelle, did you not?"

"I can't answer that. I resented her, but I loved her at the same time."

"Were you still in love with her when she was going with your father?"

"Of course! I hoped they would break up."

"Maybe you were so jealous about their relationship that you put poison in her drink."

"You're putting words in my mouth!"

"Were you alone with Michelle du Prix before the poison took effect?"

"Yes, but I went upstairs to make a call."

"How long were you gone?"

"About ten, fifteen minutes."

"You had it in for Michelle. Maybe you poisoned her drink. You had the means and opportunity."

"I object!" John Harkens bellowed. "He's badgering the witness!"

"Mr. Ackroyd, the witness is not on trial!" Judge Robinson rebuked. "He already told you that he didn't put poison in the drink. The issue isn't if he poisoned the drink but whether it can be proved that the defendant did."

Ackroyd apologized and went back to his table to glance at his notes. He returned to the podium and looked over at Bill Morgan.

"Did you hear Marty Brown and Elizabeth Ashton discussing a conversation he allegedly overheard between your father and Michelle du Prix?"

"No."

"Did you overhear Elizabeth Ashton warn your mother that Marty Brown heard them talking about poisoning your mother?"

"Yes."

"So you knew they were plotting to poison your mother?"

"Yes, but I didn't take it seriously."

"That was all you needed to know. All you had to do was switch your mother's drink with Michelle's, correct?"

"No."

"How did Michelle du Prix and your mother get along?"

"It was a toxic relationship. They loathed each other."

"Did she feel threatened by your mother?"

"I don't know."

"Objection," Harkens said. "That calls for speculation. How would he know what his mother was thinking?"

Judge Robinson agreed and instructed the court reporter to strike the question.

"Your father stands accused in connection with the death of Michelle du Prix and Martin Brown. If everyone suspected what they were planning to do, I suppose just about anyone could have slipped the poison into the drink—if that person was jealous enough, correct?"

"Maybe," Bill replied flatly.

"You were so angry about their future wedding plans, that you figured this would be the perfect opportunity to get Michelle du Prix out of the way, correct?"

"If you think I killed her, you're crazy!" Bill snapped.

"Objection!" Harkens yelled. "He's badgering the witness."

"Don't antagonize the witness, Mr. Ackroyd," the judge warned. "He's not on trial for murder!"

Bill's eyes watered. "I would never have laid a finger on Michelle. I loved her."

"Did you ever see Marty Brown drinking on the job?"

"Once in a while. But he did a great job."

"Wasn't he known for telling tall tales?"

"Well, sometimes—sometimes you had to take things he said with a grain of salt."

"So what you are basically saying is that he was known to make things up, correct?"

There was a long silence.

"He made things up, yes or no?"

"Yes."

"Nothing further."

Judge Robinson called a twenty minute recess, and visitors filed into the lobby.

# CHAPTER 29

When Claire Morgan was sworn in, John Harkens started with routine background questions and gradually led up to her current relationship with Trent.

"Did you recently divorce Trent?"

"Yes."

"How long had you been married?"

"About twenty-eight years."

"During that time, did Trent ever hit you?"

"He didn't start off that way. We really did love each other. But then he became so consumed with turning a profit, the stress got to him and he started drinking. He'd throw things at me—but he'd never hit me. Thank God!"

"Did you ever provoke this abusive behavior?"

"No, I tried to help, but he got angrier." She reached for a Kleenex and wiped away tears.

Trent rolled his eyes and shook his head. He could not believe what he was hearing.

Harkens walked over to the witness stand and gave Claire a look to let her know she was doing just fine. He let her have a moment to compose herself and continued his line of questioning.

"When did you find out he was having an affair with Michelle du Prix?"

"I knew about it from the start. That's when he stopped caring about me. That's when—that's when he started neglecting me and spending time with her!"

"How was your relationship with him at that point?"

"It was rocky, to say the least. He was drinking a lot then. When we were alone, he would just ignore me. He would just bury himself in his work. He didn't even know I existed. When we were together, he'd always be too consumed with his latest business acquisition!"

"What did you do?"

"I changed my appearance on numerous occasions. I changed hairstyles, hair colors, tried skimpy outfits—anything to get his attention. But when we were alone, he would only be thinking of her. I know it!"

"How did that make you feel?"

"I was severely depressed and started drinking a bit too much myself."

"Did you ever talk to him about her?"

"Frequently."

"How did he react?"

"We would get into shouting matches."

"Did he ever physically abuse you?"

"No, it was all mental. He played mind games. He would promise me he wouldn't see her anymore and that he would change, but he never did. His life revolved around her."

"Did you see him hit Mac Yeager at the party last May twenty-fifth?"

She shuttered. "Yes, it was horrible!"

"Where were you?"

"In my bedroom. I was so unhappy; I couldn't cope with being cheerful around the guests. I heard shouting outside. I looked out my window and saw Michelle hitting Mac. Trent came to the rescue and hit him so hard he fell down at the edge of the patio—close to the edge. It was horrible! All because of that witch!" She went on to tell about the brawl in vivid detail.

"Had you ever seen Trent act that way before?"

She sniffled and wiped away tears with her palms. "No. He does have a bit of a temper, mind you, but he would never hurt anyone. He just gets agitated when he's under pressure."

"Did Trent say that he was leaving you?"

She rocked her body, her voice squeaking. "Yes. I kept asking myself, Why did I deserve this?" Then she broke down.

Harkens went over and spoke in a soothing tone. "That's okay. Take your time."

Judge Robinson asked if she needed to take a break, but she said it was all right. She sniffled and rubbed her tear-stained face. While doing this, she checked for people's reactions. There were a few murmurs from jurors. Others looked at her with empathy. She heard an elderly woman say, "You poor thing."

John Harkens went back to the podium and smiled. "Are you okay now, Mrs. Morgan?"

She nodded and said, "Yes, thanks."

"All right, let's begin again," he said softly. "When did Trent tell you about the divorce?"

"The day after the party last Memorial Day."

"How did that make you feel?"

"I felt totally betrayed and used."

Ackroyd rose. "Objection. What does this have to do with the murder of Michelle du Prix and Martin Brown?"

"Absolutely nothing," agreed the judge. He glared at Harkens and said, "If you can fit it into the two homicides that the defendant is accused of, I will allow it."

"Yes, your honor," Harkens replied cordially. "I'm just setting up the circumstances that led to the murders. That's all." He looked at Claire and smiled. "What did you do when he broke the bad news?"

"I left. I didn't mean to be gone so long. I just started packing. Then I got in the car and started driving. I didn't know where I was going. I just knew I had to get out of there."

"Did you try to contact Trent during your absence?"

"No, I was so upset that I didn't know how to deal with it. I tried to call a few times. I would pick up the phone, but I couldn't work up the nerve to dial."

"How did Michelle du Prix react when she found out you were back in the picture?"

"She didn't like it," Claire said in a monotone.

"How did you two get along?"

"We despised each other!"

"Did you feel threatened by her?"

"No, she felt threatened by me because she knew Trent still loved me."

"Is it true that your maid thought you were in danger?"

"Yes."

"What did she tell you?"

"She told me that Marty had overheard Trent and Michelle talking about poisons."

"Why were they talking about poisons, Mrs. Morgan?"

Claire testified that Marty overheard them plotting to poison her when she refused to sign the divorce papers.

"Did you believe her?"

"With my life. She is the only person I can trust."

"Did you usually confide in her?"

"All of the time."

"Did you ever talk about your marital problems?"

"Yes, she was always supportive."

"Did Mrs. Ashton tell you how they planned to kill you?"

"Yes."

"Why did you believe her?

"I was in Michelle's way. She couldn't have him if I didn't sign the divorce papers."

"Why didn't you just sign them?"

"I didn't want Michelle to get her hands on my husband."

"How did Michelle du Prix act that night? Did she seem sickly?"

"I didn't notice."

"What happened next?"

Tears welled in her eyes when she testified about the argument that ensued when Trent shook the divorce papers in front of her and she refused to sign them. "He was furious, and we got into a shouting match. I got so angry that I yanked the tablecloth. The room was in a horrible state of disarray! Elizabeth had to come in and clean it up."

"How long did the fight last?"

She looked up at the vaulted ceiling a moment and then met his penetrating gaze. "About ten, maybe fifteen minutes. I don't know how long. I just knew I had to get out of there. So we went to the den to cool off. Michelle gave him a drink, and we just sat there, barely looking at each other. I felt like a caged animal!"

"Did Michelle du Prix appear ill at that point?"

"She was her usual bitchy self. She had energy enough to keep at it."

"What do you mean?"

"She just wanted to cause trouble, that's all. She said she didn't care if Trent was a bigamist; she was going to marry him anyway. Can you imagine that?"

There were loud murmurs around the courtroom.

"Trent and Bill got upset and stormed out of the room," Claire continued after spectators quieted down.

"What time was that?"

"About seven thirty."

"What did you two talk about?"

"We talked about Trent. And it wasn't a pleasant conversation, I'll tell you that! She told me he didn't love me, and I strongly disagreed. Then she got really angry. I pulled out my checkbook and told her I would pay her any amount of money she wanted, as long as she got out of our lives. She tore it up and threatened to kill me!"

"Objection!" Ackroyd shouted. "Your Honor, no one was privy to their conversation. It's just her word against that of the deceased."

"Sustained," Judge Robinson said. "Jurors are instructed to disregard the last statement."

"You testified that Michelle du Prix was upset," Harkens continued. "When did you notice she appeared sickly?"

Claire described in graphic detail the horrifying events that transpired but left out a few details about her blackmail threats against Michelle du Prix. "She started choking and clutched her throat. And then—and then she collapsed on the floor and started thrashing about. It was just horrible! She looked like a madwoman. I screamed, and everybody came rushing in."

Harkens asked some more questions regarding that incident, then moved on to Marty Brown.

"Was the gardener blackmailing your ex-husband?"

"I don't know."

"Did Trent tell you why he fired him?"

"No, I didn't know he had been let go until the day his body was discovered."

"Did you see Trent wandering outside on the night of Marty Brown's murder?"

"I couldn't sleep, so I got up to get a glass of water. When I looked outside, I saw him wandering around in the backyard."

"What time was that?"

"Around quarter to twelve or so."

"Was he in bed with you all night?"

"Not the whole time. You see, I have insomnia."

"Were you awake the whole night?"

"No, but I was awake for quite a while, though."

"Did you fall asleep when you got in bed?"

"Yes."

"Did you wake up at any time after that?"

"Yes."

"What time did you wake up?"

"About twelve thirty in the morning."

"Was Trent with you?"

"No."

"How long were you awake?"

"About an hour and a half. So I decided to catch up on some reading."

"Did Trent come back to bed during that time?"

"No."

"Nothing further."

# CHAPTER 30

"It is an established fact that you are a liar, Mrs. Morgan," Ackroyd began. "You admitted staging your disappearance in a national magazine. You lied to your ex-husband and son. You had them worried sick. Trent offered a $25,000 reward for information about your whereabouts. You sit there and expect the people in this courtroom to feel sorry for you? You knew that Trent was unhappy, and you kept making him more miserable."

"That isn't true!" Claire insisted.

"Trent asked you for a divorce on numerous occasions. He's a decent man and did not want to sneak around anymore. He wanted to be honest about his relationship with Michelle du Prix. And you were standing in his way."

"That isn't true!"

"Did you believe you were in danger?"

"Yes, but—"

"Elizabeth Ashton told you that Trent and Michelle were talking about poisoning you, correct?"

"Yes."

"You can't prove that Marty Brown actually heard them discussing it, can you?"

"No."

"He had a drinking problem, did he not?"

"Yes, but he was okay."

"Is it true that Trent caught him drinking on the job on more than one occasion?"

"Yes."

"Is that why Trent fired him?"

"Yes."

"Do you believe that Marty Brown had a grudge against your ex-husband?"

"I don't know."

"Do you think he had a grudge, yes or no?"

"Why I suppose so. Yes."

"If he had a grudge, he could have said anything to trash Trent's reputation, correct?"

"I suppose so."

"Is it possible that Marty Brown made up stories that he had heard them plotting to kill you, Mrs. Morgan?"

"I suppose so."

"Because you never actually heard their alleged conversation, did you?"

"No."

"You were just going by word of mouth from Marty Brown to Elizabeth Ashton, correct?"

"Yes."

"It was second-hand information that you got from the housekeeper, correct?"

"Yes."

"Marty Brown had a reputation for telling tall tales, did he not?"

"Yes, that sounds about right."

"Did you ever question the authenticity of his stories?"

"Sometimes," Claire admitted.

"Did you believe Elizabeth Ashton when she told you about Trent and Michelle's plot to murder you?"

"I trusted her with my life. She wouldn't have told me if she didn't really believe Marty. I knew Michelle loathed me. She could always get Trent to do things for her. And I knew Trent was angry about my disappearance."

"So you were warned that they might poison you."

"Yes."

"Did you talk to Marty about it?"

"No."

"Why didn't you do something to protect yourself?"

"I don't know."

"Did you confront Trent about what you knew?"

"No."

"Did you call the police?"

"No!" she snapped.

"Then you must not have really thought your life was in danger. If you were really afraid, you wouldn't have had a drink. Surely, you would have done something about it, correct?"

"Yes, I suppose you're right."

"You weren't really in danger, were you?"

"But they plotted to kill me!" she screeched. "Liz told me everything! I believe her! I trust her with my life!"

"So you were willing to let events transpire without doing anything about it. Let us suppose, shall we, that you slipped the poison into Michelle's drink."

"Objection!" Harkens shouted. "That calls for speculation."

"Overruled," Judge Robinson said. "Continue, Mr. Ackroyd."

"You were alone with Michelle du Prix at the time she got sick. You are the only one who actually knows what happened in there, correct?"

She wiped away tears with her palms and said, "Yes."

"Maybe you switched drinks."

"I didn't do it, I swear!" she insisted. "You must believe me!"

"It's just a thought. There is really little proof that my client put the poison into the drink. Especially since the maid washed the glasses. It does seem interesting that Michelle wound up with the wrong drink. After all, you were both drinking wine when you were having your private conversation. Your maid warned you that the drinks might be spiked with poison. And you were paying attention."

"I didn't do it!"

"When Mr. Harkens asked you questions, you neglected to mention that there was another incident when you were all in the family room after dinner. Is it not true that you were about to call Todd Stevens at the *Main Line Chronicle?*"

She huffed and said, "Yes."

"I have a sworn statement from Detective Frank Logan of the Townsend Police Department. Your husband and son both said they heard Michelle say, 'Go ahead and make the call. See if I care.' What were you going to tell Mr. Stevens?"

"I decided that if they were going to get married, that I would tell the whole world. I thought the newspaper would appreciate the tip."

"What if I told you I tracked down a private investigator named Wally Baker who you hired to dig up dirt on Michelle du Prix?"

"Yeah, so what?"

"He is willing to testify that you paid him a substantial fee to do you a favor."

She scowled at him and said, "What does it prove?"

"He got dirt on Michelle du Prix, and you confronted her, didn't you?"

"I figured if Trent knew about her filthy past, he'd dump her. She did nude shots! And she did a porno film!"

Trent's jaw dropped. "Oh my God," he murmured under his breath.

The crowd roared with excitement.

"Isn't that why you really called Todd Stevens?"

There was a long, uncomfortable silence. Ackroyd repeated the question.

"Yes," she finally answered.

"Were you blackmailing her?"

"I had to do it, don't you see? It was my last chance to get him back. I think any woman would have done that under the circumstances." Tears smeared her mascara.

"Why didn't you just leave him? He obviously didn't want you anymore."

"I didn't want to be alone!" she bawled.

"Michelle du Prix was so terrified you would spill the beans, she decided to get rid of you. According to the sworn statement, Trent and Bill started hitting each other, and Michelle tried to break them up. Maybe you switched the glasses during the confusion. Is that how you planned it?"

"That's impossible!" she screeched.

"You could just say they were planning to murder you, and she got the wrong drink," Ackroyd continued, undaunted. "She did it to herself. Is that how you planned it?"

"There's no way I could have done it!" Her voice sounded hoarse from shouting so much. "There wouldn't have been enough time! My glass was on the end table that my smartphone was on—I mean, I was sitting there—Michelle had her glass clear across the room—there wasn't time!"

"How long were you alone with Michelle du Prix?"

"About ten, fifteen minutes. I don't know."

"You could have switched glasses then, correct?"

"I could have, but I was drinking tea at that point. After the ruckus, Elizabeth came in and asked us if we wanted coffee or tea. I had had two glasses of wine already and couldn't drink anymore, so I had some tea. Everybody knows Michelle was drinking the wine when I was talking to her alone."

"Your son was alone with her while you argued with Trent in the dining room, is that not so?"

"Yes, but don't drag him into it!"

"He testified about being jealous of their relationship. Maybe he did it."

"Nobody did it!" her voice shook. Her eyes were wild with rage. Mascara streaked down her cheeks, and she looked like a circus clown.

"How do you know that?"

"I meant she was distraught when she thought Trent still had feelings for me. When she found out I knew about her early days, she panicked. Maybe she did it to herself!"

"Maybe, but you have to admit you certainly had the means and opportunity. So did Bill and Elizabeth."

"That's impossible! They didn't do it! I didn't do it! It was just a horrible thing that happened!"

"And wasn't it a coincidence that the gardener was found dead shortly after being fired. You never heard Marty Brown actually blackmail your ex-husband, did you?"

"No."

"And just like the alleged poisoning story, Elizabeth Ashton didn't actually hear him blackmail Trent, isn't that so?"

"Yes!" she shouted, the veins on her forehead protruding. "How many times do I have to say it?"

"It sounds like you believe everything that people tell you."

"That isn't so!"

"On the night of Marty Brown's murder, you testified that you were having trouble sleeping. You said Trent was not in bed for about an hour and a half. Is that right?"

"Yes, but what does that have to do with anything?"

"An investigator who works with my firm did some checking. After losing her job, Elizabeth Ashton was more than willing to spill the beans about her former employers who had been so good to her over the years. She said that you two slept in separate rooms that night. Is it true that you were really sleeping in the guest room that overlooks the front of the house?"

"So what if I did? It doesn't prove anything."

"It has a lot to do with the case," Ackroyd countered. "It proves that you lied. For all we know, Trent could have been in bed all night. Did you see him go out that night?"

"No!"

"Did you tell your family you were Mary Shannon when they found you at Eagle Crest Hotel in the Poconos last summer?"

"Yes."

"Did you recognize them?"

"No."

"Were you treated for amnesia at a psychiatric hospital in the Poconos after they found you?"

"Yes."

"Did you tell magazine reporter Jerry Hawke that was one of the things you lied about?"

"Yes."

"Did you tell him you staged your disappearance?"

"Yes."

"So it was a hoax, and you frightened your family for no reason other than your desire to get back at your husband, correct?"

She remained icily silent.

Ackroyd marched over to the witness stand and leaned on the rail. "Is it true, yes or no?"

"Yes."

"If you lied about all of that, why should we believe anything you have told us today?"

"I'm not lying now! I haven't lied about anything! You must believe me!"

"Did you think you were Mary Shannon?"

"Yes!"

"But you already admitted under oath that you lied about the disappearing act to Jerry Hawke. Which is it, Mrs. Morgan? Did you know who you were or not?"

Her eyes darted around the room. Jurors leaned forward their eyes fixed on her every movement. Spectators sat there with their mouths agape. The courtroom was eerily silent. Everyone was riveted on the action unfolding in front of them.

"Yes," she finally admitted.

"Were you discharged when the doctors discovered you were pretending to be Mary?"

"Yes!"

Ackroyd went over to the jury box and leaned on the rail. He looked from one to the other, silent a moment. When he decided it had sunk in, he said, "Ladies and gentlemen of the jury, we have a woman who is an admitted liar. If psychiatric professionals didn't believe her, why should we? Nothing further."

# CHAPTER 31

When it was Logan's turn to testify, he arrived at the courthouse in his uniform—with a new stripe. When he was sworn in, John Harkens stepped up to the podium.

"I guess congratulations are in order for your recent promotion to sergeant."

Logan beamed and said, "Thank you, sir."

Harkens turned to face the jurors and said, "That is a major accomplishment."

"Yes sir. It was a lot of hard work."

Harkens started asking him background information about his career and responsibilities. A few minutes later, he asked questions pertaining to the Morgans.

"On August twentieth of last year, you got an emergency call from the Morgans' residence, correct?"

"Yes sir. When my colleagues and I got to their residence, we discovered Michelle du Prix lying dead on the den floor."

"Had you seen her with Trent Morgan before?"

"Yes sir. She was always at the Morgans' residence when I was trying to locate Mrs. Morgan back in June."

"How did Trent Morgan react when he found out Michelle du Prix was dead?"

"He was in shock. They all were. It was a traumatic thing for them to go through."

"Was there anything unusual about Michelle's death?"

"Yes, there was. I watched coroner Stan Green examine her body. Her organs were a cherry-red color."

"What does that usually indicate?"

"That the victim has been exposed to cyanide."

"What did you do when you found out Ms. du Prix was poisoned?"

"I went back to the Morgans' home and investigated. I found out that Ms. du Prix had been drinking wine with the Morgans that night."

Like everyone before him, Logan testified about Trent and Claire's argument when she refused to give him the divorce he needed so he could marry Michelle. Logan mentioned that the gardener told Elizabeth Ashton about the plot to poison Claire. She, in turn, told Claire.

"Did you talk to Claire Morgan about it?"

"Yes sir."

"What did she say?"

"She told me that she feared for her life and that Michelle du Prix hated her and wanted her out of the way."

"Did you believe her?"

"No sir. I did not."

"Why not?"

"Because she admitted staging her disappearance to a magazine reporter last summer. She told him that she drove her car into a tree and punctured her fingers with a piece of broken glass and smeared blood on the car seat. When I found that out, I didn't believe her. I was angry that she made me waste my time investigating her disappearance."

"Did you suspect Bill Morgan of putting poison in Michelle's drink?"

"At one time I did," Logan admitted. "I believed he was jealous of his father's relationship with her. At one point, Bill and Michelle were dating."

"Did you ever suspect that Claire Morgan might have switched drinks with Ms. du Prix?"

"Yes, sir, that thought crossed my mind. She was talking privately with Michelle for a few minutes before the cyanide started taking affect."

"Did you believe Mrs. Morgan when she told you what the housekeeper told her?"

"No sir, I didn't believe her. I couldn't believe Mrs. Ashton. It was just secondhand information. She was just going on what someone else allegedly told her. She never actually heard Trent and Michelle talking about poisoning Mrs. Morgan. Michelle du Prix was unhappy about the Morgans' relationship. Bill told me his parents seemed to be a lot closer since she came back. He thought they were going to get back together."

"Did Trent Morgan ever show a violent side?"

"He was always calm when I was around him. I was just basing my assumptions on what the others told me. He did get upset on the day that I arrested him."

"Did you speak to the gardener, Marty Brown?"

"I talked to him when Mrs. Morgan was missing. But I didn't get a chance to talk to him after Michelle was poisoned. He was cutting the grass, and I decided to talk to him the next day. I came back the next morning, and Mrs. Ashton told me he had been fired the day before. His pickup truck was by the shed, so I went to see if he was getting his things."

"Did you talk to him?"

Logan shook his head and looked grimly at the jurors. "He wasn't in the shed, so I checked the greenhouse. And that's when I found him hanging from a support beam."

There were loud murmurs around the courtroom.

"Did he hang himself?"

"Lieutenant Harry Winters and I determined that was not the case. Stan Green confirmed our beliefs."

"Why didn't you think he hanged himself?"

"There were no fingerprints on the chair or the rope. And the marks on Mr. Brown's neck indicated that he had been murdered." He went on to explain the difference between suicidal hanging and homicide.

"I believe the murderer stood behind Mr. Brown and wrapped the rope around his neck. The murderer exerted pressure, causing the purplish discoloration at the back of Mr. Brown's neck."

Logan went on to describe what he and his colleagues discovered inside and outside of the shed and greenhouse. He went on to say that he and Flosky discovered brochures for the Greek islands in Marty Brown's apartment on King Street.

"Did you think that was unusual?" Harkens asked.

"Yes sir. I wondered why a man would hang himself, if he was planning a trip."

"Could Marty Brown have afforded a trip like that?"

"My colleagues and I didn't think so. I checked his bank statements and found out that he wasn't making enough money to make a trip like that. Elizabeth Ashton said he often blew his money on gambling."

"Objection!" Ackroyd interrupted. "Detective Sergeant Logan is making a gross stereotype against people who live in that section of town. There's no way of telling what he spent his money on."

Judge Robinson agreed and ordered the court clerk to strike the last question and answer.

"Did Marty Brown tell Mrs. Ashton that he was going to be coming into money soon?"

"That's what she told me."

"Did he tell her how he was going to get the money?"

"He just told her he had some good luck but didn't specify."

"Did you talk to Trent Morgan about this?"

"Yes. He said Marty Brown was a braggart, not to be believed. He also told me Marty had a drinking problem, and he had to let him go."

"Did you believe him?"

"I normally make it a rule never to believe anything I hear second or third-hand, without talking to the original source. But this time, there were too many suspicious circumstances. Trent fired Marty Brown. And Brown was found hanging from a rafter in the greenhouse. And someone tried to make it look like he hanged himself."

"Did you find out if Mr. Brown had the money in his possession before he was murdered?"

"No. But I found out that Trent Morgan withdrew $500,000 on the day that Brown was murdered."

There were loud gasps around the courtroom. Trent looked intently at Logan, and bit his nails.

"You don't say. Didn't you think that was an awfully odd coincidence?"

"Yes sir."

Harkens referred to his notes. A moment later, he asked, "Were fingerprint tests done on the beer bottles found in the shed?"

"That is correct."

"Did you find someone else's fingerprints on the bottles?"

"Yes sir. I determined that the murderer wiped the fingerprints off the bottles. However, there was a print at the rim of one bottle that he forgot to get rid of."

"Were you able to determine if the person was right or left-handed?"

"Yes sir. By examining the curves in groove patterns, I determined a right-handed person had been drinking the beer."

"Do you know if Mr. Brown was left or right-handed?"

"He was left-handed."

"How do you know that?"

"I asked."

"Is it true that you lifted Trent Morgan's fingerprints from a piece of a broken coffee mug he had been handling?"

"Yes sir."

"What did you find out?"

"I compared it with the prints found on the beer bottle. It was a perfect match."

"Nothing further."

Now it was Ackroyd's turn. He was ready to go for the kill. This was the moment Logan was dreading. He knew Ackroyd had a reputation for brutal cross-examinations. He had never had the misfortune of actually being interrogated by him. He had always testified for other defense attorneys. Now he would finally know what his colleagues meant when they referred to the defense attorney as "Hard-Ass Ackroyd." But it was not meant as a compliment to his firm buttocks. His once firm derriere had gone plump after years of him sitting on it. Logan tried to maintain that mental image to help take his mind off the grilling he was about to endure.

"You didn't believe Claire Morgan when she told you her life was in danger, is that right?" Ackroyd asked.

"No sir."

"You didn't believe her because she staged her disappearance," he grumbled. "Do you usually let your opinions cloud your judgments?"

"I always try to make the best judgment possible."

"You testified that you didn't believe her. She lied about being missing. That sounds like a judgment to me."

"I also based my conclusions on what the housekeeper told me," Logan replied calmly. "I don't form conclusions until I have all the facts. I had not talked to Mr. Brown yet."

"When you found out Michelle du Prix had been poisoned, did you examine the glass she had been drinking out of?"

"No sir."

"And why not? Isn't that the logical thing to do?"

"It is, but I couldn't examine it. Mrs. Ashton had washed the dishes and destroyed the evidence."

"Was that before or after they all got into the argument in the family room after dinner?"

"After."

"How convenient. That would have been a crucial piece of evidence, would it not?"

"Yes sir."

"Without it, you can't be sure who had been drinking out of which glass, correct?"

"Yes, that's right."

"So you have no proof that Trent Morgan put the poison in his wife's glass, do you?"

"No sir."

"So you also have no way of knowing that the glasses were actually switched, correct?"

"That's true."

"Were Trent and Michelle ever alone that night?"

"Elizabeth Ashton said he was never alone with her."

"We all know that Claire and Michelle were alone, don't we?"

"Yes sir."

"Was Bill Morgan alone with her?"

"Yes, he told me he was for a little while."

"Is it possible that Bill or Claire could have put the poison in her drink?"

Logan maintained steady eye contact with the lawyer and said, "I suppose so."

"They both had good reason to want Michelle du Prix out of the way, did they not?"

"I suppose so."

"You can't really believe what the gardener thought he overheard, can you? You never actually talked to him, did you?"

"No sir, I did not."

"Like you said, you also can't trust information obtained from second and third hand discussions, can you?"

"No sir. That's why I needed to talk to Mr. Brown, so I could form my own conclusions."

"You said you didn't believe Claire Morgan. You thought she was a liar. You didn't really believe her when she told you she thought her life was in danger, did you?"

Logan knew what Ackroyd was doing. He was asking the question differently each time so he could trip him up. Detectives used that interrogation method too. He often did it to confuse suspects.

He reached for a glass of water and drank heartily. A stalling tactic.

"No sir, I didn't," he said at last. "She has a flair for theatrics."

"Elizabeth Ashton testified that she and Claire Morgan were confidantes. Maybe she was just saying that to look out for Claire after all the horrible things Trent apparently did to her."

"That is possible."

"You said you talked to Marty Brown when Claire went missing. What was your general impression of him?"

"He seemed like a nice man."

"Did you smell liquor on his breath?"

"No."

"How many times did you go to the house during Claire Morgan's absence?"

"About a half dozen times, I believe."

"Did you see Mr. Brown on any of those occasions?"

"Yes."

"Did he ever appear to be intoxicated?"

"I don't know. He always did have a bright red face."

Laughter filled the room.

"He was always busy doing yard work," Logan continued. "I never got close enough to determine if he was drunk or not."

"Did he stagger when he walked?"

"A little bit. But I assumed he had a bad leg."

"Drunks often walk like that, don't they?"

"Sometimes they do."

"Did you find empty beer cans lying around the shed or greenhouse?"

"I didn't go in the shed then. I was trying to get information to help find Claire Morgan."

"You don't have proof that Trent Morgan had been drinking with Marty on the night of August twenty-fifth, do you?"

"We found his matching fingerprints. And we did a plaster mold of the shoe print we found in the greenhouse. It matched Trent Morgan's shoe size and style."

"Could Trent Morgan have left those footprints several weeks before?"

"I suppose so. But the footprints would have faded. These looked fresh."

"He could have been drinking with Mr. Brown earlier that afternoon, is that not true?"

Logan took a deep breath and exhaled slowly. "Yes, I suppose so."

"Could the fingerprints have been left earlier that day?"

"We were not able to determine that."

"Is it possible that those bottles could have been lying around the shed for several weeks?"

Logan hesitated before answering. He sensed where Ackroyd was headed. It was a trap. "I suppose so," he said at last.

"Are you saying you don't know how long the bottles were actually in the shed?"

"I guess not."

"So you have no way of knowing if the bottles had been there for a week or two or even an hour before Mr. Brown died, is that correct?"

Logan remained silent. Ackroyd went over to him and said, "You don't know how long the bottles had been there, yes or no?"

Logan was quiet. Ackroyd repeated the question.

"Is it yes or no, Detective Sergeant Logan?"

"I don't know how long the bottles had been there," Logan replied coolly.

"So you're saying there is no proof when Trent Morgan had been there. It is his shed. Shouldn't he be able to go in there once in a while?"

"Trent Morgan's fingerprints on the broken coffee mug matched the ones on the beer bottle."

"Yes, the matching right thumb and index finger—or shall I say, a portion of it. Would that give an accurate reading?"

"It takes a trained eye to make a comparison."

"But mistakes can be made?"

"I suppose so."

"You only had the top third of the right thumb and index finger on the beer bottle. And it matched the print Trent Morgan left on the coffee mug?"

"Yes sir."

"But you didn't have the remaining section of the index and thumb print on the beer bottle, did you?"

"No sir."

"So how do you know that the remaining section actually corresponds to the ones found on the coffee mug? You don't know that for sure, do you?"

"It was a match."

"Have mistakes ever been made?"

"Yes, I'm sure there have been some mistakes made in some cases."

"Why is that?"

"Fingerprint patterns can be similar."

"Ah, fingerprints can be similar," Ackroyd mocked. He stared him down and raised his voice. "Let's review the facts, shall we? You based your information on the second or third-hand conversation from a disgruntled gardener who had been fired for drinking on the job, a storyteller to boot. Is that not true?"

Logan reached for his glass of water and drank heartily to stall. "Yes."

"You testified that you don't base your conclusions on these kinds of conversations, unless you actually talk to the person who saw or heard something, is that not the case?"

Logan stirred in his chair. "Yes sir."

"Mrs. Ashton testified that she thought it was odd that Mr. Brown seemed so cheerful right after Trent Morgan fired him. Yet she didn't question him when he told her he was coming into money soon. What did you think when she told you that?"

"I thought he was blackmailing Trent Morgan. The pieces fit."

"But you didn't have any proof?"

"No sir, I did not."

"You were just basing your opinion on conjecture. Marty Brown never actually told you he was blackmailing Trent Morgan, did he?"

"No sir."

"So you are basing everything on a word-of-mouth statement, is that not so?"

Logan wiped perspiration from his forehead. He reached for his glass of water and drank a healthy swig. Ackroyd leaned against the witness stand rail and silently looked him over. His eyes were cold and menacing.

Logan remained silent as he mulled over his answer.

Ackroyd repeated the question with more anger in his voice. "Are you basing everything on hearsay, yes or no, Detective Logan?"

"No!" he shouted.

"Maybe Mrs. Ashton misunderstood. Maybe the conversation was distorted somehow. Isn't that why you don't use those statements, unless you actually talk to the person who actually saw or heard it? Don't you have to check out the statement to make sure it's accurate? You can't do that if you don't actually talk to the person, can you? Do you need to talk to the original source?"

"Yes sir!" Logan shot back.

"Are you absolutely certain that the money Trent Morgan withdrew was used to pay off Mr. Brown?"

"No sir."

"So you have no proof that Mr. Brown was blackmailing him. Trent Morgan could have just withdrawn a large sum of money for a business transaction, correct?"

"I suppose so. But you have to admit that the timing is awfully suspicious."

"In murder trials, we don't deal with speculation. You're assuming that the money was used to pay off the alleged blackmailer, Mr. Brown. But you have no proof, do you?"

"I guess not," Logan said after a long silence.

"And couldn't the scuff marks found on the back of Martin Brown's shoes been there before? He was a gardener. Maybe he got dirt on them when he was working outside, correct."

Logan shook his head. "The scuff marks matched the streaks on the grass as his body was being dragged toward the greenhouse. The Philadelphia crime lab technicians confirmed it."

"It's a lot of circumstantial evidence. Trent Morgan had access to the shed and greenhouse—on his property. And Martin Brown worked outside. He could have scuffed those shoes the day before and the grass would have still been displaced the next day. Maybe Brown was carrying something heavy into the greenhouse and dug his heels on the grass as he was doing it. Anything's possible."

Ackroyd reviewed his notes. He looked back at Logan and said, "A few minutes ago, you testified that you found footprints near the site of Mr. Brown's body. Were you able to determine whose footprints they belonged to?"

Logan drew a deep breath. "Yes sir. A plaster mold was made. It matched Trent Morgan's shoe size and style."

"Doesn't it stand to reason that Trent Morgan would go into the greenhouse on his property?"

"Yes sir."

"And didn't criminologist Lynne Tulley report that he stepped on a flower stem?"

"Yes sir."

"What condition was it in?"

"It was still fresh."

"In other words, it wasn't all dried up?"

"That is correct."

"Were you able to determine how long it had been in that condition?"

"No sir."

"So you have no proof that Trent Morgan stepped on it between one and two in the morning, correct?"

"No sir, I do not."

"If it was fresh, he could have stepped on it hours earlier, could he not?"

Logan hesitated before answering. He knew it was a trick. "He could have, but—"

"A footprint doesn't link Mr. Morgan to the murder of Marty Brown. It could have been there several hours before Marty's body was discovered, could it not?"

"I suppose so."

"Once again, you are rushing to judgment on the evidence. Just because Trent Morgan's footprint was found in the greenhouse on his property doesn't mean that he murdered that poor old man. Is that not the case, Detective Sergeant Logan?"

"I suppose so."

"Which is it? Yes or no?"

"Yes. It's true that the footprint could have been there for several days, but you can't dismiss the displaced grass leading from the shed to the greenhouse and the blood spot that was discovered on a thorn branch in the greenhouse. A DNA test was done, and Trent Morgan was a perfect match."

"Couldn't Trent Morgan have cut himself on the thorn bush a few days earlier?"

"No sir, he couldn't have. It was a fresh spot."

"But that doesn't mean Trent Morgan couldn't have ripped his jacket on it several hours earlier, does it? He probably did it at the same time he stepped on the flower."

"It proves he did it exiting the greenhouse. The toe end was pointing toward the path leading to the exit." And what about Trent Morgan's fingerprints on the beer bottle? It links him to the crime."

"You have one fingerprint from a coffee mug and another one from a beer bottle."

"That is correct."

"When you are looking at fingerprints, they can all look similar, is that not so?"

"Yes sir. It depends on the fingerprint patterns. There can be various kinds of loops. There can be different kinds of whirls. And sometimes you see arches. In most cases, there are combinations of these prints."

"It must be a painstaking task, identifying the correct match."

"Yes sir, that is true."

"So what you are saying is that fingerprint patterns look alike?"

"Yes sir."

"If they are that similar, are mistakes usually made?"

"Sometimes, but—"

"Nothing further."

# CHAPTER 32

"Cheer up, Logan," Flosky said. "You did the best you could."

"Now I know how Ackroyd got his nickname. I knew he had me when he started asking about hearsay and taking things out of context."

"Don't blame yourself. Ackroyd does it to the best of us."

"What really gets me is that Claire Morgan is probably getting away with something."

"Do you think she actually switched drinks with Michelle du Prix?"

"Don't start that up again," Logan grumbled. "More of the same questions!"

"People will probably be debating it years from now."

"It makes me wonder, though. And you know how much I hate it when a missing piece goes unsolved."

"You can't tell me that Claire Morgan didn't know what was going on. I think she did it. But there's really no way to prove it, thanks to the maid destroying the evidence. Do you think she was working with Claire Morgan?"

Logan shrugged his shoulders. "I don't know. She was just doing her job. She's a tidy woman."

"Do you think she could come clean my place?"

Logan grinned and said, "You couldn't pay her enough to do that, Flosky."

"See, I got a smile out of you after all!"

Just then, Lieutenant Winters came in carrying the *Lancaster Times*. Logan grabbed it out of his hands and skimmed the article written by Rob Watkins.

"I don't believe it!" he cried. "Under cross-examination from G. Walter Ackroyd, Detective Sergeant Frank Logan admitted he used unreliable information. The fingerprint evidence was ruled unreliable as well…it is only a matter of time before the jurors come back with a verdict."

Logan crumpled the newspaper and tossed it in the trash can.

"Hey, I haven't read it yet!" squawked Flosky.

"It's all bad news anyway," Logan moaned. "Where did Watkins come up with this unreliable crap?" He sat back at his chair and concentrated on paperwork.

"Will he be all right?" Flosky asked Winters.

Harry glanced over at him and nodded. "He'll be fine. Just leave him alone for a bit. He'll snap out of it. If not, we'll just have to make his life miserable for a while till he comes around."

They went to their desks and caught up on their own paperwork.

Logan was just finishing up about six o'clock, when he looked up to see his coworkers carrying a cake lit with candles across the room. Penny and Gramps were standing behind them, all smiles.

"Congratulations, Logan!" Flosky exclaimed.

"I don't know what to say."

"I'm sorry we didn't celebrate sooner, but the trial got in the way."

"That's fine."

Gramps gushed and hugged him. "Your father would be so proud of you right now."

"Now you have a license to boss me around," Flosky said.

Logan grinned. "I already do anyway."

Penny kissed her husband and said, "It was a lot of hard work. It's well deserved."

"Well, are you gonna stand there yapping, or are you gonna blow out the candles?" Flosky squawked.

"Well, if you weren't all talking so much, I would've done it by now." He leaned down and blew out the candles.

Everybody clapped and whistled.

"Congratulations, Sergeant," Winters said. "I hope you won't get a swelled head."

"It's already swelled anyway," Logan replied dryly.

Gwen grinned at Penny. "This has been a really good year for you two. You got married. He got a promotion. And you finally came to your senses and took that job closer to home. How's it going by the way?"

"I love it! The people are great. There are no more ten hour stress-filled days. I know most of the clients. And I'm not practically living in my car. And I get to spend more time with Frank."

"You should have done it a long time ago."

"I know."

Frank went over to them and patted Penny's stomach. "Well, now that we're going to be spending more time with each other, I guess we'll actually have to talk to each other."

"My, my, what ever will we say to each other?" Penny wondered.

"I don't know."

"How far along are you?" Gwen asked.

"Three months."

"Do you know if it's a boy or a girl?"

"No, and I don't want to know. There are no surprises anymore."

Gwen nodded and smiled. "I know exactly what you're talking about. You know who's calling on the phone. The sex of the baby should be a surprise."

"I agree a hundred percent."

"Well, it's not a secret what we're gonna name the kid," Logan said. "It's either gonna be Frank the third if it's a boy. Or Frankie if it's a girl. I guess we'll have to start looking for a bigger apartment."

\*   \*   \*

G. Walter Ackroyd and Trent Morgan entered the courtroom and sat at the defense table. Waiting for the verdict was always a nail-biting experience. Over the years, Ackroyd had gotten clients off in many sticky situations. He wasn't so sure this time. He hoped he had peppered Trent's murder trial with a lot of circumstantial evidence, but was certain that the jurors didn't buy it.

John Harkens arrived a short time later. He was confident that the jurors voted to convict the defendant. In his closing statement, Harkens admitted that there was a lot of circumstantial evidence. He hoped he had hammered the point that while one of those bits of inconclusive evidence could be circumstantial, taken together they amounted to proof that Trent Morgan murdered Marty Brown.

The room grew more crowded. When Judge Robinson appeared through the side door, everyone rose. The jurors filed in and took their seats.

Trent Morgan bowed his head and prayed. His palms sweated. He could feel his heart racing.

Claire bit her lower lip. Bill put his arm around her and whispered, "It will be all right."

"What is your verdict?" Judge Robinson asked the foreman of the jury.

A man with glasses rose and said, "For the murder of Michelle du Prix, we find the defendant Trent Morgan not guilty."

There were murmurs around the room. Trent felt a cold chill shoot down his spine.

"The charge of conspiracy to commit murder, we find the defendant, Trent Morgan, not guilty."

Harkens patted Trent's shoulder. The murmurs grew louder.

"For the murder of Martin Brown, we find the defendant, Trent Morgan, guilty."

Loud gasps reverberated around the courtroom.

Trent lurched forward, burying his face in his hands. "Oh God!" he cried. "Oh God!"

Claire slumped down in her seat and burst into tears. Bill rubbed her shoulders, uttering soothing words. He was used to calming her nerves.

"Thank you all for your hard work," Judge Robinson said. "The jury is now dismissed." He made concluding remarks and set the sentencing date for one month hence.

When the sentencing date arrived, Trent appeared visibly shaken in his orange prison jumpsuit. His eyes were vacant, and his face was expressionless.

Claire had put her makeup on in a hurry. Her cheeks were pasty looking. Her hair was sticking out from the brutal wind. She held Bill's hand so tightly he had to gently loosen her grip.

Waiting for Judge Robinson to arrive seemed like an eternity. Trent wondered how things had gotten to this point. He was a smart man. How did he get himself into this mess? His world was crumbling and there was no way to stop it.

At twenty past nine, Judge Robinson entered the courtroom and sat behind the bench. He looked over at the defendant and said, "Step forward, Mr. Morgan."

Trent approached the bench and bowed his head. His legs were so weak, that a bailiff had to help hold him up.

"You have been found guilty of murder," Judge Robinson announced. "I hereby sentence you to life in prison beginning immediately."

Trent wiped away his tears and listened to Judge Robinson make his concluding remarks. Ackroyd was quick with a response. "We can appeal!" he shouted to be heard over the roar of the crowd. "I'll draw up the papers by this afternoon."

A guard handcuffed Trent and escorted him out of the courtroom.

Claire got up and started to fall, but Bill held her firmly. They followed the crowd out to the lobby, went down the winding marble staircase, and waited in the hall for the guard to take Trent downstairs. At last, the elevator door opened, and they marched toward Claire and Bill.

Claire choked back tears. "Trent! Trent!"

"Come on," Bill said, "There's nothing we can do now."

Trent looked at Claire, his eyes pleading. "Why did you set me up? You lied! You lied!"

"I don't know what you're talking about."

Claire turned away so she did not have to watch the guard walk him out the door. Another guard made them wait. He reopened the door, and Claire braced herself for the frigid March air before going out. They stood on the front steps, watching the guard put Trent into a police car.

Bill held her hand firmly and helped her down the steps. "It'll be okay," he said gently.

"I just don't know what I'll do without him!" she wailed.

They walked under the pavilion to avoid getting in the way of the construction workers. They stopped in their tracks when they saw a patch of ice on the sidewalk.

"Wait here," he said. "I'll get the car."

Claire rubbed her hands and bundled up. "Please hurry. It's cold and windy!"

He slowly edged his way down the block, making sure he didn't slip on all the ice. She stood there shivering. The wind cut through her like knives. She pulled her hood over her head and stood under the pavilion to keep warm. She peeked around the corner to see if the car was coming. It was nowhere in sight. Another arctic blast of cold air shot up her spine.

"Come on, Bill. I don't know how much more I can take."

She saw him pulling across from the courthouse and cautiously maneuvered her way onto the sidewalk, checking for ice patches. She was looking down when she should have been looking up.

A construction worker shouted, "Look out, lady!"

She didn't hear him over the howling wind. As she was crossing the street, plywood blew off the scaffolding and smashed on top of her.

"Mother!" A look of horror flashed across Bill's face as he watched the plywood crush her.

He slammed on the brakes and parked in the middle of the street. He raced over to the accident scene and pushed himself in among the construction workers who were trying desperately to pull off the plywood.

"Mother!" he shouted over the unrelenting wind. "Oh my God, Mother!"

When they managed to pull off the plywood, a construction worker checked her pulse. "Oh my God, she's dead!"

# ACKNOWLEDGMENTS

I hope that you have enjoyed reading *Lethal Glitch*. I would like to thank my mom and dad, who have spent many hours proofreading various versions of my manuscripts in three-ring notebooks. I appreciate their help and suggestions. I also want to thank my family and friends for their constant support. Thank you Karen for reinstalling Word so I could remove track marks.

I would also like to thank members of the Rehoboth Beach Writers Guild. It is really amazing what material comes out of us at our 8:00 a.m. freewrites at the Rehoboth Beach Library before the parking meters turn on at 10:00 a.m.

I would also like to thank the Newark Arts Alliance Open Mic night group for their constant interest in my stories that I read in five-minute installments every month.

I also want to thank Dr. John Kelly for taking time to discuss criminal cases with me. I don't know where you found all those crime scene images. I especially enjoyed working on pictures from the old police magazines you brought to my house.

I want to thank Dr. Michael Duerrsen for taking time out to answer odd questions about poisoning my characters.

I also want to thank Elite Editing for all their assistance during the production process for this book.

# BIBLIOGRAPHY

Chapter 11, "Retrograde Amnesia" Wikipedia.

Chapter 17, "Morgue Scene" "Cause of Death: A Writer's Guide to Death, Murder, and Forensic Medicine," Keith D. Wilson, M.D., Writer's Digest Books, 1992, pp. 118-119.

Chapter 19, "Hanging Scene" "Cause of Death: A Writer's Guide to Death, Murder, and Forensic Medicine," Keith D. Wilson, M.D., Writer's Digest Books, 1992, pp. 114-115.

Chapter 31, "Fingerprint Patterns" "Forensics: A Guide for Writers," D.P. Lyle, M.D., Writer's Digest Books, 2008, pp. 274-278.

Made in the USA
Lexington, KY
11 September 2018